CAMPUS HEARTTHROB

JENNIFER SUCEVIC

Campus Heartthrob

Cover Design by Mary Ruth Baloy at MR Creations

Editing by Evelyn Summers of Pinpoint Editing

Pinpoint Editing – Affordable editing services for independent authors

Home | Jennifer Sucevic or www.jennifersucevic.com

Want to subscribe to my newsletter? Jennifer Sucevic Newsletter (subscribepage.com)

ALSO BY JENNIFER SUCEVIC

Campus Player

Claiming What's Mine

Confessions of a Heartbreaker

Crazy for You (80s short story)

Don't Leave

Friend Zoned

Hate to Love You

Heartless

If You Were Mine

Just Friends

King of Campus

King of Hawthorne Prep

Love to Hate You

One Night Stand

Protecting What's Mine

Queen of Hawthorne Prep

Stay

The Boy Next Door

The Breakup Plan

The Girl Next Door

Chapter One

BRAYDEN

"Yo, Kendricks, grab me a cold one when you come back," Asher Stevens yells as I walk into the kitchen.

I give him a one-fingered salute to let him know that I heard him loud and clear. That guy drinks like it's his sole mission in life. By the time he graduates college this spring, he'll be in desperate need of a liver transplant. Although, I've got to give him credit—he's at the top of his game on the field. I have no idea how he does it. It's one of the great mysteries in life that I've stopped trying to unravel.

With a yank, I open the refrigerator door and scan the shelves. What I find is a depressing sight. Other than a shit ton of beer and Gatorade, it looks more like a barren wasteland.

Bunch of fuckers.

Don't these guys realize that we live half a mile from the nearest grocery store? Hell, with a few taps on their phone, groceries would magically appear outside the front door.

We're all supposed to be pitching in with the domestic chores. One look around this place will tell you that isn't happening. The toilet on the first floor resembles a sketchy Chia Pet. Plus, it smells like the penguin house at the zoo.

I avoid it at all costs.

With a grumble, I pull out one of the last bottles of water and twist off the top before guzzling down a quarter of it. Then I grab a Miller Lite for Stevens. I've tried broaching the subject of his alcohol consumption a few times, but it's not like I'm his mom. The dude is twenty-one years old; he can do whatever the hell he wants.

Carson, one of the other guys who lives here, saunters in as I slam the refrigerator door closed.

Carson Roberts and I go way back. We're talking elementary school. He's practically part of the family. The brother I never had but always wanted. He was there when I needed him and got me through one of the toughest times in my life. Even at twenty-one years old, I realize that friends like that aren't easy to come by.

Football is what we originally bonded over. We've been playing together since second grade. First, flag football before moving on to a middle school team and then high school. Luckily, we both ended up at the same college and roomed together freshman and sophomore years before finding a house with a couple of teammates. Like me, Carson will enter the draft in the spring. He's one of the best tight ends in the conference and was an All-American last year. The guy is one smart motherfucker.

Before I can open my mouth, he says, "Heads up, Kira just walked in."

Goddamn it.

A groan escapes from me.

That girl takes crazy, psycho stalker to a whole new level. It's almost as impressive as it is frightening.

Scratch that. It's just plain frightening. There have been numerous times when I've come home, afraid I'd find our pet rabbit boiling away on the stove.

Just kidding, we don't have a bunny.

But still...

You get the point I'm trying to make. It's fucking scary. And she won't leave me alone. I've tried everything, going so far as to tell her that it's never going to happen between us.

I mean, come on. Of course it's not going to happen!

I've never even locked lips with this chick, and she shadows me around campus and turns up in my classes. I'm *this* close to taking out a restraining order. The girl needs to move on. Or move away.

Preferably the latter.

For the most part, I've enjoyed my time at Western University, but it'll be a relief to get the hell out of here after graduation. There's only so much of this crazy behavior I can put up with.

Carson's shoulders shake with undisguised mirth. "That's what you get for being so damn pretty."

"Fuck off," I mutter. Just because he's a good friend, doesn't mean he won't give me shit.

He shrugs. "Hey, I've got an idea. Take her to bed and show her that you're not as amazing as she thinks you are. Aren't you notorious for your starfish impersonation?"

Again...

"Up yours."

Not offended in the least, a smile breaks out across his face. "You know what you need?"

I'm almost afraid to ask.

My stoic silence doesn't stop him from continuing. "A girlfriend."

Is he nuts?

"No, thanks," I snort.

I have zero interest in one of those. Especially right now. I've got enough going on with school and football. This is a big year for me. The season is underway, and, so far, we're number one in the conference. The goal is to take home a championship and win a bowl game. That would be an amazing way to end my four years with the Wildcats. Then I can turn my attention to the NFL with the combine and draft in the spring.

"I'm serious," he says, pushing the subject.

Yeah, that's the scary part.

I shake my head, ready to put an end to this conversation.

Over the years, there have been a few girlfriends. What I've discovered is that they're more of a hassle than they're worth. Division I football is more like a job, and my schedule is packed tight. My life revolves around practice, lifting, film review, travel, and games. Most of the chicks I've dated get bent out of shape when they aren't moved to the top of my priority list and end up forcing me to choose.

Want to guess what gets downsized?

I'll give you a hint...it's not football.

After the first couple of times it happened, I decided having a permanent girl in my life wasn't worth the price of admission. Sure, it would be nice to find someone to spend time with, but that's just not in the cards. And quite frankly, I'm not sure it will be in the near future. Not with wrapping up my last year of school and hopefully getting picked up by the pros. It's just easier to screw around with the jersey chasers on campus. For the most part, they understand that sex is nothing more than an hour or so of mindless pleasure. They get to brag about banging guys on the team, and I get a little stress relief to take the edge off.

"Then Kira would have no choice but to leave you alone," he continues as if I haven't already nixed the idea.

Like I need to get myself entangled in one bad situation just to get out of another... What the hell would be the point of that?

"She should have backed off when I flat-out told her that nothing was ever going to happen between us," I mutter.

"Again, if you weren't so pretty, girls wouldn't lose their damn minds over you." His lips curl around the edges before he tacks on slyly, "*Mr. Campus Heartthrob*."

I wince at the title I've won three years in a row.

Talk about embarrassing.

Sure, I'll admit it—I was flattered at first. Who wouldn't be? I got a ton of pussy by winning that stupid competition. My teammates were jealous, and I didn't mind rubbing it in their faces. As difficult as it is to imagine, screwing your way through all the girls vying to sleep with you gets old after a while. Now the damn thing is just a nuisance. Like I need these chicks trailing after me, following me around all over the place.

Nope. I'm over it.

Last year, I didn't enter the contest and *still* managed to win. How is that even possible?

My lips flatten before I grumble, "I prefer to think of it as ruggedly handsome. No dude wants to be called pretty."

"Please," he snorts, "your face could be plastered on a billboard. I'm surprised there aren't more crazies coming out of the woodwork just to sleep with you."

"Bite your tongue," I grunt. I don't even want to imagine that. I've got my hands full as it is. The last thing I need is to add more bullshit into the mix.

"I don't know, man. I think the girlfriend idea is worth considering. It could be the solution to all your problems."

"Or just give me more headaches." I shift my weight and take another drink from my bottle. "There's only one flaw with your plan. There aren't any girls I'm even remotely interested in."

His brows jerk together. "Who said anything about this being a real situation? I'm talking about finding a friend who could pretend to like your ass for a couple of weeks. Someone who wouldn't mind doing you a solid." He tilts his head. "Don't you know anyone like that who fits the bill?"

Hmm. I suppose a ploy like that could work. Except...there aren't any females who I'm strictly friends with. Even the ones who pretend to be platonic end up throwing themselves at me at some point. And the ones who get all drunk at parties and start sobbing about how much they love me are the absolute worst.

"Not really." I shake my head. "Any other bright ideas?"

He nods toward the backdoor. "I guess you could always try to make a run for it. Lay low at Rowan's girl's place for a couple of hours until Kira gets bored and finally takes off."

Yeah, the last time I did that, she waited around for five hours. Let that sink in.

Five.

Full.

Hours.

The woman is seriously tenacious. Must be part of the stalker job description.

I turn the suggestion over in my head. Heading over to Demi's would give me a chance to see Sydney. And I rarely pass up an opportunity to do that. There's something about the blonde-haired, green-eyed soccer player that has gotten under my skin. Kind of like an itch that is impossible to scratch. And steroids haven't done the trick to cure it, either. If she's anywhere in the vicinity, my attention is locked on her.

My guess is that it's because she refuses to give me the time of day. There's definitely something to that old adage about wanting what you can't have. And what I can't have is Sydney. That girl wants nothing to do with me, which is precisely why I never miss an opportunity to mess with her.

Trust me, I'm more than aware that I'm not doing myself any favors. But still, I get perverse satisfaction in provoking her ire. All I have to do is open my mouth and she goes off the deep end. The girl has a real temper. I've seen it rear its head on more than one occasion. My guess is that she would be a real wildcat in the sack. Not that I'll be finding out anytime soon.

Or, more than likely, ever.

As tempting as it is to flee our house for the next couple of hours, I have a test to study for. I might have every intention of taking my game to the next level by getting drafted to the NFL, but it's still important I do well in school and leave with a degree in hand. Even the most talented players are only one career-ending injury away from being let go. I'm taking every precaution to make sure that my future goes off without a hitch. Even if that means doing something other than playing professional football.

So, ducking out of here isn't really a choice. I drag a hand through my hair and consider my options before blowing out a steady breath. "All right, I'm going to need you to create a distraction so I can sneak upstairs without her noticing."

A smirk curves Carson's lips as he folds his arms across his chest and leans against the counter. "How am I supposed to do that? She's sitting in the living room with the perfect view of the front door and staircase."

Christ...this girl.

I shouldn't have to sneak around my own damn house. "I don't know," I snap in frustration, "just think of something. I need about twenty seconds to get upstairs."

It doesn't escape me that I'm taking out my aggravation on someone who doesn't deserve it, which isn't like me, but I'm over this situation. I want this girl to leave me alone. If I honestly thought sitting down and having yet another conversation with her would put an end to this infatuation, I'd do it in a heartbeat. But I've done that several times and she refuses to move on. It doesn't seem to matter that I'm not interested.

He shakes his head as if I'm the crazy one for going to such lengths to avoid her, and I'll tell you what—I'm beginning to feel like it. "I'll do my best, but I'm not making any promises."

As soon as Carson exits the kitchen, I realize that we didn't come up with a code word. I almost leap after him but stop myself at the last moment.

Damnit! How am I supposed to know that the coast is clear without a code word?

I seriously can't believe this is what my life has come to. I'm skulking around my own house to avoid some chick.

But what else can I do?

Waste the next hour or so fighting off her unwanted advances?

No way. I don't have time for that.

Grumbling under my breath, I tiptoe across the kitchen like it's boobytrapped before arriving at the wide entryway that leads to the dining room. The only furniture in the space is a scarred table that has seen better days—more like better decades—and four chairs. Everyone is crammed together, chilling in the living room. The loud, rowdy babble of voices fills my ears.

Just as I work up the courage to peek around the corner, Carson materializes on the other side. We both startle, and my heart slams against my ribcage.

"Fuck, dude...you nearly gave me a heart attack." I point to the living room. If he's with me, then who the hell is occupying Kira? Even more frighteningly, he might be drawing her attention in this direction. That's exactly what I don't need. "What are you doing in here?"

"It's not necessary," he says with a shrug. "She's gone."

No way.

My brows shoot up at that unexpected bit of good news. "Really?" Well, hot damn! Looks like I've lucked out for once.

"Yeah. I did a total sweep of the first floor. She's not in the living room, and I checked both bathrooms. They're empty. She must have gotten bored and taken off."

Huh. That was way easier than anticipated.

All of my muscles loosen with relief. Until now, I hadn't realized how tense I'd become. "Thanks, man." I slap Carson on the back. "I owe you one."

"No worries." He shoots me a grin. "I'll think of some way for you to repay me." Before I can respond, he swings around and strolls into the living room.

I grab my bottle of water along with Asher's beer before following him. Once the beverage has been passed off, I do a cursory inspection of the immediate vicinity just to make sure Carson isn't fucking with me. Although, it's doubtful he would do that. We've been friends for way too long for that kind of bullshit. If there's one guy I trust, it's him. Rowan Michaels would be a close second.

A quick scan of the room as I beeline to the staircase solidifies that Carson wasn't yanking my chain. Kira is nowhere to be seen.

Carson is right about one thing—I need to do something about this situation before it spirals any further out of control. I refuse to spend the rest of senior year looking over my shoulder and avoiding my own house. I need that chick to understand that we are never getting together. At this point, there's no way we can even be friends.

"Kendricks, where you going?" Crosby Rhodes shouts from his sprawled-out position in an armchair.

I flick my gaze at him. Like most of the other guys, he's surrounded by a handful of females. Being on the football team will get you all the chicks you could ask for. Having a lip ring and a sullen attitude will get you twice as many.

Go figure.

"Got a test to study for," I call back, trudging up the steps.

"Come on, Kendricks, let me kick your ass in a little GTA," Easton adds from the couch he's stretched out on.

It's a tempting offer, but still...

"If memory serves, aren't I the one who kicked yours the last time we played?" I shoot back.

Easton smirks before shoving his chestnut-colored hair out of his bright blue eyes. If I'm not mistaken, a few girls in the room sigh. "Maybe. How about a rematch, then?"

"Sorry, not tonight."

It might not seem like it, but I've never been a slouch in the partying department. Freshman year is nothing more than a blur. I spent most of it shitfaced, attempting to drown the grief that had been my constant companion.

Big surprise—it didn't work.

What did end up happening is that I almost flunked out of college and got my ass kicked off the football team. Coach Richards pulled me aside at the end of the season and told me that I had a choice to make —either pull myself together or get the hell out of his program.

I could do one or the other, but not both.

That conversation had been a rude awakening, and it had been exactly what I needed to hear. The year before, I'd lost one of the most important people in my life. Losing football on top of it wasn't a choice I was willing to make. I returned home and dried out over the summer. I focused on working out in the gym and getting stronger so I could prove to Coach that he hadn't made a mistake in recruiting me. When I returned to Western for my sophomore year, I swapped out the alcohol for pussy. I guess if you can't drown your sorrows in beer, girls are a close second. Except...it doesn't actually solve anything or make your problems disappear. You just run the risk of an STI.

"Lame ass," Easton shouts after me.

Knowing that I don't have anything to prove, the taunt slides easily off my back. My accomplishments and the records I've broken over the years speak for themselves. "Yup."

As I disappear onto the second floor, I swing right and pass by two doors before arriving at mine. Now that Kira is no longer a concern, my mind gravitates to the exam I need to cram for. I grab hold of the handle and push open the thick wood before crossing over the threshold. I probably have three solid hours of work ahead of me. After doing my damnedest to flunk out freshman year, it's taken a lot of focus and determination to raise my GPA. The fact that, two years later, it's over a three point zero is a source of pride for me.

I'm jerked out of those thoughts by a noise as my gaze cuts to the queen-sized bed at the far end of the room.

And the naked girl lying on top of it.

"Hey, Brayden," Kira coos, shifting on the comforter as she spreads her legs wide. "I've been waiting for you."

Well, hell.

Chapter Two

SYDNEY

"Are you absolutely sure that you can't squeeze me in?" I plead, phone shoved against my ear as I search the Union for my bestie. It's noon and the place is packed with hungry students making a pitstop.

"Sorry, sweetie. If you had gotten ahold of me a few days earlier, I might have been able to slide you in, but someone else beat you to it and booked the last of my free time. I just can't do it," Marco finishes.

Damn.

Damn.

Damn.

"No worries," I say with forced lightness before spotting Demi and Rowan camped out at a table in the corner. "I'm sure I'll find someone else."

Hopefully.

"I really am sorry, Syd. You know how much I love working with you."

Marco has modeled for me several times throughout the years, and he's the absolute best. We usually end up laughing and joking around the entire time.

Even though he can't see me do it, I wave a hand. "Seriously, don't worry about it. I'll find another model. I've got time."

Sort of.

"Okay, girl. Talk soon."

"Yup." I hit disconnect and drop onto the bench opposite them.

Demi and Rowan have turned into one of those couples who sit on the same side of the table, even when they're alone. It's super barfy. As much as I'd like to roll my eyes, I can't. If anyone deserves happiness, it's Demi. Her last boyfriend put her through the wringer. The guy was a real jerk. Not only did she find him in a compromising situation with his pants around his ankles with one of our teammates, Annica—what a bitch—but he then proceeded to spread around campus that *she* was the one cheating on *him*.

The only good to come out of that situation is that Rowan was finally able to win Demi over. And the rest is relationship history.

As much as I hate to admit it, I'm a little jelly of what they have. My last relationship was a veritable roller-coaster of emotions. High-highs and low-lows. It was a constant whirlwind of breakups and makeups before we finally pulled the plug and decided to go our separate ways. I can't say that the making up part wasn't a blast, but the constant bickering was exhausting. What I learned from that epic fail is that sometimes it's just not possible to make a relationship work—no matter how much you both want it. Ethan was a great guy, but we weren't meant for the long haul.

The second thing I discovered?

That I need to take a legit hiatus from men.

Ethan wasn't my first break up. I've had a long string of ill-fated relationships. I have a nasty habit of extracting myself from one disastrous situation only to dive headfirst into another. After the latest debacle, I'm taking a little time to get to know myself and figure out what I really want.

And you know what?

It's kind of nice.

All right, the lack of sex isn't great. But other than that, I'm happy.

Fine, if not entirely *happy*, then at least content.

We'll just go with that.

Anything less and I would be venturing into pathetic territory, and

I'm unwilling to go there. I don't need a man to be satisfied, and that's what I'm set on proving to myself once and for all. I'm perfectly content on my own.

Except when I'm around these two lovebirds. And all their obnoxious canoodling.

They're seriously too cute for words.

It makes me want to puke. Or cry into a pint of Cherry Garcia.

Rowan whispers something in Demi's ear and a light blush blooms in her cheeks. I can just imagine what he's saying. Or promising.

Ugh.

See what I have to deal with?

I'd be better off eating lunch by myself.

"All right, you two," I grumble, "break it up before I have to get out the hose." And contrary to popular belief, I will, indeed, hose these two off. Their sexual chemistry is enough to induce immaculate conception.

Demi straightens before shoving Rowan back a couple of inches. Although, let's face it, he's not going far. The guy is completely enamored by her. I suspect it's been that way for years. There was once a time when Demi professed to hate her father's star quarterback and did everything in her power to avoid him. I had no idea how Rowan did it, but he managed to break through all her barriers, and now they're Western's most swoonworthy couple.

"Hey," Demi greets. There's a breathless quality to her voice. "What's up?" She does her best to blink the sexual haze from her eyes before inspecting me with more care. "That's a whole lot of unhappiness going on there," she says, pointing to the general vicinity of my face.

"It's nothing." I shrug and attempt to downplay the desperateness flooding through me. I'm practically drowning in it. "I need to find a male model for an art class project. Unfortunately for me, all of the usual suspects have been snapped up." My voice drops as I reluctantly admit, "I should have done this weeks ago, but I was so bogged down with my accounting course. I've made a few calls, but everyone is booked up tight."

"No worries, Syd. I'll model for you," Rowan offers. "How hard can it be to strike a pose?" Looking robotic, he makes a few gestures with his hands.

A genuine smile lifts my lips.

Have I mentioned how much I adore Rowan?

The first-string QB is a real sweetheart. If he and Demi weren't so stinking cute together, I'd make a play for him myself. But the guy only has eyes for my bestie. Amusingly enough, everyone else could see that but her.

I glance at my roommate before smirking at him. "Why thank you, Rowan. That would be incredibly helpful. You're cool with modeling in the buff, right?"

He blinks, blue eyes widening before he gives his girlfriend a bit of side-eye. Her lips tremble around the edges.

"Umm...like, naked?" he asks, shifting uncomfortably on the bench.

"Yup, we're talking full-on nudity. And you'll have to pose for at least a couple of hours so I can draw every inch of you."

"Oh." There's a pause as ruddy color rushes into his cheeks. "Sorry," he mutters, "I'm gonna have to retract my offer. There's only one girl who gets to see the goods."

A gurgle of laughter escapes from me as Demi presses a kiss against his cheek.

"You're so adorable when you're embarrassed," she chuckles.

She might be laughing, but it's doubtful she'd be cool with her hot boyfriend posing naked for me. Even if it is for a school art project.

Just as my phone lights up with an incoming call, a hard body slides into the booth next to me. I pounce on my cell, shooting a glance at the guy now invading my personal space as his hip bumps into mine.

"Hello?" My gaze becomes ensnared by Brayden's dark one as I answer the call. He's way too close for comfort. I blink and attempt to focus on the conversation. It turns out to be another model who isn't able to sit for me.

Crap.

This is turning out to be more problematic than I assumed. I should have realized all the good ones would get snapped up. Honestly,

I only meant to put it off for a week or two until a bigger chunk of my accounting project was completed and I could turn my attention to art. Except the class consumed more time than I thought, and now that I'm ready to get to work, everyone I normally partner with is otherwise engaged.

Where are the procrastinators when you need them?

Apparently, I'm the only one.

When Brayden's gaze takes a leisurely stroll of my body, I shoot him a dirty look before refocusing my attention on the call.

"Are you sure?" I wheedle. "I promise it'll only take four hours of your time. Five, at the most. You know how quickly I work."

From the corner of my eye, I watch as Brayden shifts toward me. The guy doesn't even attempt to disguise the fact that he's listening intently to my private conversation. I can practically feel the burn of his gaze. As much as I try to stifle it, a sizzle of awareness slides through me. It starts in my fingertips before gradually working its way through my body until it reaches my toes. My entire being feels electrified by his perusal. I lock my jaw and steel myself against the unwanted sensations coursing through me.

If there's one guy on this campus that I refuse to be attracted to, it's Brayden Kendricks. Unfortunately, someone needs to give that memo to my hormones. Anytime I'm around the guy, my body goes haywire. It takes effort to stomp out the flames attempting to ignite in my core.

Barely do I hear the model on the other end of the phone explain that he's already working with two other art students and can't possibly take on anything more with his schedule. If I thought that pleading would change his mind, I would happily do it. I'm not above groveling.

It's a little disconcerting when I realize that I'm once again staring at Brayden. And that he's wearing his usual smirk. The one that makes me gnash my teeth every single time he flashes it my way.

I force my gaze from the dark-haired football player and concentrate on the conversation at hand. "No problem, I understand. Just," I bite my lip before lowering my voice, "let me know if anything changes with your schedule. I'm kind of desperate here."

That's the third model I've struck out with. As I hit disconnect, a disheartened breath escapes from my lips.

When Brayden's knee bumps into mine, another unwanted sizzle of awareness shoots through me. "What was that about?"

My gaze flickers in his direction before skittering away. I find it easier to hold a conversation with the guy if I don't have to stare at him for too long. He's not just good looking, he's stupid pretty. We're talking chiseled cheekbones. Long, Romanesque nose. Broody mouth. Dark eyes that feel like they can see straight down to your very soul. Perfectly tousled hair that begs female fingers to tunnel through it.

And I haven't even mentioned his body. He's like a Greek god carved from marble. The artist in me would delight in sketching him. Especially in the nude. Can you even imagine his sinewy musculature?

It's for that very reason I refuse to go there.

Plus, he irritates the crap out of me.

"Nothing," I mutter, wanting to shut down any further conversation. Had I realized Brayden would be gracing us with his presence, I would have politely declined the invitation and grabbed something to go. I refuse to spend any more time with him than absolutely necessary. It's bad enough that we're stuck together in a class and somehow got partnered up for our accounting project. Do you have any idea what that's been like?

In a word—aggravating.

Plus, with Demi dating one of his roommates, we're thrown together even more often than before. Avoidance has become almost impossible.

Sure, he's charming as hell. I've watched him in action for the past three years. My conclusions on the subject are that he's nothing more than a fuck boy, and I have zero interest in getting caught up in that.

"Syd needs a model for her art project," Rowan pipes up rather unhelpfully when I remain silent.

I narrow my eyes and shoot him an icy glare. He's well aware of my feelings for his friend and teammate. One side of his mouth hitches in response as he shrugs.

Forget what I said earlier about Rowan being a sweetheart. He's the furthest thing from it.

"Really?" Brayden says with interest.

"Naked," Rowan adds.

"Well, I have to admit you had me at *model.*" There's a pause as he slides closer until all of the distance between us is swallowed up, and he fills my entire line of sight. "Throw in naked and I'm all yours, sweetheart."

Air gets clogged in my throat when I realize that I've become trapped in his predatory stare. Liquid heat pools in my core. It takes effort to tamp down my body's natural reaction as my palms flatten against the solid strength of his chest and I push him away.

"No thanks." I make sure to add the right amount of contempt to my response. There's no way in hell I want Brayden to suspect that he can turn me on so easily. We're talking the flick of a switch. Before I could blink, he'd find a way to use that weakness against me. And I know exactly how he would do it. Even the thought is enough to make me break into a cold sweat.

"You're not interested in drawing all this?" He does his best impersonation of Vanna White while waving a hand down his body.

"Nope." Yes! A hundred percent. He's gorgeous. The guy didn't win Campus Heartthrob three straight years in a row for his uncanny likeness to the Hunchback of Notre-Dame.

He shrugs. "Your loss."

Probably.

"Hardly," I respond in a haughty tone.

"If you can't get one of your models to do it, why not get your boyfriend?" Brayden asks, settling against the seat. He stretches out until his arm can drape across the back of the wooden bench we're squeezed into. "Voilà. Problem solved."

Even though his fingers are gentle and barely rest against my skin, I feel his touch down to my bones. It's impossible to ignore. Every bit of my attention becomes centered on it.

Why?

Why him?

Why does my body react to him like this?

It's as irritating as it is disturbing.

Demi's brows beetle together as she opens her mouth.

"Ethan is busy with baseball," I blurt before she can set him straight. "He's not able to do it."

"Hmm." His gaze stays fixated on mine. It's as if everything around us ceases to exist. I feel trapped in place, like a butterfly pinned to a Styrofoam board. All of the oxygen gets sucked from the atmosphere, making it impossible to breathe. His voice dips, turning raspy. "If you were my girlfriend, I wouldn't let some dude model naked for you. I'd be the only guy you were catching an eyeful of."

"Then it's lucky for me that I'm not your girlfriend, isn't it?" Where that comment comes from, I have no idea, but I'm thankful for it. Verbally sparring with Brayden comes second nature to me. I've had a ton of practice over the years.

The humor filling his eyes drains away, leaving a steely glint in its place as we continue to stare. Just when it becomes almost too much to withstand, I force my gaze to Demi. Once my attention is focused elsewhere, the air rushes from my lungs in a burst.

Questions fill her dark eyes. They're ones I don't necessarily want to answer. Brayden doesn't need to know that Ethan and I broke up about a month ago. It's just easier if he assumes my ex-boyfriend is still in the picture. The guy hits on me all the time; I can't imagine how much more intense his attention would become if he realized I was single. It's not something I'm interested in discovering firsthand.

"So," he says, cutting into my thoughts and drawing my attention reluctantly back to him, "what time are we hooking up at the library tonight?"

A change of topic is exactly what's needed.

Even if it's this one.

"We are not *hooking up*," I growl. "We're working on our project." With any luck, we can wrap it up so we no longer have to meet on a regular basis. I've had just about as much of Brayden Kendricks as I can withstand for one semester. More like the rest of my life.

The hard edge filling his eyes vanishes as he flashes me a grin. "Semantics, baby."

Ugh.

I have no idea why Brayden enjoys needling me, and I've stopped trying to figure it out. Avoidance seems to be the best tactic to employ with him. Not that it's done me much good.

"After practice," I tell him. "Around seven. Does that work?"

Honestly, it would be better if—

"I'll be there. Ready and willing."

I huff out a breath.

Yeah, that's exactly what I'm afraid of.

Chapter Three

BRAYDEN

Unable to help myself, I swipe my phone off the table for the twentieth time and look at it before glancing around the third floor of the library. Sydney is nowhere to be found. She's ten minutes late and counting.

The realization that I'm being stood up flickers through my brain. Even though we have work to plow through, I wouldn't put it past her to be a no-show. My ability to piss off the green-eyed soccer player is almost impressive. I have no idea what I did to Sydney to earn the number-one position on her shitlist. It's like she took an instant dislike to me and nothing I've done has been able to turn that frown upside down.

And I must be a glutton for punishment, because I'm unwilling to let it go.

Another three minutes slowly tick by and there's still no sign of her.

It's official.

I've been ditched.

Hell, she's probably making out with her boyfriend somewhere. That thought is enough to piss me off more than I'd like to admit.

Fucking Ethan.

Those two are all wrong for each other. One day they're together and the next, all hell is breaking loose. I've stopped trying to keep tabs on their relationship status. It changes as often as the weather. Just when I think it's safe to swoop in for the kill, they're back on again and sucking face right in front of me.

No. She needs a different kind of guy. Someone more like...

I shake that thought loose. Just as I'm about to pack up my computer and get the hell out of here, Sydney drops onto the chair across from me. Her face is slightly flushed, and her hair is damp from her shower.

"Sorry," she says by way of greeting, "practice ran over by about twenty minutes."

When her phone chimes with a message, she pulls it from her pocket before glancing at the screen and then setting it in front of her. As soon as it hits the table, I pounce.

"Hey! What are you doing? Give that back!" Her voice escalates with each word that falls from her lips as she makes a swipe for the slim device. But I'm too stealthy and lean back in my chair. Unless she's going to dive across the table, she's not getting her hands on it until I'm done. With quick movements, I tap the home screen and access her phone app before punching in my number. When mine buzzes with an incoming call, I hit end and hand back the cell. She scowls and rips the electronic device from my fingers. If looks could kill, I'd be dead on the spot.

Much to Sydney's chagrin, that doesn't occur.

"Now I have your digits," I say with a smirk.

"Ever think that I didn't want you to have them?" she shoots back, upper lip curling with irritation.

Yup. All the time.

When I continue to smile, her lips tighten into a grim line. My guess is that she's on the verge of exploding. Less than thirty seconds in my presence and she's ready to lose it. This might be an all-time record for me.

"We should get to work," she finally grumbles. "I've got other assignments to finish up tonight."

"The grind never ends," I say lightly, because it's the truth. It's pressure I feel on a daily basis. My bet is that Sydney does as well. Being student athletes at Western University means that we need to be on top of our time management game. Most professors don't give a shit if you play a sport. For them, academics are the be all end all.

"Truth." Her shoulders loosen, falling from the general vicinity of her ears.

In silence, she pulls her computer from her backpack. Only now that I'm taking a closer look at Sydney's face do I notice the dark purple smudges decorating the fragile skin beneath her eyes. A rush of sympathy arrows through me.

I shift in my chair, wondering if there's anything I can do to lighten her load. Even though I'm the last person on the face of this Earth she would willingly accept help from, that doesn't mean I'm not going to offer. She might vehemently disagree, but I'm not a complete dick. "If you've got other stuff to do, we can work on this another time. There are two more weeks before it needs to be turned in, and the bulk of the project is already finished."

It's a surprise when her expression softens. Some of the lines of tension straining her face drain away as she shakes her head. "It's fine. We can put in a few hours here and then I'll head home and study for my quiz."

With a nod, we delve straight in. We're looking at what causes financial instability among business giants. It's an interesting topic with plenty of material to pour over. Our biggest issue has been narrowing it down to our thesis statement. We could easily write a book on the subject. Hell, dozens of them have already been published on the issue. It's research rich.

It's vaguely that I recall ending up in the same section of an introductory accounting class with Sydney freshman year. This is the second course we've had together. To say it was a surprise to learn that she's an accounting major is an understatement. Her personality doesn't quite fit the stereotype. The girl is a real firecracker. I have a difficult time imagining her hunched over a desk, crunching numbers all by her lonesome for sixteen hours a day during tax season.

After about two hours of shoring up our research, I found a few more references that back up our assertion. With a stretch of my muscles, I glance up. That's all it takes for my gaze to fasten on the girl across from me. Her brows are furrowed in concentration as she pours over a document on her computer. For just a few moments, I'm able to study her while she's unaware of my perusal. If she realized what I was doing, the intensity would be replaced with a dark scowl. I don't think I've ever met a girl who was so hostile to my advances. Usually, I can charm the panties right off the opposite sex.

That's not the case with this one. She's liable to bite my hand off if I even try.

I've often wondered what it is about Sydney that has captured my interest so completely. She's pretty with long, blonde hair and vibrant, green-colored eyes. They're almost the exact shade of freshly-mowed grass. If you look closely enough, there's a delicate smattering of freckles across the bridge of her nose. She's probably around five-foot-six with a tight, athletic body and muscular legs from years of kicking around a soccer ball.

And her breasts...

My gaze unconsciously drops to them.

She's wearing a turquoise Dri-Fit T-shirt that hugs the roundness of her chest. Most guys are all about the tits and ass. The more curves, the better. I don't necessarily feel that way. Sure, I like breasts. What red-blooded, college-aged guy doesn't? But I don't need to be smothered to death by them when a chick is riding me. And yeah, there's been a few times when I thought that asphyxiation was a genuine possibility.

It wouldn't be a bad way to go, I'm just saying...

But Sydney isn't built like that at all. Her breasts would be the perfect palmful.

Not that I would know. As much as I'd like to find out for myself, that's not going to happen. The girl would probably take me out if I were to accidently graze her boob.

I'm still lamenting the fact that I'll never get my hands on her when movement from the corner of my eye catches my attention. Since we're camped out on the third floor of the library, there isn't much student traffic. It's quieter up here. People aren't constantly stopping by the table, wanting to shoot the shit about the football season and our chances of bringing home a conference championship. I have no problem talking about that, but not when I'm with Sydney. This is about as much alone time as I'm going to get with her, and I need to take advantage of it.

My gaze flickers to the couple who has now settled at a table on the other side of the space.

Wait a minute—

Is that Sydney's boyfriend *Ethan*?

No way.

I've known Ethan Price since freshman year. We lived on the same floor in the dorms. It's grudgingly that I'll admit he's a decent guy. He's not one of those boyfriends who conveniently forgets he's in a relationship when he's out with the bros. I've known plenty of dudes like that. Not only do they want their cake, but they want to devour it, too. They want as much fucking cake as they can stuff in their pie holes.

Ethan has never struck me as that type.

So, what the hell is he doing here with another chick?

By this point, I'm craning my neck, watching them with open interest. Ethan hasn't even bothered to glance in our direction. He's focused on the tall brunette parked across from him. There's lots of smiling and laughing. A few touches here and there.

My brows rise, recognizing flirty behavior when I see it.

Hmm. Is it possible that I'm jumping the gun here? Just because Ethan is at the library with a girl, it doesn't mean jack shit. Sydney and I are doing the same thing, and we're totally platonic. There is absolutely no flirting going on at all.

Much to my disappointment.

Just as I'm about to disregard the situation as wishful thinking on my part and get back to work, Ethan leans across the table and plants a kiss on the girl's lips.

One Mississippi.

Two Mississippi.

Three Mississippi.

Four—

What the actual fuck?

A kiss like that definitely constitutes cheating.

And right out in the open at the damn library, no less?

This guy is un-fucking-believable. I'm half-tempted to stomp over there and knock him upside his head. Doesn't he realize that his girlfriend is sitting on the other side of the room? Sydney could swing around at any moment and see them making out.

What a jackass.

I'm knocked from those thoughts when the girl across from me clears her throat. My distracted attention slices to her.

"Did you say something?" she asks.

I certainly hope not.

"Umm," *what to do—what to do*, "yeah. I think we've plowed through enough for the night. We should probably head out so you can study for that quiz before it gets too late." I'm rambling, and it's not a good look for me. "We can pick this back up tomorrow or whenever you have a couple of hours of free time." When she continues to stare like a horn has sprouted on my forehead, I slam my laptop closed. I want to get out of here before she catches sight of her cheating asshole of a boyfriend. Honestly, I should be delighted to point out what's going on behind her back.

Literally.

I know exactly how the situation would play out. She'd dump his ass in two minutes flat. Maybe then I'd have a real shot at fucking Sydney out of my system. Where she's concerned, I'm not picky. I'd be more than happy to be rebound sex. This chick has lingered in my thoughts for way too long.

But still...as well as this situation could work out for me, I'm reluctant to take that approach. The last thing I want to do is hurt her.

If her brows weren't pinched together to begin with, they're practically touching now. "You want to leave already? We've only been here for," she glances at her phone, "two hours, and there's still more to do."

I shrug as my gaze flickers in the couple's direction. Hopefully, they're no longer sucking face.

Nope. They're still going at it like two cats in heat. Any moment, he's going to crawl across the table and mount her for all to see.

"Brayden?" Impatience simmers in Sydney's voice.

My gaze snaps back to hers. A frown tugs at the edges of her lips as she swings around and glances in the direction I've been staring. I know the moment she catches sight of them. Her muscles tense.

Mine do as well, waiting to see how this situation will play out. I'm half expecting her to jump up, storm over there, and punch Ethan in the face before beating the crap out of the unlucky chick. If there's anyone who could do it, it's Sydney. She's not afraid to throw down.

That probably shouldn't be so hot.

Instead of doing exactly that, she calmly twists toward me on her chair. Her face has morphed into an expressionless mask. For the first time in three years, I have no idea what she's thinking. It's disconcerting to say the least.

"Let's get back to work," she murmurs.

Well, that's certainly not the reaction I was expecting.

It takes a moment to find my voice. "Correct me if I'm wrong, but isn't that your boyfriend over there?" Not that I want to rub the situation in her face, but I need a little clarification as to what's going on.

A long silence stretches between us as her teeth scrape against her lower lip. She mumbles something under her breath that I can't quite make out.

I tilt my head and cup my ear. "Sorry, I didn't catch that. What did you say?"

Hot color stings her cheeks as she repeats, "We broke up a month ago."

I blink, my mind drifting back to our previous conversation at lunch. "But this afternoon—"

"I said he was busy," she grumbles, "not that we were together."

My eyes narrow. "You know what that's called?" I don't give her time to respond. "Semantics. Why is this the first time I'm hearing about your breakup?" A goddamn month later.

A month!

She jerks her shoulders and avoids all eye contact. I bet she's wishing she'd taken me up on my offer to get out of here. "Because my personal life is none of your damn business."

Wanna bet?

Whether Sydney realizes it or not, this bit of information changes everything between us.

It's oh-so-tempting to rub my hands together with anticipation. Since I'm not in the mood to get punched in the face, I refrain.

Just barely.

Chapter Four

SYDNEY

With the back of my head resting against the cool marble of the grave marker, I stare at the trees in the distance. By now, they've lost all of their leaves and the branches look strangely barren. The vast stretch of sky is a bright azure color as puffy, cotton candy looking clouds pass overhead. A warm October breeze wafts against my skin as birds chirp and bees drone nearby, buzzing from one flower to another. They must have figured out that there's always an endless supply of fresh bouquets here.

As much as I hate coming to the cemetery, I do it twice a month like clockwork. Just like I have been for the past four years. I can't imagine what it would be like to stop. It would probably feel like a limb that had been freshly amputated. The phantom pain would serve as a perpetual reminder that something integral was missing from my life.

It's not like I can't talk to my brother anywhere, but it always feels like he's with me when I'm sitting against his headstone. Almost like there's a direct line of communication between us. Even though the idea of him being buried six feet beneath the ground fills me with sadness, I think that's the reason I end up here. It's the last place I saw him before he was laid to rest.

Is he resting now?

Sometimes I wonder about that.

It's a depressing thought.

Peter was always so full of life and restless energy. He could make me smile against my will. And I loved him for it. Mom always joked that there was an invisible motor tied to his butt. He never stopped moving. My brother was four years older than me and graduated high school the year before I started as a freshman. Even though a handful of years separated us, we were close. Out of my four brothers, we had the most in common.

It was his love for soccer that prompted me to pick up a ball and kick it around in the backyard. Even as a small child, I wanted to be exactly like him and attempted to emulate everything he did. Soccer is what we bonded over, and, in the end, it's what got me through the pain of his loss.

People say that time heals all wounds. I think it's a lie we tell ourselves to make it through the grief. The realization that it never gets easier would be too much to bear.

"Remember last time, when I told you I thought Lucus had a girlfriend?" I pause as if waiting for him to pipe up with a response. Instead, the cemetery remains eerily silent. "Turns out that my suspicions were right on the money. Mom swung by the Stop and Shop the other day to pick up some groceries and there they were, in the checkout area, heads bent together, whispering to one another." A chuckle slides from my lips. "You know Mom, she took it upon herself to make introductions. Apparently, the girl's name is Holly, and she lives with her parents. She just started working at the grocery store. Trust me when I say Mom got all the deets. Now that the cat is out of the bag, Lucus is talking about getting his own apartment so they can move in together. Mom is trying to hold him off until the summer, but he has a one-track mind. It's kind of cute. Kids," I murmur, picking at a blade of grass before folding it like an accordion. "They grow up so dang fast."

I share everything going on with the family and then in my own life. There's a natural ebb and flow to my voice. Sometimes I'll lapse into silence before picking up the thread of my previous conversation.

I tell him about soccer, knowing he would take pride in my accomplishments. Peter died before he could graduate from college. It's disconcerting to realize that I'm now the same age as him when he passed away.

Instead of dwelling on that uncomfortable thought, I fill him in on my classes. He's the only one I've told about my growing fears that accounting isn't the right career for me. Every day that passes, more doubts mushroom up until it feels like I'm being suffocated by them. Most of the time, I'm able to shove the uncertainties aside and ignore them.

I've always had a good head for math. It comes easy to me. And accounting is the same way. Even though I excel in my classes, I don't particularly find pleasure in them. By the time I realized this, it seemed too late to backtrack and major in something else. If I want to graduate on time, then I need to stay the course. At this point, I'm hoping that I'm wrong and once I start working, everything will fall into place. The prospect of ending up in a career that I hate for the rest of my life is a scary one.

Once I get all my fears off my chest, the tension knotted in my shoulders loosens and I can finally relax. My eyes close as bright sunlight pours down, warming my skin.

Sitting against my brother's gravestone in the cemetery on such a gorgeous autumn afternoon feels wrong. The days I visit should be dark and gloomy, overcast with the threat of severe storms. Sometimes, I search through the upcoming forecast, trying to seek out the most miserable day.

It's like a cosmic joke. No matter what I choose, it turns out to be gorgeous. Always sunny. Even in the dead of winter when everything should look bleak and desolate, the sun will throb in the blue sky and the untouched snow will look like it's sparkling with diamonds. There are times when the tree branches ice over and shimmer in the light. It's resentfully that I'll admit how magical they look.

Nothing in a cemetery should be beautiful.

Even though Peter has been gone for a while, it's still strange that life carried on without him. Wasn't the world supposed to grind to a halt on its axis? Didn't people realize that a vital part of our family had been cut off and removed?

Maybe we managed to pick up the shattered pieces and stumble on without him, but, in a way, we're just like Humpty Dumpty. None of us will ever be put back together again. How is it possible to not fall completely apart when someone is ripped from your lives?

Peter's death rocked the very foundation of our family. There were times when I didn't think I could bear the loss. And my parents...

They were steeped so deeply in grief that it was difficult to witness. There is nothing worse than watching your mother and father—the very same people who are pillars of strength—sob like babies. There were times when I couldn't remember what Mom's face looked like without a constant river of tears flowing down her pale cheeks. Dad retreated quietly into his work. For the first couple of months, it almost seemed like we would splinter apart. Mom was the first to pull herself together before forcing Dad into counseling along with the four of us.

As painful as therapy was, I'm not sure we would have survived the ocean of grief that surrounded us without it. It's all too easy to feel like you're alone and drowning in the darkness.

Even though coming to the cemetery is a lot like picking at a healing scab and making the wound bleed all over again, there isn't a choice in the matter. I refuse to forget about Peter. And talking to him, telling him about all the family gossip makes me feel like he's still here, listening to every word. I can almost imagine his responses, and they make me laugh.

And that's exactly how I want to remember him.

Laughing and full of life.

Chapter Five

BRAYDEN

Harsh breath escapes from my lungs in a rush as I push open the front door and walk inside the house I share off-campus with four other guys. Almost immediately, voices assault my ears. There's nothing uncommon about that. It would be strange if they didn't. Five signatures might be on the rental agreement—Rowan, Carson, Asher, Easton, and yours truly—but at any given time, there's at least a dozen people hanging out. Sometimes guys from the team crash at our place if they need to get away from the dorms or their roommates. There's also usually a handful of die-hard groupies, looking for any lap to settle on.

I'll fully admit that I took advantage of the pussy situation freshman year and delved straight in, sleeping with as many girls as possible. When you're an eighteen-year-old guy and all these females are hanging on you, spreading their legs without the least bit of encouragement, it's hard to say no.

Even after I stopped drinking, the girls remained a constant. But last year, something began to change, and I curtailed all the fucking around. That doesn't mean I stopped dipping my wick completely, but it no longer held the same appeal as it once did. Now, I'm more discriminating. Plus, a dozen or so guys on the team tested positive for chlamydia because they all bang the same groupies. As much as I enjoy screwing, it's not worth an STI. Not even a curable one.

"Hey Kendricks, take over for me," Carson calls out, eyes laser focused on the game he's playing. "I gotta take this call."

I shake my head and point to the guy across from him. "Give it to Asher. I'm sweaty from my run."

Carson's gaze flickers to one of our roommates before he scowls. "No way, he's shit at this game, and he's totally baked."

Asher grins. He can barely crack open his eyes. The guy could easily be blindfolded with dental floss. "He's right, dude. I am *sooo* baked."

I shake my head. "Fine."

As soon as I step into the living room, I notice Kira tucked around the corner on the couch.

Goddamn it.

I shoot Carson a scowl. The motherfucker could have warned me that she was here, lying in wait. I would have avoided coming home at all costs. That's when I remember that I didn't take my phone on my five-mile run.

This girl is the last person I want to deal with. The plan was to hit the showers and delve straight into homework. I'm trying to nudge my GPA up as much as I can before graduation. With six semesters under my belt, I've got my work cut out for me.

I force myself into the living room. As soon as I'm close enough, Carson passes off the controller. I drop onto an empty couch cushion and focus on the screen. Maybe if I ignore her long enough, she'll give up and leave me alone. After I kicked her ass out of my bed the other night, I'm hoping she finally got the hint that I'm not interested in what she's offering up.

I almost snort, knowing that it's an unlikely scenario.

Even though my attention is fastened to the television, I notice her rise from the corner of my eye. A second later, she settles next to me. When her slender hand brushes against my thigh, I know I'm in trouble. I also realize that I need to do something drastic, otherwise this will never end.

But what?

What the hell am I supposed to do?

This chick refuses to take no for an answer.

"Hi, Brayden."

It's tempting to ignore her. Although, it's not in my nature to be a dick. But maybe that's what I need to do. I'm running out of options, and desperate times call for desperate measures.

"Hey," I say in a clipped tone. Hopefully, my whole *I'm not interested in talking to you* vibe is coming across loud and clear.

When I don't keep the conversational ball rolling, she clears her throat and makes a second attempt. "I was wondering if we could talk."

"I'm kind of in the middle of something," I mumble.

Persistence is an attractive quality in the opposite sex, but not to this degree.

Hasn't she ever heard that no means no?

"How about after?"

My lower jaw locks. "I've got to take a shower and hit the books. I don't have time tonight."

Her slender shoulders collapse as she rakes her teeth across her lower lip. A wounded look enters her eyes.

Fuck.

I just want to get out of here.

Hell, I'd leave the damn house if there were someplace else to go. Maybe I should gather up my books and hit the library for a while. Best case scenario, she'll take off when I don't return. Worse case, I'll find her waiting naked in my bed again.

Where the hell is Carson?

Seriously, who the hell is he talking to on the phone? Who would call that guy?

He needs to get his ass back in here so I can leave.

The moment my blond teammate steps into the living room, I jerk to my feet and pass off the controller. I make it three steps before slender fingers lock around my bicep, halting me in my tracks.

"Please, Brayden?" Her tongue darts out to moisten her lips. "I just want to talk for a few minutes."

Air escapes from my lungs in a slow hiss as I plow my hand through my hair. I'm so damn tempted to shake her off. Instead, I keep all of my frustration bottled up inside.

"Kira," I say patiently, "we've been through this before and nothing has changed."

Her blue eyes turn glassy as wetness fills them. The tears somehow manage to simultaneously piss me off and make me feel like a grade A asshole. I have a sister who is two years younger than I am and a sophomore at Western. I'd beat the piss out of any jerk who caused her a moment of heartache. That being said, I hope she would have enough self-respect not to throw herself at a guy who has made it perfectly clear that he's not interested.

"Why don't you want me? Aren't I pretty enough for you? Smart enough? What is it? What do I have to do so that you'll give me a chance?" Not only does desperation fill her eyes, it wafts around her like a stink. "Just tell me what I have to do. I've been in love with you since freshman year."

Fucking hell.

How am I supposed to answer that?

"You don't love me," I mutter as heat stings my cheeks. I glance at the guys sitting around in the living room. Carson and Easton are smirking. Crosby is doing his damnedest to hold back his laughter. "You don't even know me." Not really. The guy she wants to be with is Brayden Kendricks, wide receiver for the Western Wildcats. The football player who will most likely get drafted by the NFL this spring.

All Kira sees is a handsome and popular façade. This girl doesn't know the first thing about me. We've talked a handful of times and they've all been surface-level conversations. It's ridiculous that she would even think she has such strong feelings for me.

I shift my weight, wishing that she wasn't so intent on forcing this uncomfortable discussion. Especially in front of a roomful of teammates. I'll never live this down.

"If you gave me a chance," she steps closer, her fingers squeezing my arm, "I could make you happy."

My heartbeat picks up speed. This girl is really starting to freak me out. I've jokingly thought about taking out a restraining order. I might actually have to go through with it.

"Yo Kendricks, maybe you should give her a chance," Asher calls out. "She seems like a real sweetheart."

I shoot him a scowl. Of all the fucking times for him to wake up and take part in the conversation, it would have to be now.

It feels like a thousand-pound weight has settled on my chest and the walls are closing in on me. I have no idea where the words come from, but they're shooting out of my mouth before I can stop them.

"I'm already dating someone," I blurt.

"What?" She straightens to her full height, which is still a good eight inches shorter than I am. "You're going out with another girl?" Before I can respond—with what, I have no idea—she fires off another question. "When did this happen and why didn't I know about it?" Her eyes narrow to slits. "I haven't seen you with anyone lately."

It's like she can smell my deceit a mile away. Maybe this was a mistake.

No, this is my only chance to break free. No matter what happens, I need to stick to the lie.

"Well," I improvise, "we've been, you know, keeping it on the downlow. We didn't want to go public until everything was for sure." I need this girl to swallow this down—hook, line, and sinker. What I don't need is for her to fire off more questions that I don't have answers to. "So," slowly I inch away from her, "as you can see, there's no—"

"Who?" Her hand falls away from my arm before her fist settles on her cocked hip.

"*Who?*" I echo, gaze darting away.

Whose name can I pull out of my ass?

This whole lying thing is more difficult than it appears. Sweat breaks out across my brow as my mind goes blank.

"Yeah," her voice escalates, "I want to know who this girl is."

Most of the guys in the other room turn and stare. They're all ears. You think one of these assholes could jump in and help save me from myself?

Nope. Not a damn one.

"Does it really matter? The point here is that I'm in a committed relationship and couldn't be happier."

"Actually, it does. I want to know her name." The way she tilts her head while eyeing me up reminds me of one of those sly raptors from the dinosaur movies. Kind of scary. "Is there a reason you don't want to tell me?"

No, crazy pants. No reason at all.

It's all together possible that I've made a tactical error in judgment. I've got two choices here—I either abandon this sinking ship and admit that I made the whole thing up or I rally and put on a convincing show, so she'll leave me alone once and for all.

Hey, it worked for Sydney. She pretended to be dating her ex-boyfriend for a damn month and I was never the wiser.

Sydney.

"Sydney Daniels," I blurt.

"Sydney Daniels?" The corners of her lips sink into a frown as she silently racks her brain.

That was probably the last name I should have thrown out. "Yup."

Just when I think she might drop the subject and leave me alone, she snaps, "Wait a minute, isn't that the soccer player from our accounting class?"

"Yeah," I admit weakly, "that's her."

"Hmm." She shifts her stance and taps her pointer finger against her lips. "Looks like I'll be having a little chat with her for stealing my man."

Oh...fuck. Well, that's not good.

I scrunch my face and shake my head. "I don't think that's necessary, do you?"

"It's *completely* necessary," she growls. The tears have dried up as anger dances across her features.

Why the hell did I let Sydney's name slip out?

Any other girl on this campus would have been thrilled to be my pretend girlfriend.

Sydney, on the other hand?

She'd rather gnaw off her own arm to get away from me. Make that both arms.

This situation has disaster written all over it. And I have no one to blame but myself.

Chapter Six

BRAYDEN

For the umpteenth time, I glance around the crowded party, searching for Sydney's blonde head. Why isn't she responding to my texts or calls?

I need to find her before Kira does. What irritates me most is that you know damn well that girl will be all over Sydney in order to verify the information. Like she can't just take my word for it.

Like I'm some kind of liar who makes shit up.

Well...maybe in this case.

My first mistake was trying to pull off this lie. The second was dragging a chick who hates me into this mess. Instead of enjoying the party, my head is on a constant swivel. I have no idea if she'll go along with the tiny fib I've told. Although, if I were a betting man, I'd say probably not.

If Kira discovers that I lied, it will be game over and I'll never shake her loose. That thought is enough to send icy tendrils of panic scampering down my spine. There's no way I can put up with eight more months of her stalker-like tendencies. I'll have to move home just to get away from her.

What a fucking mess.

From the corner of my eye, I catch a glimpse of long blonde hair and my head whips in that direction. I'm about to take off like a man on a mission when the girl turns toward me, and I realize that it's not Sydney.

Damn!

Everything inside me deflates.

Twenty more minutes drag by without a sighting. I've taken up sentinel near the entryway so I can keep an eye on the door. My gaze is coasting over the crowd for the millionth time when it skims over a dark head.

Wait a minute.

My attention resettles on the girl in question.

What the hell is Elle doing here?

All thoughts of Sydney disappear from my head as I shove my way toward my sister.

When she was a senior in high school, she applied at several state universities, but I encouraged her to attend Western. How else could I keep an eye on her?

Most of the guys around here understand that she's completely off-limits. And if they don't, I'm more than happy to help them come to that realization.

With my fists.

I crane my neck, attempting to catch sight of who she's talking and laughing with. More than likely, it's one of the girls from her dorm floor. She's made a few good friends and they usually travel in a pack, which is smart. A lone female makes for an easy target at one of these parties.

Her head is bent close to whoever she's speaking with. I push a few people out of my way until I'm able to catch sight of a broad shoulder and muscular arm.

Yeah...that's not going to happen. I'll be breaking up this little love fest before this asshole can get any ideas in his head. Just as I shove another person out of my way, the dude in question comes into view and relief instantly floods through me as my footsteps slow.

Carson.

False alarm. If there's anyone I trust with my sister, it's him. The guy is like family. He hung out at my house while we were growing up more than he did at his own. Carson is an only child, and his parents work a shit ton of hours. I always got the feeling that he was lonely. Mom would joke that he was her unofficial third child. Elle is more like a sister to him than anything else.

"Hey," I greet, pulling up alongside them and interrupting their conversation.

They both startle at my unexpected appearance.

Almost nonchalantly, Carson takes a step away from her before shoving his hands into the pockets of his shorts. "Hi. What's up, man?"

"Not much," I mutter, glancing around.

Now that I realize there's nothing to be concerned about, thoughts of Sydney rush back in to fill my head. The only positive in this situation is that I haven't caught sight of Kira. I thought for sure she would be here by now, waiting to pounce. I'm not naive enough to think that my announcement has finally done the trick. There's no way she's going to roll over and give up at this point. She's too invested. "You haven't seen Sydney around, have you?"

Carson's brows slide together. He knows exactly why it's imperative that I nail down her location. "Nope. Still haven't been able to get hold of her, huh?"

I shake my head. "She's avoiding my calls."

"Strange that she would do that," Carson says with a smirk. "She really seems to enjoy your company."

"Who's Sydney?" my sister cuts in, gaze bouncing between us.

My attention flickers to her. There's no way in hell I'm telling Elle about this situation. She'd probably laugh herself silly. And then she'd turn around and tell our mother. Like I need that.

No, thanks.

Instead of answering, I pull out my phone and text the blonde for what feels like the dozenth time in the past two hours. Do you think she could bother with a response?

Of course not. She'd much rather ignore my ass and make me sweat.

A big smile breaks out across Elle's face. "Well, well, well." She turns her attention to Carson as laughter bubbles up in her throat. "It looks like my brother has a crush."

Oh, for fuck's sake.

Before Carson can open his trap—because the last thing I need at the moment is him egging her on—I grumble, "I do *not* have a crush."

Mirth dances in my friend's eyes. I can almost see the temptation to add kerosene to this particular fire.

"Does Mom know about this?" Elle asks.

I'm reminded once again why I prefer not to party with my sister. I don't need her watching every move I make and reporting back to our parent with her findings.

When she arches a brow, I roll my eyes. "She's my partner for a project. It's nothing more than that."

Elle tilts her head. The suspicious look in her eyes says that she's not buying what I'm attempting to sell. "And you need to talk to her about a class project on a Saturday night while celebrating your win from this afternoon?"

Fair enough. That sounds lame even to my own ears. Obviously, I should have come up with a more plausible explanation. This one isn't going to cut it.

How has this become my life?

No, I'm serious.

Taking out a restraining order would have been a hell of a lot easier than all this subterfuge. Clearly, I'm not good at it.

With a glare, I turn the conversation around on her. "What are you doing here? I thought we agreed you would stay away from the football parties."

Not to mention, the football *players*.

Make it guys in general and we'll call it a day.

Something flickers in her dark eyes before being snuffed out as she lifts a slender shoulder. "Do you remember my friend Madison?"

Nope. Not at all. I couldn't pick her out of a lineup that consisted of two girls.

When I shake my head, she gives an impatient huff. "Anyway, her boyfriend is on the football team. I think his nickname is Sausage."

Right.

The dude's actual name is Kevin Anders. One of the first practices of his freshman season, he inhaled so many damn sausages for breakfast that he ended up barfing them up all over the turf. Coach Richards just shook his head and ordered him to clean up the mess. It doesn't matter how many years—or decades—pass, he will never live down that poor decision which is exactly how he earned his nickname.

If the guy is lucky, Coach will send him onto the field during the last quarter for a snap or two if we're up by enough points. From what I've gathered, he's not working with a lot of brain cells. And he's definitely not the type of guy I want hanging around my sister. Then again, I can't think of any dudes I'd want her spending time with. Luckily, that hasn't been a problem. If she's messing around, it's not in front of my face. And I've never caught wind of any gossip making the rounds on campus either.

"Did you come with friends?" I glance around, wondering how she ended up with Carson.

She waves a hand toward the kitchen. "They went to get something to drink. They'll be back soon."

Just what I need to deal with—a bunch of underage girls getting drunk off wine spritzers or some equally sugary drink. Cleaning up their puke will be the perfect cap to this disastrous evening.

I narrow my eyes. "Are they bringing a beverage back for you?"

Elle meets my stare head on. She isn't easily intimidated. Not even by me. "Is that a roundabout way of asking if I plan to drink tonight?"

I give her a tight-lipped smile. "Yup, that's exactly what I want to know, squirt."

When a flash of grief fills her eyes, guilt swiftly slices through me.

She draws herself up to her full height before saying stiffly, "You know I don't drink."

No, she doesn't. Not after what happened to our father. Elle doesn't even like it when Mom has a bottle of wine in the house.

Fuck. This situation with Kira is making me lose my damn mind. I'm tempted to drag a hand across my face.

"Sorry," I mumble, feeling like an asshole.

An awkward silence falls over the three of us. I'm about to apologize for a second time when a flash of wheat-colored hair catches my attention. Relief instantly floods through me.

"All right, gotta go." I take two steps before swinging back around.

My gaze locks on Carson as I stab a finger in my sibling's direction. "Keep an eye on her."

"I don't need a babysitter!" she yells.

Since I'm not about to get drawn into an argument, I don't bother with a response. Elle might not think she needs someone to look out for her, but she does. My sister is too damn pretty for her own good. When she showed up on campus freshman year, I had to knock more than a few skulls together before word caught on not to mess with her. I'm happy to report that the guys now steer clear. She's no longer on their radar and that's just the way I like it.

Whatever choice words Elle continues to spew get lost in the raucous noise of the party as I shove my way through the thick crowd in order to reach Sydney. Who knows, maybe she'll surprise me and help me out of this sticky situation.

Then again, maybe pigs will fly out of my ass.

Statistically speaking, the chances of swine taking flight are astronomically higher.

Chapter Seven

SYDNEY

It's Saturday night and I'm more than ready to cut loose. I need a drink to help shake off the heaviness of visiting my brother's grave. It's like this every time. It'll take a couple of days to tamp down all of the sadness and grief attempting to break loose beneath the surface. There would probably be less emotional upheaval if I didn't visit quite so often. But how can I do that?

The guilt alone would eat me alive. And part of me likes sitting against the smooth surface of his headstone. Sharing my life makes me feel closer to him. For a few minutes, I can pretend that he's not really gone. I keep waiting for the pain of his loss to fade, but it's been four years and that has yet to occur. I'm beginning to doubt it ever will. I think the grief is something I'll carry around with me forever.

So, yeah...I need a drink. Pronto. Maybe a couple of them to take the edge off and help me forget.

Arm in arm, Demi and I stroll up the sidewalk to the football house. As much as I don't want to be here, my bestie told Rowan that we would make an appearance at some point in the evening. She also assured me that we wouldn't have to stay long. I plan on holding her to that.

My phone vibrates in my back pocket for the umpteenth time

today. Irritation swiftly bubbles up inside me as I grit my teeth, not bothering to pull out the cell and glance at the screen. There's no need to. I already know who it is.

Brayden Kendricks has been blowing up my phone for the last two days.

What the hell is that guy's problem?

Does he think we're suddenly friends and he can talk to me whenever he likes?

No, thanks.

Since he refuses to comprehend what my silence implies, it looks like we'll need to have a discussion as to what it means when someone ignores your advances. Although, that won't be happening tonight. I have zero interest in dealing with him at the moment. Not when I'm already feeling emotionally raw.

He tried to catch me at class the other day, but I slipped out of the room a few minutes early so I could meet up with my advisor to discuss my credit situation. All she did was reconfirm that if I scrap the accounting degree and get out of business all together, it'll end up tacking on an additional year of classes. There is no way I want to stick around Western for that long. For all intents and purposes, I'm stuck. I keep reassuring myself that it won't be as bad as I think. I'm actually a whiz at crunching numbers. The question is—how much will I enjoy doing it forty hours a week?

It's yet another problem to wash away with a massive glass of alcohol. Just like when it comes to dulling my grief, it'll be a temporary measure. A flimsy Band-Aid until I can work through everything in my head.

When my phone buzzes thirty seconds later, Demi asks, "Aren't you going to answer that?"

Not a chance in hell.

"Nope." I have zero intentions of responding to Brayden's texts or calls. This is exactly why I was reluctant to give him my digits in the first place. If he thinks he can wear me down and we'll hook up, he couldn't be more wrong.

"What if it's important?"

"It's not."

With a curious expression marring her brow, she shrugs and drops the subject.

It's oh so tempting to block his ass. The thought brings a smile to my face. That would serve him right for making such a nuisance of himself. Maybe some girls—all right, most girls—clamor for his attention, but I'm not one of them. Not after what happened freshman year. As soon as that thought pops into my head, I shove it away. It's just another thing I refuse to dwell on.

After climbing five steps onto a rickety front porch, we wait to be admitted inside. The freshman football player who is supposed to be manning the door is making out hot and heavy with a girl. His tongue is shoved so far down her throat that I'm pretty sure he's touching her tonsils.

I clear my throat, hoping they'll splinter apart, but that doesn't occur. If anything, the sucking action becomes more voracious. I'm almost impressed with his hoovering skills. But also slightly repulsed. It's doubtful there's a drop of spit in that girl's mouth.

Eww.

Demi gives me a little side-eye. "Maybe we should just walk in?"

"Probably." We slip inside while their mouths are still fastened. "I think Rowan needs to find someone a little more dedicated to his job."

Demi snorts. "I'll be sure to pass that along."

We don't get more than four steps inside the packed first floor when someone wraps their arms around Demi. That someone—in case you're wondering—is Rowan. A smile springs to her lips as he moves in for a kiss.

And that would be my cue to leave.

You would never know it from Demi's behavior that there was a time in the not-so-distant past when she couldn't stand to be in the same room with Rowan. It's almost amazing how much has changed in such a short span of time.

"I'm going to grab a much-needed drink," I shout, attempting to be heard over the pulsing beat of music. "You want anything?"

It's not a surprise when Demi shakes her head. She's never been much of a drinker. With a shrug, I take off through the mass of students packed in here like sardines. Is it too much to hope that we only have to stay for thirty minutes before taking off? I'm sure there are a ton of other parties happening around campus. I'd rather be anywhere but here. Plus, I'm actively trying to avoid Brayden, and that's difficult to do at his own house.

At this point, it's become a game.

Let's see how long it takes for him to track me down. Fingers crossed he'll grow bored and move onto easier prey.

I pass by the congested living room on my way to the kitchen. I wave and say hello to a couple of people I recognize. A handful of my teammates have shown up to help celebrate the victory on the turf this afternoon. They don't care which Wildcat team won, they're just happy to toss back a few drinks and get their party on. And then there are two girls I recognize from my classes. I've been here enough times to know that a makeshift bar will be set up at the back of the house, stocked with cheap liquor. I'm looking forward to an icy cold drink. Normally, when I'm out, I'll have a beer or two, but tonight calls for something more potent.

We're talking shots.

After five minutes of fighting my way through the unwashed masses, I've almost reached my destination. Just as the brightly shining beacon that is the keg comes into sight, a girl with long, tawny-colored hair steps in front of me, effectively blocking my way. Since there are so many people crammed in the space, I don't think much of it. As I try to sidestep her, she quickly shadows the motion so I can't move past. When I slide in the opposite direction, she follows suit. That's when I realize that this chick is deliberately messing with me.

What the hell?

I give her a quick once over. Other than looking vaguely familiar, I have no idea who she is. What I do know is that she'd better move her carcass before I lose my shit. I'm not in the mood to mess around.

Not tonight.

"Excuse me," I raise my voice over the pumping music, "I'm trying to get through."

"Is your name Sydney?"

"Yeah." With a frown, I search her face more carefully. That's when recognition hits. This girl is in one of my classes. Coincidentally, it's the same one I have with Brayden. Accounting. I've never spoken to her before, but I've noticed the way she hangs all over him. It would be hard not to. She'd probably crawl into his lap and burrow there if he allowed her to do it. Her behavior has always struck me as needy and clingy. Although, Brayden is such an attention whore, I'm sure he gets off on it.

Eww. I just vomited in my mouth. The last thing I want to think about is what Brayden gets off on. I shift my stance, willing away the horrific image.

Before I can ask any further questions, she says, "I was wondering if we could talk for a few minutes."

Talk? About what? I don't even know this girl.

"You want to speak with me?" With a frown, I press a hand to my chest as the party continues to rage on around us. "Why?"

Her tongue darts out to moisten her lips as she sidles closer. "I wanted to discuss the Brayden situation with you."

The Brayden situation?

What is she talking about?

More strangely than that...how am *I* involved in it?

Is this chick drunk? Maybe high?

I tilt my head and scrutinize her pupils. I'm not a medical professional, but they certainly don't look dilated, and she doesn't smell like a brewery. I do a careful sniff test. There's no skunky scent permeating from her either.

Well, I'm stumped.

"Just to be clear, there is no," I use my fingers to make air quotes, "*Brayden situation*. Honestly, I'm not even sure why you'd want to discuss the guy with me."

A hopeful glint enters her eyes as she steps even closer, invading more of my space. "Wait a minute—aren't you dating Brayden Kendricks?"

A bark of laughter explodes from my lips. As I open my mouth to tell her that I am most certainly *not* dating the dark-haired football player—that I would *never* date him—firm lips collide with mine, cutting off any further protest.

Chapter Eight

BRAYDEN

Every muscle in Sydney's body goes rigid as my mouth crashes onto hers. One arm snakes around her waist as I haul her close. Her eyes widen before narrowing when she realizes who has a firm hold on her.

That would be when her struggles begin in earnest.

I almost shake my head at my own stupidity. This girl is going to fight me tooth and nail.

Undeterred by her response, I sweep my tongue across the seam of her lips. When she presses them together, I pull away enough to whisper, "Open for me."

"Are you insane?" she snarls in response.

Bingo.

The moment she snaps at me, I take the opportunity to delve inside.

Am I taking my own life into my hands?

You bet your damn ass I am. But it's a risk I'm willing to take.

My tongue sweeps inside to tangle with her own. This is where I need to be cautious. A quick retreat might become necessary. I wouldn't put it past Sydney to bite me.

Hard.

I give Kira a little side-eye, hoping this affectionate display will be enough to satisfy her curiosity and that it won't become necessary to take this charade any further. The entire issue can be laid to rest, and we can all move on with our lives.

What?

It could happen.

Kira continues to watch us like a hawk as I lock lips with Sydney. Her arms are folded across her ample chest and her eyes are narrowed in speculation. She doesn't look the least bit convinced.

Which is a problem, because I'm not sure how much longer I can keep the blonde subdued. Any moment, she's going to break loose, and then I'll probably be sporting a black eye as a party favor. Just a little reminder not to tangle with this chick ever again.

Sydney's steely palms slap against my chest before she gives me a hard shove, attempting to fight her way free of my embrace. Left without further recourse, I break contact. Her wide gaze searches mine in confusion.

"I need you to go with this," I mutter under my breath.

Before I can explain the situation, a perturbed voice interrupts. "So, you two really are a thing?"

Kira.

Damn. I was kind of hoping she would have taken off by now.

I clear my throat as my gaze stays fastened onto the feisty female in my arms. "Yup, it's official. We're together."

Sydney's eyes widen. "*What—*"

"Are you being serious, dude?" Asher's deep voice booms over the crowd and cuts her off. "Like you're legit seeing someone? When did you decide to be monotonous?" That guy always seems to appear exactly when I don't need him to.

"I think you meant to say *monogamous*," I mutter.

"Same damn thing," he says with a snort.

I glance reluctantly at him. Given the fact that we're a few hours into this party, he looks surprisingly clear-eyed. He has a chick tucked beneath each brawny arm. Their hands are pressed against his chest as they stare up at me owlishly, as if even they can't believe I've decided to get serious about someone.

For fuck's sake. Is it really that difficult to believe I might be interested in settling down?

Sydney tries again. "I think—"

I crush her stiff body against mine before dropping a kiss against the top of her head. "That it's time for everyone to know the truth? I couldn't agree more, babe."

With a huffed-out breath, she tilts her head to meet my gaze before narrowing her eyes.

Asher shakes his head as if he's still having a hard time wrapping his brain around this new development. "I never thought I'd see the day. First Michaels and now you. One by one, we're all falling to the wayside. It's like an epidemic. When the hell did this happen? Why all the secrecy?"

With each added question, more people take interest and gather around like we're a circus sideshow act. For fuck's sake, my dating life isn't *that* interesting.

Go back to your lives, people. There's nothing to see here.

Someone needs to give Asher a beer. He's entirely too sober if he's bombarding me with this many questions. It's a real shocker that he can remain so focused.

"That's exactly what I was wondering," Kira pipes up. "Why keep it a secret?"

I glare at the tawny-haired girl, hoping she'll shut her pie hole. I've had about as much as I can take from her. She's the reason I'm in this mess to begin with. Now she's just adding to it for shits and giggles.

"Looks like congratulations are in order, dude. If you're looking to be tied down, then I'm happy for you. I guess that means more chicks for me. See? Sometimes you gotta look at the bright side of things." There's a pause. "Although, I don't think I'd mind being strapped down and restrained by that one." He winks at Sydney. "Hey, beautiful."

A growl rumbles up from my chest. I would be more than happy to knock those thoughts from Asher's head. I don't give a damn if he's joking around or not.

Just as I'm about to break up the growing crowd, Elle pushes her way through the throng.

Her wide gaze bounces from me to Sydney and then back again. "I knew it!" she crows. "I *knew* something was going on with you and this girl! Project my butt!"

I glance at Carson, who has sidled up behind her. His shoulders shake with silent laughter. He's the one who put this cockamamie idea in my head. If there's anyone to blame for this mess, it's him.

"We need to talk," Sydney hisses, "*in private*."

"How about I get you a drink and we talk after?" More like a few drinks to dull the anger burning brightly in her eyes. Although, I'm not even sure alcohol will douse those flames.

"Now, Brayden."

Well, damn.

Chapter Nine

SYDNEY

Holy shit, did that actually happen?

My fingers brush across my lips where the faint taste of him continues to linger. I'll admit— albeit privately— that I've secretly wondered what it would be like to kiss Brayden. That being said, I never imagined I'd actually find out.

This feels more like a dream.

Or maybe a nightmare.

All I know is that I need to get to the bottom of what's going on before it can spiral any further out of control.

Like it hasn't already?

I almost groan.

The moment his fingers wrap around mine, a little sizzle of electricity dances down my spine. Before I can blast him into next week, he's dragging me through clumps of people toward the staircase. A few brave—or drunk—ones clap him on the back and congratulate him. Most aren't interested in being run over by two hundred pounds of muscled man barreling through. I have to hasten my steps to keep pace with him as we head to the second floor. My head spins. I can't believe this is happening. I throw a furtive glance over my shoulder at the gathered crowd. A good number of them continue to watch us with ardent interest. A few hold up their phones to snap photos.

Do you know what these people are probably thinking?

That we're going upstairs to have sex.

Ugh.

The sooner this situation is cleared up, the better. There's no way I can deal with everyone on campus thinking we're a couple.

Brayden moves steadily up the staircase until we hit the second-floor landing and turn to the right before walking down the hallway. We pass by two doors before he reaches for a handle and pushes it open. When I stutter to a halt over the threshold, he huffs out a breath and yanks me into the room. Once sealed inside, the music and noise from downstairs fades. It's a relief when he releases my fingers and my hand can drift back to my side. I stare at him and wait for a rational explanation as to why he would tell people we were together.

Seconds creep by. When he remains silent, I throw my arms wide and explode. "Oh my god! What the hell was that about?"

He winces before plowing a hand through his hair. "Look, I'm sorry. It got a little out of control."

"*A little out of control?*" I echo with disbelief. Is this guy for real? "That scene was *totally* out of control!"

"You do realize," he says mildly, "that none of this would have happened if you had returned my calls."

My eyes widen until they feel like they might fall right out of my head. I jab a finger at him. "Are you actually trying to blame *me* for your lies?"

The nerve of this guy!

He sucks in a deep breath before gradually releasing it. As he does, his broad shoulders collapse. "No, I'm not. For what it's worth, I'm sorry that I dragged you into this mess. I didn't expect everything to go down like that."

"Like what? What didn't you expect?"

Instead of answering the question, he asks one of his own. "You know the girl you were talking to downstairs? The one from our accounting class?"

I jerk my head in a nod.

"Her name is Kira, and she's been after me for a while. I've told her a thousand times that I have zero interest in doing anything with her, but she refuses to take no for an answer. The chick is relentless."

Uh-huh. I still don't understand how this affects me.

When I remain silent, he blurts, "She won't leave me alone. It's turned out to be a real problem."

"Seriously? One of your fangirls has become a little overzealous and suddenly this is an issue?"

"I found her in my bed the other night." When I fail to react, he snaps, "*Naked.*"

"Awww...that sounds terrible. Girls are literally falling onto their backs and spreading their legs wide for you." I cock my head to the side. "However do you deal with it?"

His lips flatten into a tight line as he narrows his eyes. "That's the issue, Sydney. I don't *want* to deal with strange girls sneaking into my room and lying in wait. Wouldn't you be unsettled if you found a naked guy in your bed?"

"I don't know," I say with a shrug. "I guess it would depend on who the guy was."

If it's possible, his lips smash together even more. When he continues to glare, I shift my stance, uncomfortable under his relentless scrutiny.

"Fine, I would be upset," I grumble reluctantly. "There. Are you happy now?" Although, I'm still confused as to how I got dragged into this mess.

"I'd hoped after I kicked her out of my room that she would finally get it through her head that nothing was ever going to happen, but she was back at my place the other night, confessing her love for me and wanting to know why I won't give her a chance."

All right, so maybe I can understand his concern. Those are definitely stalker vibes I'm beginning to feel.

"So," I say carefully, piecing everything together, "you told her you were dating someone."

Me.

Brayden told this girl that he was dating me.

As bad as I'm starting to feel for him—because clearly that girl is cuckoo for Cocoa Puffs—there is no way I'm getting sucked into a situation that has nothing to do with me. "Forget it." When he opens his mouth to argue, I shake my head. "I just got out of a relationship. I'm not interested in having people think that I'm delving headfirst into another. And even if I was," I add, wanting to make sure we're both on the same page, "it wouldn't be with someone like you."

"Excuse me?" His brows shoot up. "Did you just say *someone like me*?"

Do I really need to explain this to him?

By the pinched expression on his face, apparently so.

"Come on, Brayden...you're not the kind of guy I would ever go for. You're a manwhore." I hold up my hands and quickly add, "That's not judgment on my part, it's just the unvarnished truth. You're free to sleep with as many girls as you want. Have sex with the entire university, for all I care. But do us both a favor and don't pretend you're something that you're not, all right? You don't do serious."

"I am not a manwhore," he says in halting tones as if I've truly offended him, which is rich.

Laughter bubbles up from my lips.

Brayden folds his arms across his chest and glares. "All the girls I've slept with knew the score up front. And they were cool with it. Don't act like I'm out there, taking advantage of these chicks."

He's missing the point entirely.

"I never said you were taking advantage of anyone. I simply pointed out that you like to sleep around and share the love. Maybe it shouldn't be so surprising when some psycho chick gets obsessed."

"For your information," he grits out, "I never slept with Kira."

"Maybe it would help if you did," I snicker. "She'd probably lose interest by the third thrust."

"Hardy-har-har. You're hilarious, you know that?"

Now that I've made my position perfectly clear, I inch toward the bedroom door. "You seem to have gotten yourself into a real quandary, and I don't want any part of it. So...I'm just gonna—"

As I reach for the handle, he blurts, "Wait!"

I glance over my shoulder, impatient to get the hell out of here. "What?"

"Please," he swallows, desperation flashing across his face. "I really need your help. It would only be for a couple of weeks. That's it."

It's official—Brayden has gone off the deep end. We're not even friends; why would I entertain the idea of helping him out for even a minute?

If anything, he's dragged me into a mess I want no part of. And if he won't clear up the situation, I will. And then I'll do what I should have from the very beginning and block his damn ass on my phone. From here on out, we can work solo on our project. It's not like there's a ton left to do.

"Sorry, this sounds more like a *you* problem than a *me* problem. But don't worry, you're a resourceful guy. I have total faith that you'll figure something out."

For a second time, I reach for the handle. Before I can make a clean getaway, Brayden springs forward and wraps his fingers around my shoulders before swinging me around. My eyes widen and I stifle a yelp of surprise at the way he's manhandling me.

"I've already told Kira that we're dating. If you go downstairs and say differently, she'll never leave me alone." His grip tightens. "Would you really do that to me?"

"Yes." It's not even a question.

His jaw locks, but he still doesn't set me free. "I can help you."

Other than staying out of my way, there's nothing I need Brayden's assistance with.

Just as I'm about to demand that he remove his hands or risk losing digits, he asks, "Were you able to find a model for your art project?"

My brows shoot up into my hairline.

How the hell did he—

Oh. Right. Lunch. He overheard me on the phone. More like he was listening intently.

"Not yet, but I've got plenty of feelers out," I say airily as if I'm not concerned in the slightest. "I'm just waiting for the responses to roll in." The truth of the matter is that I'm waiting on one more call. The fact that Leo hasn't bothered to get back to me isn't a good sign. For obvious reasons, I won't be sharing that information with Brayden.

He drags me closer. "I'll model for you."

"You?" I scoff. My belly hollows out at the thought of seeing him naked. "Model?" I shake my head, unwilling to entertain the idea.

"Sure, why not?"

I twist out of his arms and break his hold before blowing out a long breath. "Have you forgotten that I need someone who's willing to sit for me in the nude?" I allow that bit of information to sink in before adding, "The best pieces from the portfolio will be displayed at the art gallery on campus at the end of the year."

Indecision flickers over his expression before he straightens to his full height. "Is that supposed to be a deterrent? FYI, there's no shame in my game."

I'm sure there's not, but that doesn't necessarily mean he wants hundreds of people to see naked sketches of him. That's one of the reasons the fine art students use professional models.

Who don't attend Western University.

And certainly aren't high-profile football players looking to turn pro.

Unconsciously, my gaze drifts over the length of him, starting with his handsome face. Brayden has high, chiseled cheekbones and thick eyelashes. His mouth is full and his chin strong. As if that wasn't the most arresting part of him, there's his muscular body. Broad shoulders, a wide chest and tapered waist. My hunch is that there's not an ounce of fat on him.

Fine. Speaking strictly from an artistic perspective, the guy would be an absolute pleasure to draw.

No doubt about it.

But...

That would mean spending more time alone with him. When he tugs me close enough to feel the heat of his body, I snap out of the dangerous thoughts attempting to take root inside my brain.

"You're contemplating it," he says, eyes sharpening on me.

"No," I lie, "I'm not."

With a tilt of his head, he squints as if he's able to pick through my innermost thoughts. It's a disconcerting sensation. "Yeah, you are. Just remember that this situation can be beneficial for both of us."

I'm startled to realize that he's right—I'm actually giving serious consideration to his proposal. Bottom line, I need a model. My project is due in less than a month. Not only am I running out of time, I'm running out of options. Brayden needs someone to be his girlfriend.

His *fake* girlfriend.

The solution neatly solves both of our issues.

"What's the problem?" he asks. "Not sure I'll measure up in that department? Need a little proof that you'll have more than enough to draw? Maybe a preview will tip the scales in my favor." His fingers settle on his waistband.

I throw up a hand and shake my head. "No, that's not necessary."

There's no way I can tell Brayden that I don't want to spend time with him because deep down, I'm attracted to him. I don't even want this guy to know that I like him as a human being, much less find him good looking. It would only feed his already massive ego, and that's the last thing I want to do. There are already enough females on campus fangirling over him. It'll be over my dead body that I'll be thrown in with that lot.

What I need to do is decline his offer. If I agree to this, it won't end well. I'll end up strangling him or—

"What's it going to be?" he asks, voice turning gravelly.

Tell him no.

Do it now.

Tell him—

"Okay." The word pops out of my mouth before I can rein it back in. "I'll do it."

A wide grin breaks out across Brayden's face. Before I can second guess the spontaneous decision, he wraps his arms around my waist and pulls me against the hard lines of his body before swinging me around in a tight circle.

"But only for a couple of weeks!" I wheeze as he forces all of the air from my lungs. "That's it."

"Not a problem. It'll be more than enough time for Kira to see that I'm involved with someone else and back off."

For his sake, I hope he's right. I refuse to get sucked into anything more long term.

My feet are still dangling a few inches from the ground when I grunt, "All right, you can put me down now. The deal is done. For the short term, I'll pretend to be your girlfriend. And you'll model for me."

Carefully, Brayden sets me on my heels. The smile that dances across his face somehow makes him even more handsome. My belly trembles in response and I find myself taking a hasty step in retreat in order to put some distance between us. As much as I hate to acknowledge the truth, even to myself, Brayden Kendricks is way too good looking for his own good. Mine as well. Over the years, I've done my best to tamp down any attraction from sparking to life between us and causing any more unwanted problems. He's the one guy I refuse to mess with.

You know what they say—once bitten, twice shy?

That's become my mantra when it comes to the hot football player.

I wince.

Damn.

Brayden might be all kinds of sexy, but I don't want to think of him along those lines. It'll only mess with my head. Probably other parts of me as well.

And that, I don't need.

"In order for this to work, this little agreement needs to stay between the two of us," he says, cutting into my thoughts.

Once every last bit of desire has been ruthlessly stomped out, I glance away and force a puff of air from my lips. "Oh, come on. Is that really necessary?"

"You know how it is around here," he insists. "Gossip travels at the speed of light. You tell one person a secret and suddenly everyone on this damn campus is talking about it."

Well, he's not wrong about that. Although, it's not like I'm going to broadcast it to the entire soccer team. There's only one person I'd shared this with, and that's Demi. Who would she tell?

Okay...so maybe she'd blab this little bit of ridiculousness to Rowan. I'm sure they're at that stage of their relationship where they tell each other everything. But it's not like he'd open his mouth to anyone else...

All right...I see what he means.

"Fine," I reluctantly agree. "Can we head back downstairs now?" If

I'd been craving a drink when I walked through the front door earlier, it's even more so now. I need something that's going to make me forget that I just signed a pact with the devil.

More than that, I need to get away from Brayden so I can regain my equilibrium. Even if we're pretending to be a couple, it's not like we'll be joined at the hip, right?

Exactly. He can go one way, and I'll go the other. If people question the status of our relationship, I'll answer in the affirmative and that'll be the end of it. Two weeks from now—three at the most—we will quietly part ways. We'll uncouple as quietly as one of the Kardashians. It's not like they make a big deal out of these things, right?

If I'm lucky, Brayden's overzealous fangirl will lose interest before then and I can go on my merry little way even sooner. Yup, it'll all work out in the end. There's no need to get my panties in a twist.

"Not quite yet. Let's give it a few more minutes."

I frown and reach for the handle. "Why can't we just leave?" I'm tired of being stuck in this tiny room with him. I need out.

Now.

With a slight frown, he glances at his phone before shoving it back into his pocket. "We've only been up here for ten minutes. Give it a bit more time."

I don't understand what his problem is. "Brayden," I snap, "what's the hold up?"

"Look, I can't have people thinking that I pop off like a shot. It would damage my rep, if you know what I mean."

My mouth falls open. I really hope he's not serious. Unfortunately, I can tell by his earnest expression that he is.

When I fail to respond—because, really, what am I supposed to say—he points to the mini fridge situated in the corner of his room. "How about I get you a cold beverage to enjoy while we wait?"

I blink. Holy shit, this guy is offering me a drink until an appropriate amount of time has passed for us to engage in make believe sex. That realization is all it takes for a heavy wave of regret to crash over me. Is it too late to back out of this stupid arrangement?

"I've got water, Gatorade, lime La Croix, and a few Diet Cokes for the ladies." He gives me a wink.

"I'll take a water," I say through thinned lips.

As soon as he swings around, hunkering down to peer in the fridge, I grab the handle, rip the door open, and stalk into the hallway before slamming it shut so it rattles on its hinges.

Brayden Kendricks can shove that bottle of water up his ass for all I care.

If fact, if he bends over, I'll happily do it for him.

Chapter Ten

BRAYDEN

I really should have anticipated that last maneuver. I know Sydney well enough by now to realize that the final bit probably shoved her right over the edge. It only takes a few seconds for me to catch up as she stomps down the staircase.

"Clearly you're impatient to spread the good word." I throw an arm around her shoulder and haul her close. "I can see it now...football legend and soccer all-star crowned Western's most adorable couple."

"I think Demi and Rowan have that title locked down tight," she says, keeping her attention focused in front of her.

Well, she's probably right about that. Those two are so damn cute that my teeth ache just looking at them. The quarterback finally had the balls to go after the coach's daughter. And he didn't get killed or benched. Looks like it all turned out for Rowan.

I snake my arm around Sydney's waist before dragging her closer. "Oh, I think we could give them a run for their money."

She snorts. "Except they're the real deal and we're...*not*."

True, but still...

As soon as we come into view, a loud cheer rises from the assembled crowd. It's like they were waiting for us to make an encore appearance. Sydney stumbles. It's a good thing my arm is wrapped around her, or she would have tripped and fallen.

"Hey, that was quick!" some asshole yells.

"What was that? Like two seconds, Kendricks?" another guy shouts.

Ha-ha. Very funny, fuckers.

"See? I told you," I grumble near her ear. "Now you've done irreparable damage to my reputation by not waiting five damn minutes."

Sydney narrows her eyes and gives me a well-honed death stare. If I'm smart, I'll tread lightly. She's liable to get so pissed that she blows our cover to smithereens. But I can't help myself. For some perverse reason, I enjoy riling her up. It's a challenge to see just how far I can push her before she snaps. It would seem like tonight, her patience is stretched thinner than usual.

"Aww, poor baby," she says with a faux pout. "Would you like to end this now? I'd be more than happy to part ways before it ever starts," she grits through clenched teeth and points. "Oh look, there's your friendly neighborhood stalker. Should I inform her that it was all a joke to make her jelly?"

My eyes narrow. "You wouldn't dare."

What am I saying?

Of course she would.

I wouldn't put anything past Sydney when she gets fired up. Strangely enough, it's one of the things that attracts me. The girl is a real firecracker. You never know what she's going to do.

"Try me," she growls.

"Fine," I mutter, backing down. I'm afraid of what her reaction will be if I call her bluff. "I'll just tell them that you drive me crazy, and I can't control myself around you. Happy?"

"Thrilled."

Funny...she doesn't sound it.

As soon as we step off the last tread, people gather around the staircase, bombarding us with questions.

My sister shoves her way through the mass of bodies before throwing her arms around Sydney and pulling her in for a quick hug.

"OMG, this is so exciting! I can't believe my brother is actually dating someone! He never said a word! Our mom is forever trying to fix Bray up with her friends' daughters." Elle pulls back enough to search Sydney's dazed expression. "Maybe you can meet her next weekend? Does that work for you?"

I have to bite back a groan.

Sydney looks completely shell-shocked. Like she doesn't know what to make of the girl who now has her in a death grip. It's amusing in a not-so-funny kind of way. There is no doubt in my mind that she would probably punch me in the face if I started laughing.

"Ummm," she says, looking like a deer trapped in the bright glare of oncoming headlights.

"You know what, squirt," I cut into the conversation, "how about we hold off on that for the time being?"

"Why?" She frowns. "Mom is dying to meet her."

"How can Mom be dying to meet someone she doesn't even know about?" My eyes narrow. "Unless you already opened your big mouth?"

An innocent smile curls around the edges of my sister's lips as she lifts a shoulder. "Does it really matter how she found out?"

"Please tell me you didn't call her."

Oh, for fuck's sake. Could this get any worse?

"Of course I didn't!" she shoots back, as if offended. "I texted. She's thrilled, by the way."

Sydney makes a choking sound deep in her throat.

Elle blinks, excited gaze bouncing between us. "Let's not talk about how Mom found out. I'd rather discuss how you two lovebirds got together."

Sydney's wide green eyes flicker to mine in alarm. I suppose that's something we should have discussed before trekking downstairs. And we probably would have if Sydney hadn't been in such an all-fire rush to escape my evil clutches.

I shoot her a look that says—*See? It would have been far safer to remain upstairs.*

Before either of us can respond, Elle says, "I can't remember the last time Brayden was in a relationship." She scrunches her face as if deep in thought. "Maybe junior year of high school? Wasn't it Clarissa Hodges?"

I drag a hand over my face. This situation is careening further out of control by the second, and it's my own damn flesh and blood leading the charge. How's that for a kick in the ass?

"I can't remember," I mutter. "Maybe."

Dropping the subject of my spotty dating history, Elle claps her hands together with unrestrained enthusiasm. "This is so amazing!"

Every time Elle explodes with another burst of excitement, Sydney flinches, her face draining of more color. She looks pale as a ghost. If she wasn't regretting her impromptu decision to go along with this charade before—and I know damn well that she was—she sure as hell is now. I should probably hustle her ass out of this party before she decides this is way more hassle than it's worth. Although, by the hunted look on her face, we flew by regret about five minutes ago going ninety down the freeway.

From the corner of my eye, I catch Kira in the crowd, watching us with a frown and watery eyes. If this doesn't put an end to her single-minded obsession, I don't know what will. Maybe I'll have to forget about the NFL and go into hiding for the rest of my life.

"You better believe that we're going to talk about this later," Sydney mutters under her breath so only I can hear.

"Smile, love muffin. Act like you couldn't be more blitzed out of your mind."

The way her lips lift looks forced and painful. Like she's constipated.

"Is that the best you can do?"

"It's the best you're going to get," she growls.

I raise my voice, knowing we need to get the hell out of here. "So, we're gonna—"

"What? You can't leave yet!" my sister chirps in protest. "I haven't had a chance to talk with Sydney and get to know her!"

Before I can manufacture an excuse, Elle loops her arm through the blonde's. "Come on. Let's grab something to drink and then we can chat. I have a feeling you and I are going to be best friends."

"Ummm..." Sydney's pleading gaze locks on mine before she's dragged away by my younger sibling.

"Hey, make sure to bring her back in one piece, squirt!" I yell after them.

Sydney throws one last confused look over her shoulder as she disappears from the room.

"Well," Carson says with a snicker, "looks like you jumped from one frying pan straight into another."

Fuck. He's right about that.

At this point, all I can do is hope that Sydney doesn't kick my ass for what I've set in motion. We've been a couple for less than twenty minutes and our fake relationship has already taken on a life of its own.

Chapter Eleven

SYDNEY

There's a light knock on the bedroom door before it creaks open. Unwilling to surface from this state of slumber just yet, I burrow deeper into my blankets. My subconscious is telling me to stay blissfully ignorant for as long as possible. Over the years, I've grown to rely on my instincts. They rarely steer me wrong. Unless it has to do with guys. Then all bets are off.

"Syd?" Demi whispers. "Are you awake?"

Ugh.

"No," I grumble, flipping onto my side so that my back is turned toward her. Hopefully, Demi will take the hint and leave. I love this girl like a sister, but not at the butt crack of dawn. "Go away."

Instead of doing exactly that, she settles on the edge of the mattress. "So...last night was pretty crazy, huh?"

Last night?

What's she talking about?

My brain is barely functioning at the moment.

"*Whatdoyoumean?*" My words come out all slurred together.

There's a pause before she says carefully, "You and Brayden."

Is it possible that Demi consumed more than I thought she did and is still smashed from the party last night? Although that's unlikely. My roommate doesn't really drink. A beer or two at the most. She likes to stay in control. Plus, her father is Nick Richards, head football coach for the Western Wildcats. She doesn't want any unsavory gossip making its way back to him. Can't say I blame her for it. Demi has been the topic of the rumor mill here at Western enough times to know how damaging it can be.

If she's not drunk, then maybe I'm the one who got a little too crazy. Wouldn't be the first time and probably won't be the last.

Wait a minute...did she just utter my name with Brayden's in the same sentence?

Why would—

Oh, shit.

That's when everything from last night crashes back into my brain at warp speed.

Brayden.

The crazy fangirl who won't leave him alone.

Me rather stupidly agreeing to fake date the guy.

No...it wasn't a bizarre dream. It actually happened. I drag the pillow over my face and smash it down, attempting to smother myself. It doesn't work. Demi gently pries the fabric from my white-knuckled grip until she can meet my gaze.

"Exactly how long has this been going on for?" she asks.

"What?" It takes effort to blink away the last remnants of sleep.

Demi rolls her eyes impatiently as if I'm too dense for words. "How long have you and Brayden been secretly seeing each other?"

"Oh."

Me and Brayden.

Seeing each other in secret.

Right.

That's an excellent question. Unfortunately, at the moment, I don't have an excellent answer. We'll have to get our stories straight if this has any chance of working. Otherwise, there'll be more holes in this fabrication than Swiss cheese. Barely do I recall his sister—I can't remember her name—grilling me for information. "Umm, it hasn't been very long," I say vaguely, hoping we can move on from this line of questioning.

One of her dark brows slants upward. "Well, that's not evasive at all."

I huff out a breath. Ambiguous is exactly what I was going for. I'm not a good liar under the best of circumstances, and certainly not when I'm staring my bestie in the face at the crack of dawn, and I'm still hung over. I drag myself up to a seated position. I really wish we'd hit a different party last night. Maybe then none of this would have transpired.

Is it too late to tell Brayden to forget it?

It's not like Leo ever got back to me. I should probably make a last-ditch effort to reach out. If he's willing to model, then I don't need Brayden. And if I don't need him...

Then I can back out of this stupid arrangement. He can find another girl to fake date for the next week or two.

Less than twelve short hours later, I'm chock-full of regrets and could kick my own ass for agreeing to this. I should have known better. If I remember correctly, news of our faux relationship spread through the party like wildfire. By the time I took off, everyone was talking about it. I think people were discussing possible ship names.

A groan slides from my lips. Even if it's possible to extract myself from this unpleasant situation, it's going to be a mess. What am I talking about? It's already a disaster and it hasn't even been a full day.

"I don't understand how this happened," Demi says. "You hate Brayden with the passion of a thousand burning suns."

She's not exaggerating. I really do. But I can't agree openly with her spot-on assessment, now can I?

"Hate is such a strong word," I mumble weakly.

Her eyes narrow as she frowns. "Is it?" Clearly, given my past aversions toward Brayden, Demi is skeptical.

Ugh!

"You know what they say..." my voice trails off. When her brows rise, I force myself to continue. "There's a thin line between love and hate."

She snorts as a smile trembles around the corners of her lips. "It must be a barely perceptible one."

"Oh, trust me, it is." I run my hand through my hair. It feels like it's standing on end. Much like my life, it's a complete mess. Before I can say anything else, my phone dings with an incoming message. I practically pounce on it, swiping it from my nightstand and glancing at the screen.

It's from Leo.

Everything inside me lifts.

This right here could be my way out of this mess!

I tap the screen before punching in my password and pulling up the message.

Sorry. All booked up at the moment.

There's a sad face emoji to rub a little more salt in the wound.

Damnit!

That leaves Brayden as my only viable option. I can't afford to push off this project any longer. With everything else going on, I'll need at least a month to prepare a portfolio of drawings.

Unwilling to accept defeat just yet, I fire off one last text.

Are you sure? I just need a few hours of your time.

I tack on the pleading emoji so he realizes how desperate I am.

"I thought after Ethan, you were going to take a break from guys. What happened to dating yourself for the time being?"

I shake my head, unable to come up with a plausible explanation. I really hate when people use my own words against me. Now I have to backtrack without sounding like a boy-crazy flake. When it comes to guys, I have a terrible track record. My relationships inevitably tank. And I end up hopping from one guy to another. This thing with Brayden makes me look like I'm reverting back to old patterns of behavior.

"What can I say?" It's almost painful to force out the next words. They taste like bitter ashes on my tongue. "When the right one comes along, you just know it."

Demi's eyes grow wide. Just as she opens her mouth to respond to that absurd statement, my cell dings with another text. I say a quick prayer that Leo has taken pity and relented.

Instead, I find a message from the very last person I want to hear from.

Let's meet at Denby's Diner in an hour to hash out specifics.

A third text rolls in five seconds later.

Sorry, love. Can't do it.

With no other choice in the matter, I reluctantly agree to meet Brayden.

Chapter Twelve

BRAYDEN

Looking pale and grumpy, Sydney drops onto the seat across from me at a diner that's a couple of blocks away from campus.

"Hey," she greets in a monotone voice.

"Nice to see you, too," I shoot back easily.

She glares before rolling her eyes.

Before either of us can delve into this much-needed conversation, a waitress sidles up to the table to take our breakfast order. Sydney picks up the menu and peruses it. "I'll take oatmeal, a side of fruit and," she purses her lips, "a yogurt with a large coffee."

The girl flicks her gaze in my direction. It only takes a moment before recognition dawns across her face, and she beams. "You're Brayden Kendricks!"

I force a polite smile to my lips. It's not uncommon to get recognized both on and off campus. At the moment, though, it's not helping matters with Sydney. She's already irritated. Having some overzealous fan gush in front of her will only make matters worse. "Yup, I am."

The waitress edges closer before dropping her voice. "Can I get your autograph before you leave? My boyfriend would kill me if he knew that I waited on you and didn't ask. All he talks about is how you'll turn pro at the end of this year."

"Sure, no problem." I shift uncomfortably on my seat, just wanting her to take my order and move it along so I can talk with Sydney. When she continues to stare with a perma-grin plastered across her face, I clear my throat. "I'll have eggs and lightly buttered wheat toast. Coffee, black. Thanks a lot." I flash a tight smile, willing her to take the hint and walk away before this situation can turn any more awkward.

It takes a long, drawn out moment for her to snap to attention before scribbling on her notepad. As she takes a reluctant step in retreat, her gaze stays pinned to mine. "I'll be right back with your breakfast."

Sydney cocks her head. "All the hero worship must be exhausting."

There's not much I can say to that. If I bitch about people bothering me, then I'm an asshole. If I flash a smile and tell her that it's all part of the job, I look like an egomaniac asshole who loves the adoration.

Either way, I look like an asshole. It's a no-win situation.

Yeah, I know. Boo-hoo, Brayden. Life is tough.

And Sydney, unfortunately, already thinks I'm a gigantic asshole. I don't need to do anything that will further confirm her suspicions.

When I fail to respond, she clears her throat and glances away. "So, I'm here. What was so urgent?"

I jerk my shoulders. I had a whole plan in place and now that she's sitting sullenly across from me, I have no idea what to say. I just want a chance to smooth over what happened last night. To say that she was less than thrilled to be my girlfriend is an understatement. It doesn't escape me that any other chick would be jumping at the chance to say they were with me.

Not this one.

If the look on her face is anything to go on, she'd rather gouge her own eyeballs out than continue with this farce. At this point, I'm not sure there's anything I can do to change her opinion.

I've always known that Sydney didn't like me, but I'm unsure as to the reason why. I've never done anything to inspire this kind of intense dislike. Sure, I enjoy giving her shit, but it's all been in good fun.

Just as I'm about to broach the subject, a group of college-aged students saunter past on the way to a table in the back. When my gaze flickers to them, they grind to a halt beside us.

"Hey, Brayden," one of the guys pipes up, "great game yesterday. Congratulations on the win." His gaze slides to Sydney. "And congrats, I saw on Snap last night that you two are now an item."

"Yeah," one of the girls chirps, "now you need a ship name. I was thinking something like Brayney. That's super cute, right?" Her enthusiastic gaze bounces to Sydney.

I wince.

This girl is way too peppy for ten o'clock on a Sunday morning. She needs to tone it down. And for everyone's sake, stay away from any more caffeine.

Sydney must agree because her only response is to silently burn holes into the girl.

I clear my throat when it becomes obvious that the blonde across from me isn't going to respond. "Yeah, that's a definite keeper. Thanks for stopping by."

"No problem, man," the guy says. "See you around."

"Sure will."

Once they depart, our waitress returns with our cups of steaming hot coffee. She leans closer and lowers her voice as if she's spilling state secrets. "I put a rush on the order. It should be out in a minute or so."

"Great," I say. "Appreciate it."

She gives me a wink before rushing away.

"This is a nightmare," Sydney grumbles, looking distinctly uncomfortable with the unwanted attention. "If I'd realized last night that this would be such a big deal, I wouldn't have agreed to it." She glances at the table of people who just stopped by. They all wave when they catch sight of her looking at them. If she's not careful, they'll take that as a silent invitation to join us. I've had it happen before. "Why do they even care?"

I shrug. Honestly, I have no idea, but it's been this way since I stepped foot on campus. What I've discovered is that the glare of the spotlight can be blinding. Especially when you're not used to it. If Sydney thinks this is bad, it'll be ten times worse once I make it to the NFL. That'll be on a national scale. The fandemonium isn't necessarily something I enjoy, but it comes with the territory. You can't have one without the other. Over the years, I've come to accept it.

"After a week or so, I'm sure it'll settle down."

"Great. Just in time for us to—"

"Here you go! Hot off the griddle!" The waitress slides my plate of eggs and toast in front of me before doing the same with Sydney's oatmeal, fruit bowl, and yogurt. She flashes a smile at both of us. "Is there anything else I can get for you, *Braydey*?"

Sydney's mouth falls open.

"Nope," I say hastily. "We're all set! Thanks."

"No problem at all! I'll be back to check on you in a couple of minutes. Otherwise, just wave me down if you need anything."

"Will do!" I say, only wanting her to disappear.

This is going much worse than I imagined. As if to prove that point, an oppressive silence falls over the table as the waitress takes off.

Is it too much to hope that Sydney is just hangry?

Maybe if she gets a little grub into her belly, it'll improve her disposition. Although, that's probably wishful thinking on my part.

With a sigh, she mutters, "Are you sure we need to go through with this?"

When she glances around the restaurant for a second time, I find myself doing the same. As soon as my gaze connects with a table of four girls, they all giggle and wave in unison. I jerk my attention back to Sydney.

She grumbles something indecipherable under her breath before digging into her bowl of oatmeal. Once she plows her way through most of her breakfast and I've demolished mine, it feels like we should get down to business so we're both on the same page if people start poking around and asking questions. Even though I had to talk her into the situation last night, it feels like I've got to do it all over again. If I don't play my cards right, she'll end up walking away, leaving me high and dry. And I can't afford for that to happen.

"This doesn't have to be difficult," I say. "Hell, it might even be pleasant."

Her expression flattens as if she doesn't believe that's within the realm of possibilities.

In hindsight, I probably shouldn't have led with that.

"Anyway," I clear my throat when she remains silent, "here's what I'm thinking—we walk around campus together, sit by each other in class, hit a couple of parties over the weekend, engage in a little PDA to make it look legit—"

"What?" She pokers up on her seat before shaking her head. "PDA? That wasn't part of the original agreement."

I lift a brow. "What's the problem?" I've seen this girl make out with tons of guys throughout the years. She's no stranger to public displays of affection. So maybe there's no affection on her part, but still...is swapping spit with me really that big a deal?

She jerks her shoulders before her gaze falls to my mouth. "I just don't think it's necessary. That's all."

I press against the table, swallowing up some of the distance between us. "Trust me, it's *completely* necessary." My mind tumbles back to the party and what it felt like to lock lips with her. It's definitely something I want to do again. Sooner rather than later. "We need to make this look real. I want Kira out of my life once and for all."

"Fine, but I'm not happy about it," she mutters.

"Noted." I tilt my head. "Although, you sure didn't seem to have a problem with it last night."

Color floods her cheeks. Have I ever seen Sydney blush?

I don't think so. It's kind of adorable.

"I'd be more than happy to provide a refresher. All you have to do is say the word."

She shakes her head. "No, thanks. We'll just save it for when we need to put on a show."

"Your loss," I say with a shrug, leaning back against the booth.

After last night, I'm itching to get my hands on her again. I've had a hard-on for that girl for years. If I can sweet talk her into bed, it just might do the trick in purging her from my system. Although, for obvious reasons, that will be a challenge.

All this conversation has done is confirmed my earlier suspicions that she can't stand the sight of me. Under normal circumstances, it would be water off a duck's back, and I wouldn't give a shit, but for some reason, with Sydney, it bothers me.

I've never been able to figure it out. Now that we're going to be stuck together for a couple of weeks, it seems as good a time as any to get to the bottom of her disdain.

"You don't like me very much, do you?" There's a pause. "Why is that?"

As much as I hate to admit it, air gets wedged in my throat as I wait for a response.

Chapter Thirteen

SYDNEY

My gaze jerks to Brayden in surprise.

What exactly am I supposed to say?

The truth? That I don't like him. Or do I brush off the question and keep everything surface level like I've done for the past couple of years?

It's not like Brayden and I are friends. We're barely acquaintances. Even though I've tried to avoid him, it hasn't done much good, or I wouldn't be stuck in this predicament. Spending the next couple of weeks together won't make us besties. Much like the accounting project, we're stuck together and have to make the best of the situation.

There's only one thing we have in common. And that's our friends dating.

Other than that?

Absolutely nothing.

Brayden isn't anything more than an attention-seeking whore. And I don't have time for that.

When I fail to respond, he presses even closer to the table. "Are you going to give me an answer?"

The question spurs me into tossing one back at him. "Does it really matter how I feel about you?"

Hurt flares in his eyes before being quickly snuffed out. It's enough to prick at my conscience.

His shadowed jaw hardens. "I suppose not, but it would at least be nice to know the reason."

This isn't the conversation I expected to have over breakfast. If I could bolt from the booth, I would. My gaze meanders to the large picture window we're parked in front of and the deserted streets beyond.

Is there really any point in dredging up the past?

Will it solve anything?

Nope. I should change the subject and move on to the only reason I'm sitting here with him.

"Sydney?" he says, interrupting the whirl of my thoughts.

My gaze skitters to his. The words escape from my mouth before I can stop them. "You really don't remember, do you?"

He blinks, looking as thrown off by my shift in conversation as I was by his. "Remember what?"

Seriously?

Was I that forgettable?

Somehow, that only makes matters worse. Heat floods my cheeks and I wish it were possible to snatch the question from the air. But it's much too late for that.

There's a headache brewing at the back of my skull. It feels like tiny men with hammers are persistently chipping away at a block of stone. Tylenol and Pedialyte haven't done a damn bit of good. And this mortifying conversation is only making matters worse. My first mistake was getting out of bed this morning. The second was agreeing to meet Brayden. And it was all downhill from there.

Actually, if we want to trip back further in time, the mistake that started all of this was showing up to that damn party last night. That's where everything went wrong.

After Brayden announced that we were Western's newest item, I tossed back a few drinks. There was a chorus of *aren't you lucky* and *I wish I were you* from the females present. Since I was irritated about being forced into the situation in the first place, it was more than I could withstand. So, I made a game out of it. Every time some stupid girl sighed and said *you're so lucky*, I downed a drink. Needless to say, I lost track after an hour. I vaguely recall Brayden taking me home at the end of the night. If memory serves, he might have carried me in his arms.

That part is fortunately murky.

Brayden's dark stare burns into mine. He's showing no signs of relenting. I hold it for a few heartbeats before shifting uneasily on my seat and glancing out the window for a second time. What happened between us freshman year isn't worth dredging up. It's obvious from the confusion on his face that he has no idea what I'm talking about, which only makes matters worse.

My mind spins, attempting to find a way to backtrack from this mortifying conversation. Unfortunately for me, I'm not running on all cylinders.

It's painful to admit that I'd had a bit of a thing for Brayden first semester of freshman year. Even thinking about it makes me wince. My only consolation is that I certainly wasn't the only one. To this day, girls crush hard on the handsome football player. The guy wasn't crowned Campus Heartbreaker three years in a row for nothing. With his dark hair and eyes, it's not difficult to fall straight into lust with him.

And I had.

Hard.

I'd sighed and stared every time I caught sight of him across campus like a giddy schoolgirl. One night at a party, we ended up talking. One thing led to another and suddenly we were making out. When the petting turned hot and heavy, I'd pumped the brakes, not wanting to go any further. Even in my alcohol-infused state, I'd realized that I didn't want to have sex at a frat house. Brayden had seemed cool with that. He'd asked for my number, told me he would text the next day and...

Never bothered.

In all honesty, I could have lived with that. Guys are notorious for pulling that kind of crap all the time. What was more difficult to swallow was seeing him at a party the next night, making out with another girl.

Here's the kicker—he'd looked me straight in the eyes and acted like he didn't know who the hell I was. At the time, I'd assumed he was being a dick. Like it was some kind of game to see how many girls he could tag and bag in a weekend. If I'd been looking for a way to rid myself of the unwanted crush, that had done the trick.

I've made it a point to steer clear of Brayden like an incurable STI ever since.

Can you blame me?

I'm startled back to the present when strong fingers fasten around my chin and manually turn my face until I have no other choice but to meet Brayden's unwavering stare head on. Unwanted attraction sizzles through me at the innocuous contact. I'm so tempted to rip my chin from his grip. I don't want him touching me, forcing me to feel sensations I'd prefer didn't exist.

What doesn't make sense is that I dated Ethan for six months and he never stirred these kinds of emotions inside me. Neither did the long string of guys that came before him. There was never this combustible energy that hummed beneath the surface like a live wire.

Brayden Kendricks is the last man I want to find myself drawn to.

And yet...I am. There doesn't seem to be a way to extinguish the combustible chemistry between us. Even after freshman year and all the manwhoring I've been privy to. I want to shake my head in disgust. Not at him, but at myself for being one of those stupid girls I like to glare at.

Why him?

The question is asked almost desperately.

Why am I so attuned to a guy who sleeps around like it's his job and treats girls like they're throwaways?

It only makes me feel more pathetic. And that's the last thing I need while battling a raging hangover.

"Hey," he says when I fail to respond, "what's happening here?" A strange urgency fills his voice. "Tell me what's going on in your head."

I realize by the steely look in his eyes that he won't be dropping the subject until I give him the answers he's searching for, but that doesn't stop me from trying. "There's nothing going on."

His dark eyes sharpen. "That's doubtful. If I've learned anything about you, it's that there is *always* something going on up here." He gently taps the side of my head with his finger. "How about you tell me, and I'll decide for myself."

When I huff out an irritated breath, his grip tightens on my chin, holding me firmly in place. We stare silently as the tension ratchets up until it becomes almost unbearable. Any moment, I'm going to burst into flames. This unwanted attraction that floods through me at his barest touch is ridiculous. "We hooked up freshman year."

Shock washes over his features. "We slept together?"

I shake my head and glance away. "No, it never went that far. We fooled around for a while and then you asked for my number and told me you would text. Shocker, you never bothered. The next night, I saw you making out with someone else." My tone is clipped. The last thing I want is for him to realize how much it wounded me.

His fingers turn slack before his hand falls away and he leans against the seat, almost as if he's trying to put as much space between us as possible. Emotion flickers across his face as his eyes turn cloudy. "I'm sorry, Syd. I don't remember."

I almost snort. That much is embarrassingly obvious. The fact that I was entirely forgettable makes me feel like even more of a pathetic loser.

I jerk my shoulders, attempting to play off the incident even though it's much too late for that. If it didn't matter, I wouldn't have brought it up. It would be a non-issue that we could joke about. But we both realize that's not the case.

Brayden lays his hand over mine, swallowing my smaller one up. Even though I don't want it to, the unwelcome energy we always seem to generate sparks to life. Attempting to tamp it down doesn't do a damn bit of good.

Another heavy silence crashes over us. If I didn't know better, I'd suspect he might actually be filled with remorse. But I'm sure that's more wishful thinking on my part than anything else.

"I was really messed up freshman year." There's a pause. It's almost as if Brayden is attempting to pick and choose his words carefully. "A year before that, I lost someone really important to me. Instead of dealing with the grief the way I should have, I attempted to numb it with alcohol and girls." He gives me a slight smile that doesn't quite reach his eyes. In no way is it a full-on, panty-dropping Brayden Kendricks smile. The very same one that leaves a trail of broken hearts in his wake. "It didn't work. In fact, it only made everything worse."

His brutal honesty takes me by surprise. This is in no way the bullshit excuse I was expecting from him.

Not even close.

The air gets sucked from my lungs, making it impossible to breathe. It's painful to realize that we have more in common than I ever imagined. The difference is how we dealt with our grief.

I immersed myself in soccer. The only time I felt whole was on the field. It didn't matter if it was for practice or a game. When I was on the turf, I could forget about everything. I was forced to set all of my heartache aside and live in the moment. I couldn't get lost in the thorny tangle of my thoughts. I couldn't rail at a higher power for stealing my brother. Without soccer, I have no idea how I would have made it through that difficult period in my life.

"I'm sorry," I murmur. If there's anyone who understands what it feels like to lose a piece of your heart, it's me. It's a pain I'm intimately acquainted with.

Now it's Brayden's turn to jerk his shoulders and act like it's no big deal when clearly nothing could be further from the truth. He shifts awkwardly on his seat as if already regretting the overshare. I've been there too many times to count. Grief and loss make people uncomfortable. Especially those who haven't experienced it.

Sympathy floods through me, prompting me to admit, "I lost someone, too." I blink away the moisture that attempts to gather in my eyes. "It sucks. Everyone tells you that it gets better, but it doesn't. Not really."

His eyes change, losing some of the guardedness that fills them as he focuses on me with sharp intensity. "No, it doesn't."

Another quiet moment falls over us, but this one isn't racked with tension.

His gaze flicks away before resettling on mine. "The death was sudden, and I didn't handle it well. There were so many coaches, counselors, and teachers who reached out, but I pushed them away. I couldn't deal with all their stupid platitudes. Like that made anything better."

I snort out a mirthless laugh and shake my head. "I can't tell you how many times someone said *he's not really gone. He'll live on in your heart forever.*"

His lips flatten. "Yeah. What the hell kind of thing is that to say? Guess what? I don't want him in my heart. I want him in my life. Is that so difficult to comprehend?"

"No." I shake my head, understanding exactly what he means. "Or how about *he wouldn't want you to be sad?*"

"Right." He rolls his eyes. "I guess I shouldn't be sad then. I'll just move it along so that my grief doesn't make you uncomfortable."

"Someone actually had the balls to tell me that, in the end, this experience will make me stronger."

His brows rise. "Did you punch them in the face?"

"No," my lips tremble at the corners, "but I wanted to."

"I probably would have," he says, after considering it for a long moment. "That's a shit comment."

My head spins as we lapse into silence. I never expected to show up here and share an intense moment with Brayden. It feels almost surreal. How do we have something so tragic in common? How is it that he's one of the few who understand exactly how I feel about an experience I don't share with other people?

It doesn't make sense.

"Freshman year was such a blur. Sometimes, I'm not sure how I made it through without flunking out and losing my athletic scholarship. I partied too much and at one point, stopped attending classes."

My mind tumbles back to our first year at Western. Every weekend, Brayden was out partying, living it up. Girls hung all over him and there was always a smile plastered across his handsome face as if he were enjoying his college experience to the fullest. It was easy to arrive at the assumption that he was just another obnoxious athlete, content to sit back and soak up all the adoration his position on the team afforded him. I attended every home football game. He performed on the field as if life was perfect. If he hadn't told me about this tragedy, I would never have suspected that Brayden was drinking and sleeping around in an attempt to numb his grief.

But that's what people in pain do, right?

They ignore it. Bury it. Find things to make them forget. I'm guilty of doing the same. The only difference is that I threw myself into soccer. I also had to be strong for Lucus.

It's only now that I realize he isn't the fuck boy I originally pegged him to be. I've spent the last three years despising the dark-haired football player and doing everything in my power to avoid him. It's jarring to realize that I just might have to alter my perception.

"Look, Sydney, I'm sorry if I hurt you. I guess your behavior makes a lot more sense." He tilts his head. "I could never figure out why you hated me so much."

I release a steady breath, unsure how to respond. When he squeezes my fingers, my gaze drops to them, surprised to find his larger hand still holding mine.

"If it were possible to go back and change the past, I would do it in a heartbeat."

"If we could go back and change the past," I say lightly, "I think we'd both change more important things."

His expression turns somber as he nods. "You're right, we would."

Thick emotion wells in my throat until it becomes unbearable. Brayden and I have conversed countless times before, but this is the first time it feels real. Like we've inadvertently stripped away all the pretenses we usually arm ourselves with. It's a disconcerting sensation and I'm not sure what to make of it.

"Do you think it's possible for us to start over with a clean slate?" he asks quietly.

My teeth sink into my lower lip as I slowly turn the idea over in my head. Can I really say no? Even more telling than that, I don't want to.

My heart goes out to Brayden for the loss he suffered. "Yeah, of course. Let's forget about it."

He nods. "Good."

Even though I'm not ready for our relationship to morph into something new, it feels like we're entering uncharted territory.

Chapter Fourteen

SYDNEY

"Coach and I were going through game film yesterday," Demi says as we move across the cement path that cuts through campus on our way to class. "I think USC will be tough to beat. They're more prepared than they were last season. Plus, they recruited a star player from Connecticut. Even though she's a freshman, the girl is insane."

I nod, attempting to focus on the upcoming game. Like Demi, I met with Coach yesterday to pour over game film. On every team, there are always a couple players that we need to watch out for. So far this season, USC has won all their conference games. Demi's right, it'll be a tough match, but I think we're prepared.

"Now that Annica is out with an injury, the team is gelling better and we're more focused."

When the auburn-haired girl came in as a freshman two years ago, Demi took our younger teammate under her wing. They were an unstoppable duo on the field. But then jealousy got in the way and Annica did everything in her power to rip Demi down. Not only did she attempt to turn the younger girls against her, but the little bitch went after all the guys Demi spent time with. Just when you thought that Annica's behavior couldn't sink any lower, she took it a step further with those rumors.

I've never been one to put too much stock in karma, but in the end, that girl got exactly what she deserved. And that would be a broken ankle from a night out drinking. Now that she's no longer on the field, causing havoc, most of our younger teammates have fallen into line. Without Annica constantly talking shit and stirring up trouble, there's once again peace in the kingdom.

"I overheard Coach tell the trainer that Annica's doctors aren't sure if she'll be able to play at the same level she did before the accident. It'll take a lot of physical therapy and hard work on her part to even have a shot."

I shrug. As far as I'm concerned, you reap what you sow. And that girl sowed a whole hell of a lot of deceit and trouble.

"Even if she does come back," I say, "we'll be long gone. We'll never have to worry—"

I squeak in surprise when a brawny arm is slung around my shoulders, and I'm hauled against a rock-solid body.

What the—

Before I can make sense of what's happening, firm lips crash into mine. When I gasp and my mouth opens, a velvety soft tongue slips inside to tangle with my own. The way they mingle together is almost enough to make me forget we're in the middle of campus. In fact, I'm a little embarrassed to admit that all of the noise and chatter surrounding me instantly fades to the background.

It's only when the catcalls and whistles grow more insistent that they finally penetrate the thick haze that has descended, clouding my better judgment before propelling me back to the present with a painful thud. I blink and attempt to find my bearings. It's only then that Brayden pulls away enough to search my gaze.

Demi clears her throat when I continue to stare. "So," she hitches her thumb over her shoulder, "I'm gonna get moving."

"All right," I mumble, still feeling stunned, which is ridiculous. It's not like I haven't been kissed before. "Are we still planning to meet up for lunch?"

"Are you sure you'll be free?" she asks with a smirk, humor threading its way through her voice.

Heat slams into my cheeks and I nearly wince. I really need to get a grip. "Yeah, I'll be there."

Brayden grins as if realizing how easily he was able to muddle my thoughts.

It takes everything I have inside me to tamp down the rioting emotion attempting to break free. Our conversation at the diner has only complicated matters. It was so much easier to keep my attraction in check when I thought Brayden was nothing more than a conceited jackass who enjoyed nailing as many girls as possible. Now that I know the truth and everything he's struggled with over the years, my heart has undeniably been cracked open. Whether he realizes it or not, he's managed to crawl inside and burrow there.

And that cannot be allowed.

Maybe we've straightened out the past and I've let go of my anger, but it doesn't change the fact that this isn't a real relationship. We aren't going out. In a couple weeks, we'll pretend to break up and life will go back to normal. It would be smart to remember that and not read too much into the affectionate gesture. That kiss was nothing more than the PDA we agreed to.

With his arm wrapped around me, we stroll toward our accounting class. It's disconcerting how people's heads swivel in our direction as we walk by. Students call out greetings to Brayden, attempting to grab his attention before waving. We might both be Division I athletes at Western, but I'm able to move around campus without a hint of fanfare. Brayden, on the other hand?

He can't walk ten steps without attracting interest. The guy is recognized everywhere. Probably even the bathroom. It used to aggravate the hell out of me that the male athletes around here received so much love. And not just the football players either, although they do receive the most. Hockey, baseball, basketball, even lacrosse...they all have their fair share of jersey chasers, cleat sniffers, and puck bunnies.

Now I'm experiencing this craziness firsthand and realize how much I dislike the intense scrutiny. I enjoy moving through the crowd anonymously. I wouldn't always want to be *on*. People are always watching, waiting for something to happen, something that will feed the gossip mill. Even at the diner, people were stopping by to say hello or talk about the game. It was annoying, but Brayden handled it with ease and humility, never seeming bothered by the attention. Maybe he didn't want the waitress to hover over us, but he was never rude about it.

Ethan was a baseball player, and his fandom wasn't nearly at this level.

And that, I remind myself, is precisely why Brayden kissed me in front of everyone. He knows that it'll spread like wildfire and hopefully get back to Kira, helping to give this sham of a relationship authenticity.

Once my heart stops racing, I clear my throat. "Was that really necessary? A peck on the cheek would have gotten the job done."

"Are you kidding?" he scoffs good naturedly, beaming a smile in my direction. "When I'm trying to sell something, I go all the way. There's no half-assing it for me."

If I needed anything more to confirm my suspicions, that comment does the trick.

"Nine o'clock," Brayden murmurs. "There she is."

My gaze roves over the groups of students loitering outside the business building. It only takes a moment to seek out Kira in the crowd. Her gaze is already trained on us. The closer we get to the building, the more her brows pinch together.

"Well, damn. I was hoping that after this weekend she would have gotten the hint loud and clear." All of his previous lightheartedness disappears.

By the intensity of her expression, I'm guessing that's not the case.

"I'm sure after a week or two, she'll move on," I murmur.

"I don't know." His arm tightens around me, drawing me closer. "I've run into some pretty persistent chicks, but nothing like this. Honestly, I'll be glad to graduate in the spring just to get away from her."

Wow. That's really sad. Guilt flickers through me. And here I'd thought he would probably be basking in all the female attention. Instead, he's attempting to deter it.

My mind goes to what it will be like when Brayden gets drafted.

"Don't you think it'll be ten times worse once you're playing in the NFL?"

He jerks his shoulders. "I don't know. Probably. I try not to think that far ahead. Right now, I'm concerned about making it to the next level. Once I get there, then I'll worry about it. If it even happens."

Is Brayden serious?

With his looks and skills on the field?

He'll be propelled to super stardom. It's a sure bet that women will be crawling out of the woodwork, attempting to capture his attention.

"Who knows," I joke, "maybe she'll follow you wherever you go."

The look of horror that flashes across his face is enough to make me laugh. "Aww, it's so hard to be Brayden."

He tugs me close enough to bury his face against my neck. When his teeth sink into the delicate flesh, I squeal and attempt to push him away. For a moment, I forget all about the stalker-girl watching us.

"Brayden?" a soft voice interrupts.

We both still, not realizing that Kira has separated herself from the group of girls she'd been standing with.

Her tongue darts out to moisten her pink-slicked lips as she whispers, "Can we talk before class?"

If my body weren't pressed against his, I probably wouldn't notice the tension that now fills his muscles.

"Ummm..." He gives me a bit of side-eye. "Now isn't really a—"

Before he can force out the rest, I untangle myself from the death grip he has on me before stepping toward the tawny-haired girl. "I think you and I should have a conversation."

Kira's blue eyes flare as if she wasn't expecting me to take control of the situation. To be honest, I wasn't expecting it either. The words popped out of my mouth before I could stop them. But then again, maybe this is exactly what needs to happen. Maybe it would be easier for Kira to hear this from me, girl to girl.

I loop my arm through hers and continue walking. When her feet remain rooted in place, I tug her along until we're far enough away from the football player that he can't overhear our conversation. Even though she's unwittingly dragged me into this situation, I'm not looking to embarrass her.

And neither, I realize, is Brayden.

He could have easily been cruel or told her to get lost, and he hasn't. Quite the opposite. He probably could have banned her from his house. Instead, he's been keeping her at a firm distance, hoping that she would eventually turn her attention elsewhere. As much as I don't want to unearth any admirable character traits in him, I can't deny that I've already found one.

Maybe even a few.

Since I wasn't expecting to have this chat with Kira, I'll have to wing it. "I know we spoke a little bit at the party on Saturday but—"

"You and I don't have anything to say to each other," she cuts in, color riding high on her cheeks.

That might be so, but she's going to hear me out.

"Then let me do all the talking," I continue, undeterred by the anger wafting off her in heavy waves. "I know my relationship with Brayden looks like it came out of the blue, but we're together now and I would really appreciate it if you could respect that." There's a beat of silence. "Just like I would respect it if you two were involved."

Kira nibbles at her bottom lip. Instead of holding my gaze, hers skitters away. Emotion flickers in her expressive blue eyes. "It's hard. I've liked Brayden for a long time. There are always so many girls vying for his attention, I thought that if I were," she pauses, as if trying to find the right words, "bolder, he would give me a chance."

I nod. At any given time, there are dozens of girls buzzing around Brayden like drunken bees. In a way, I can understand why she felt the need to draw his attention with outrageous behavior. There's a lot of competition when it comes to the guys on the football team. They're like the rock stars of Western University.

Personally, I've never felt the need to chase after anyone like that. Maybe it's because I'm also an athlete. And it's kind of irritating to watch all these girls clamor for their attention. My life has always revolved around my sport, not chasing guys who play them.

But to each their own, right?

"I'm sure it hurts to see him get serious with another girl," I say carefully. I'm not a totally heartless bitch. I get it.

More importantly, I want *her* to get it.

Kira's gaze jerks back to me. "It sucks to be hung up on someone who doesn't want you."

The more I talk to this girl, the less crazy she sounds.

"You're right," I sigh, "it does. I've been there." And here I thought that Kira and I wouldn't have anything in common. Turns out that we do. We both, at one time, crushed hard on Brayden.

Her eyes widen as she scoffs, "Oh, come on. You couldn't possibly know what that's like! Not only are you gorgeous, but you're a really talented soccer player. You can have any guy you want!"

I almost snort. "It might seem that way on the outside, but trust me, that's not the case. I've struggled with relationships. In fact," I admit, "I wasn't interested in getting together with anyone after my last boyfriend. I was going to take a much-needed break from men."

Her eyes go a little dreamy. "And now you're with Brayden."

Umm, right.

I blink, remembering that this is nothing more than a part I'm playing. "I guess what they say is true—when you're least expecting someone to come into your life, that's when it happens." When she remains silent, I continue. "There are plenty of guys on this campus who would be thrilled to be with you. Do yourself a favor and don't chase after someone who can't see how amazing you are."

Kira draws in a deep breath as her gaze meanders to something—or, more than likely, someone—over my shoulder before she jerks her head into a nod. Emotion flickers across her face before her gaze returns to mine. "Thanks, Sydney. I appreciate you talking to me."

"Just remember, you and I aren't adversaries." I shift my weight and say gently, "At least, we don't have to be."

One corner of her mouth hitches as she nods. "You're right. We're not enemies. I'm going to head to class. I'll see you inside."

"Sounds good. Bye, Kira."

She raises her hand in a wave before walking up the wide stone stairs and disappearing through the glass door inside the brick building.

I don't realize that Brayden has snuck up on me until he says, "Wow. That went better than expected. I was half-afraid a cat fight was about to break out." There's a pause. "What did you say to her?"

I spear a glance in his direction. “That you were on your third round of antibiotic treatment for a particularly stubborn case of chlamydia, and that she can do better.”

His mouth falls open but not a sound escapes. It takes everything I have inside to rein in the laughter that bubbles up from my lips before walking away.

I get about three steps when he calls out, “You better be joking.”

“You wanted her to leave you alone. I’m pretty sure that did the trick.” I give a little bow. “You’re welcome.”

With a smile simmering around the edges of my lips, I follow Kira into the building, leaving Brayden to stand outside all by his lonesome.

Chapter Fifteen

SYDNEY

The light rap of knuckles against the door has the nerves bursting to life inside the confines of my belly as I jump from the couch and jog to the tiny entryway before pulling open the door. It's not a surprise when I find Brayden standing on the other side of the threshold.

"Hey," he says in greeting, dark gaze piercing mine.

I tamp down any attraction attempting to fight its way to the surface, all the while pretending it doesn't exist. Every time we see each other, it becomes increasingly more difficult to do. Brayden and I have never spent this much time together. When we've been forced into close proximity, I've always made a concerted effort to battle back the unwanted feelings he rouses inside me. Now, it's happening on the daily, and it's a little more than I can handle. Everything feels like it's building inside me and I'm afraid of what will happen once it reaches a pinnacle.

I blow out a breath and push those unruly thoughts away. Nothing will happen that I don't want. "Thanks for coming over."

He shrugs. "Got to hold up my end of the deal, right?"

Yes. That's *exactly* what this is. *A deal*. I'm not sure why I have to keep reminding myself of this. It shouldn't be difficult. I spent years hating on Brayden. Snarling at him whenever he wandered too close.

Now that it's no longer the case, my emotions are strangely scattered and I'm uncertain what to make of them. There's a part of me that detests the confusion. It was so much easier when I knew what to expect or how to react to him.

Brayden shifts his stance before clearing his throat. "So, you gonna let me in or what?"

I snap to attention and hold the door open so he can walk inside the apartment. As he moves past me, his body brushes against mine. He steps inside the small hallway before moving further into the cramped dining/living room combination. There's a small, round table stuffed into the space. Brayden removes his backpack from his shoulder before setting it on the wood surface. It lands with a thud.

For a heartbeat, we stare before his fingers grip the hem of his navy T-shirt and yank it up his chest, revealing a tantalizing strip of washboard abdominals in the process.

My eyes widen. "What are you doing?"

"Stripping." His brows draw together in confusion. "Why? What does it look like?"

A gurgle of nervous laughter bubbles up in my throat as I wave at the living room. "Oh my god, not here!"

As soon as he releases the cotton material, it falls back into place, covering his hard, sun-kissed flesh. "All right. If not here, then where?"

I point toward the open door. "Let's do this in my bedroom."

When a slow smirk curves his lips, I roll my eyes. "So I can sketch you properly, perv. Get your mind out of the gutter."

The knowing smile remains in place. "Please. You're just trying to get me naked so you can have your wicked way with me." He taps the side of his head with his finger. "I know exactly what's going on inside that dirty little mind of yours."

It's reluctantly that I snort out a laugh.

Had he accused me of this even a week ago, I would have taken offense to the comment and snapped at him. Now, I understand that Brayden is doing nothing more than goofing around. "In your dreams." Although, he's closer to the truth than I'm comfortable admitting, even to myself.

The humor dancing in his eyes dies a quick death as they turn flinty. "Maybe."

That one word, murmured in a deep voice, is all it takes for desire to ignite within me. Almost mercilessly, I stomp it out before it can settle like a heavy stone in my core.

I need to focus on the sole reason Brayden has turned up at my apartment this afternoon. And that's so I can do a preliminary sketch. This isn't a date, and we're not friends hanging out. Just like he quipped earlier, he's holding up his end of the deal.

I trail behind him at a safe distance as he saunters into my room. We both fall silent as he studies my personal space. It's a little surreal to have him here. Who would have ever thought I would willingly invite Brayden into my bedroom?

Certainly not me.

The normally spacious area shrinks around his large form, making it feel surprisingly small and cramped. It's almost as if there isn't enough space for the both of us. Instead of staring at him, I rip my gaze away. It skitters around, taking in everything he must see.

There's a queen-sized bed pressed against the far wall. Next to it is a nightstand with a fuzzy turquoise lamp shade that I've had forever. Fairy lights are strung across three of the walls and a fluffy greenish-blue comforter covers the bed. I love the color. It makes me think of the Caribbean Sea and I find that soothing. Especially when I'm working on my art.

A white desk that doubles as a makeup area is situated across from the bed. Framed posters of the Louvre and MoMA decorate the plain white walls along with a few of my own pieces that Mom was especially proud of. Brayden gravitates closer to one of the sketches before carefully studying it.

His silence is enough to have my nerves growing taut. If they stretch any further, they'll fray and snap. It shouldn't matter what Brayden thinks of my artwork. We aren't friends. We're not...anything, really. Our relationship has morphed into something new, but I'm unsure what label to slap on it.

It's disconcerting to realize that his opinion actually matters. Maybe it's because I'm going to draw him, and I want Brayden to be impressed by my skills. I want to assure him that he won't turn out looking like a stick figure.

When he glances over his shoulder, his dark gaze skewers me in place. "Is this yours?"

I jerk my head into a nod as my mouth grows cottony, making it impossible to swallow.

"It's really good." He leans closer as if trying to absorb the details.

"Thanks." Forcing out that one word takes a Herculean effort on my part.

It's like Brayden is at a museum as he moves from one framed piece to another before studying it with an equal amount of intensity. My fingers twist as I keep my lips clamped together. Standing by idly while people judge my work has never been comfortable. Even though I tell myself that it doesn't matter what they think, deep down, it does. Art comes from within and to have someone form unfavorable opinions or criticize a piece that has taken hours to create can be brutal. I've spilled a lot of tears because a teacher tore apart a painting or drawing. A few times, I've even been tempted to quit. The problem is that the passion you carry around inside you doesn't just go away. It stays with you, searching for an escape route. Being creative isn't a choice. It's a necessity.

"I had no idea that you were this talented," he says with his broad back to me.

"I'm really not," I reply hastily, air leaking from my lungs. It's a kneejerk reaction. I've always been uncomfortable accepting praise when it comes to my work.

He twists around to capture my gaze before tipping his head toward the wall. "This says differently."

I shrug as heat engulfs my cheeks. I hate that he makes me feel so unsure of myself. Why does everything have to feel different with Brayden?

He turns fully toward me so that we're once again facing each other before cocking his head. There's about ten feet of space separating us, and I need every inch of that distance. "Why aren't you majoring in art?" He points to the drawings. "This seems like a lot of talent to waste."

My breath escapes in a slow leak as I break eye contact. When did this conversation morph into something genuine?

Instead of giving him a bullshit excuse, I tell him the truth. "My parents didn't think it would pay the bills." And after hearing it enough times, I believed them and gave up the dream of being an artist. "Since I've always been good with numbers, accounting seemed like a good fit. My father owns an accounting firm, and one of my older brothers has been working there since he graduated college. I'll still have time for my art." Then I tack on the refrain I've heard hundreds of times before. "It's more of a hobby than a way to make a living."

He regards me with an excruciating amount of intensity. I imagine it must be similar to the way he studied my artwork only a handful of moments ago. It's so tempting to squirm beneath his scrutiny. "Is that what you want? To work in an office and for your art to be a hobby?"

The question is like a knife to the heart. It's unexpectedly painful. It's also something I would prefer not to dwell on. Especially when I'm already having doubts that accounting will make me happy in the long run.

I clear my throat, not understanding how we veered so far off topic. "What I think is that I'll have a well-paying job waiting for me after graduation." It's a pat answer. One I've rattled off dozens of times. One I've tried to convince myself is the truth. It's only now, as I inch closer to graduation, that more doubts are mushrooming up, creating uncertainty. But Brayden doesn't need to know that.

"Hmm." A skeptical expression settles on his face as if he's not convinced.

My eyes narrow. I don't need him prodding beneath the surface of our relationship. He needs to do us both a favor and stay in his lane. "What?"

"I didn't say anything," he says innocently.

Too innocently for it to be sincere.

"You made a noise," I point out.

He presses a hand to his chest. "Oh. Am I not allowed to do that? Is that a rule or something?"

Irritation bubbles up inside me as I fold my arms across my chest. "Look, I don't want to talk about my degree or my future plans."

Am I being defensive and acting like a bitch?

Probably.

But I can't seem to rein myself in. Brayden has picked up on an issue that hits a little too close to home. I haven't spoken to my family about this. I sure as hell don't want to talk to him.

"I didn't say a word about it."

"You're judging me," I mutter.

Oh my god, since when do I care about anyone—let alone Brayden —judging me?

He's twisting me up inside and I don't like it. More than that, I don't want it. I need to work harder at keeping him at a safe distance. That's the only way I'm going to get through this.

"Nope, not at all." There's a beat of silence. "You're just really talented." Again, he points toward the wall. "I'm surprised you couldn't find something where you can incorporate and utilize your talent."

His explanation has some of the stiffness draining from my shoulders. "Talent doesn't always cut it. And it certainly doesn't make money."

"That's true, but it would be a real shame to waste this. Maybe you need to explore your options while it's still a possibility."

His words circle viciously through my head before I pick up my sketch pad, but I push it away, refusing to dwell on it. He's not telling me anything I don't already know. "It's getting late. We should probably get to work. I'll need at least two hours, maybe more."

Instead of continuing the conversation, he drops it. Brayden doesn't know me well enough to understand what my art means to me or to realize that I'm having doubts about my chosen career. I'm in my last year of classes and majoring in accounting with a minor in fine arts. It's a little late to change course at this point.

Had I arrived at this decision freshman—or even sophomore—year, I could have done something about it.

Now?

I'm stuck. An imaginary weight settles on my chest. Before I can get mired in thoughts of the future, Brayden yanks his shirt up his chest and over his head. The material lands with a soft whoosh near my feet.

When my gaze collides with his, he smirks. "Sorry, were you expecting more of a striptease? I just assumed you'd want me to remove everything as quickly as possible."

This guy...

Sometimes I don't know what to say to him. At every turn, he knocks me off balance. I should be used to it by now.

Clearly, I'm not.

Brayden grins before shoving the athletic shorts down his thighs until they pool around his ankles. He picks them up and tosses them onto the growing pile of clothing.

When his fingers hover over the elastic waistband of his black boxer-briefs, I blurt, "You can leave them on. I'll use my imagination for—"

"Nah." His smile widens, his expression turning predatory. "I'm not shy about the goods."

Before any further protest can escape, the boxers disappear, leaving Brayden in all his naked glory.

Almost hastily, I avert my gaze as the atmosphere in the bedroom turns oppressive. It's almost enough to choke on.

"I'm pretty sure you'll have a hard time rendering a likeness of me if you refuse to look in my direction." Even though his voice has deepened, traces of humor tinge the edges.

Ugh.

Why am I acting like this? I've sketched plenty of naked figures over the past three years. I've always been able to act professionally.

So why does this feel so different?

Why am I acting like such a newbie?

Snap out of it!

This isn't any different than if you were sketching Marco. Or Leo. Or even Jon.

Except...it is.

"Where do you want me?" he asks, breaking into my muddled thoughts.

"Umm—"

"Like this?" He ambles closer before lifting his foot and placing it on the chair. With his leg raised, he positions his elbow on his muscular thigh before settling his chin on his fist and sending a broody look in my direction.

Oh, god.

I compress my lips and quickly shake my head.

"No?" He straightens to his full height and glances around the room. "How about something more along these lines?" He flexes his arms until both biceps bulge. My mouth dries.

Holy hotness, Batman.

When I remain silent, he says, "Not quite right? Okay, give me a moment here." Then he saunters to the bed before bending over and throwing a heated look over his shoulder. "Better? More modelish? Are you getting *Zoolander* vibes from this pose? Because that's who I'm channeling."

His ass is totally on display along with his—

I jerk my gaze away.

Oh my.

It's only been three minutes and I've already caught way more than an eyeful.

"Stop!" I can't take much more of this before I totally self-combust. I set the sketch pad down and force myself to close the distance between us before grabbing his arm and towing him to the middle of the room. "Just...stand there." I huff out a breath. "Okay?"

"What should I do with my arms?"

"Just let them hang at your sides." My heart is jackhammering a painful staccato beneath my breast. If I'm not careful, it'll explode right out of my chest.

"Sure, whatever you think is best. You're the professional," he says.

Well, that remains to be seen after this debacle.

Once he does that, I stand back and take him in, tweaking his stance until he's exactly how I want him. At least for the time being. Positioning him allows me to remove myself from the situation and stop noticing things about him that make me think of the man he is instead of the beauty of his form and bringing it to life on paper. I've drawn good-looking men before. Silently, I admit that Brayden is in a class all by himself.

Michelangelo couldn't have done a better job sculpting David. The artist in me can appreciate every slab of finely honed muscle. From a distance, he's always looked to be in peak physical condition, but it's so much more than that.

For the first time since we entered the bedroom, my fingers itch to pick up my pencils and sketch. I settle on the chair near the desk as Brayden holds his position. The silliness from moments ago vanishes as I study the lean lines of his body. That's all it takes for the charcoal to fly over the thick paper. After about twenty minutes, I grab a different pencil and shade in the image slowly taking shape. I fill in the ridges of his chest, making sure to contour all of his musculature.

Once a good likeness of his front has been rendered, I stand and stretch, moving around to capture the tall football player from a different angle. Brayden watches me until I disappear from sight. He doesn't move a muscle or say a word. I settle on my bed with the sketch pad and flip the page before getting to work. This project will be a three-hundred-and-sixty-degree perspective taken from several different angles.

Honestly, I was less than thrilled with the idea of Brayden modeling for me, but if my preliminary work is anything to go off, this project will turn out exceptionally well. He's the perfect specimen. His body is flawless with thighs that are thick and powerful. There's a smattering of dark hair sprinkled across his body. And his ass...

I'm tempted to run my fingers across the firm flesh to see if it's as taut as it appears.

Do I actually give in to the urge?

Hell, no.

That would be begging for trouble.

With Brayden's back to me, I'm able to look my fill as my fingers fly across the thick paper. It doesn't take long to lose myself in the familiar strokes of charcoal until an illustration takes shape. It's only when I notice the slant of the sun outside my bedroom window that I become aware of how much time has passed.

I rise to my feet and walk around to the front again, flipping from the fifth drawing back to the first. My gaze drifts over him, taking in every minute detail until arriving at his cock. Even in repose, it's long and thick. The length is curved, nestled against dark curls. He really is gorgeous.

Artistically speaking, of course.

My fingers still as my gaze lingers, drinking in the sight of him. The man really should be sculpted and displayed in a museum to be admired. I almost lose myself in his masculine form. The lines and ridges that bisect his body. It's only when his cock stirs, stiffening up, that my wide gaze jerks to his. Air gets wedged in my throat as my mouth turns cottony.

With a smirk, he shrugs. "There's only so much I can take of you eating me up with your eyes."

If I was expecting an apology or even a hint of embarrassment, I don't get it.

Quite the opposite.

Nudity has never embarrassed me, but it does with Brayden. Which makes no sense. I'm not the one who's standing around in his birthday suit. And yet...my entire body feels flushed and achy.

"That's not what I was doing," I mumble, because yeah, that's *exactly* what I was doing.

Hell, I'm still doing it.

Brayden Kendricks is magnificent, and I was totally ogling him. But there's no way I'll admit that. The guy is cocky enough without me adding to his swollen head.

Either of them, as the case might be.

Heat slams into my cheeks as I swing away and move toward the desk to set my materials down. The more distance between us, the better off I'll be. "You can get dressed now. We're done for today."

Hopefully, by the time I turn around, he'll be fully clothed and ready to take off.

"Sydney." His voice drops, becoming low and gravelly. It strums something deep inside I'd rather not acknowledge. Or inspect too closely. I'm afraid of what I'll find.

My nerves ratchet up with every creak of the floorboards. By the time his hands settle on my shoulders, I'm ready to jump out of my skin. He's so close that I can feel the heat of his larger frame against my backside. His warm breath ghosts over my ear and an unwelcome shiver scampers down my spine. Arousal explodes in the pit of my belly before settling in my core.

No.

No.

No.

Brayden is the last guy on Earth I want to feel this way about. I hate that he can affect me so easily. I want to feel nothing where he's concerned. I want to be stone cold. Instead, I'm ready to melt into a puddle at his bare feet. It's demoralizing.

His fingers curl around the tops of my shoulders before drawing me close enough for my back to align with the rigid lines of his chest. Lines that I studied and practically committed to memory as I brought them to life on the page.

Instead of breaking free of his embrace and scrambling away, my feet become rooted in place. I'm incapable of movement. The brute male strength that radiates from him in powerful waves is heady and intoxicating. My eyelids feather closed, and I feel myself falling. Tumbling into a dark abyss.

"Sydney," he growls again, fingertips burning my flesh as they skim down my arms. The way he bites out my name has liquid heat gathering between my thighs. The echo of it leaves me breathless and hungry with need. Whatever is about to happen, I no longer have the strength of will to fight against it.

I'm ripped from those dangerous thoughts when my bedroom door flies open and Demi screeches to a halt over the threshold. "Hey, I was—"

Her eyes go wide as her voice abruptly falls off. "Oh! I'm...ah...sorry! I didn't realize..."

I'm sure my expression mirrors the stunned one she's wearing. I shake my head. Violent little movements that leave me feeling dizzy. "No, we're not—"

I try to explain, but she's already springing forward and grasping the handle before slamming the door shut with a resounding thud.

A tortured sound of humiliation escapes from my lips. "She thinks we were about to have sex."

"It does appear that way," Brayden says, humor replacing the thick desire in his voice.

"I'm, ah, leaving now!" Demi's muffled voice comes from the other side of the door. "So...carry on with whatever was about to happen!"

Oh.

God.

This is truly horrific. And there's nothing I can do to rectify the situation. If anything, I owe her for the timely interruption. It's shocking to realize that there's a good possibility something would have happened between us if she hadn't barged in. As painful as it is to admit it, Brayden is like the pied piper of pussy, and I was so damn close to falling under his spell.

"Guess we don't need to worry about people thinking this is a fake relationship, now do we?"

No.

We certainly don't.

Chapter Sixteen

BRAYDEN

"That practice sucked ass," I huff, shoving my way inside the locker room along with the other guys. Everyone is bitching and complaining. The closer we get to the playoffs, the harder Coach works us. After four years, I should be used to it. Sweat is beaded across my forehead, has soaked through my pads, and dampens my hair. A hot shower is going to feel so damn good.

Rowan shrugs, looking no worse for the wear. "What are you talking about? It didn't seem so bad. I barely broke a sweat."

My eyes narrow. "You know why that is?" I don't bother to wait for a response. "Because all you do is stand around like a fucking prima donna waiting to unload the ball. My ass is the one running routes and getting into position."

Not taking offense to my complaint, a grin slides across his face. "Guess you should have been a quarterback. Best position on the team."

I give him a one-fingered salute.

In all honesty, I can't criticize the guy. No matter what conference you're looking at, he's the best QB in Division I college football. There's no way he won't be a first-round draft pick. And if there's anyone who deserves it, it's Rowan. He's worked his ass off to be the best.

That being said, I enjoy giving him shit from time to time. Can't have him getting too big for his britches, now can I?

By the time I peel off my pads, Rowan is already out of the shower. It's like his damn ass is on fire. What's he in such a hurry for?

Never mind. It probably has something to do with Demi. Those two went from spending as little time as possible together to practically being conjoined twins.

"Come on, man. Get a move on it," he urges, grabbing his boxers from the locker and hauling them up his thighs.

Excuse me?

I hike a brow. "Why?"

He shoots me an exasperated look. "The game starts at seven, and I don't want to miss any of it."

"Game?"

What the hell is he talking about?

The only game I'm focused on is the upcoming one this Saturday. Thankfully, we'll have home field advantage. The cheer of our fans always helps to heighten the energy in the stadium. It's a point of pride to step on the turf and stare up at the ocean of red and black that surrounds us. There's nothing more that gets me pumped than the excitement of our fans. It's electric.

"If you're gonna go out with Sydney, then you need to step up and show some support. Trust me, it won't go well for you if your ass isn't in the stands tonight." Rowan shakes his head as if I'm a complete moron. "How is it that you get all the chicks but don't know a damn thing about them?"

I almost snort.

Trust me, I know enough to make them happy. I open my mouth to tell him exactly that when it hits me.

"Oh, right," I improvise with a nod, "the soccer game. Sure, Sydney mentioned it earlier." Actually, Sydney didn't utter one damn peep. Why that should send an arrow of hurt slicing clean through me, I have no idea. We might have cleared the air at the diner, but that doesn't mean our relationship has changed. She holds me at just as much of a distance as she always has. The girl has so many walls up, she's like an impenetrable fortress.

Rowan waves his hand. "Great. Now get moving." He glances at his phone. "We've got ten minutes. Coach is already there, waiting for us."

"All right, all right," I grumble, realizing that my plans for the night have veered in an unexpected direction. Looks like I'll be checking out women's soccer. Should be interesting. Or not. "Let me hop in the shower and then we can take off."

Twenty minutes later, we're both freshly washed with our asses parked in the bleachers. The game is just about to get underway. Both teams are out on the field, warming up and taking shots at the net. It doesn't take long to find Sydney. My gaze homes in on her blonde head. Her hair is pulled up in a ponytail as she moves through a defensive drill.

"Nice to see you at the game, Kendricks," Coach says from the other side of Rowan where he's seated.

"Yup, just coming out to support the Wildcats."

He nods, his gaze refocusing on the field. In the three plus years I've been at Western, I don't think Coach has ever missed a game. He's always here, supporting his daughter.

Everyone rises for the National Anthem before the announcer goes through the starting lineup for each team and then the game gets underway. I've never attended a women's soccer match. I'm a little surprised to realize how fast paced the action is. Both the ball and the girls are in constant motion, running from one side of the field to the other. My head is on a swivel with the continuous movement. And these girls aren't afraid to get a little physical. Especially Sydney. A smirk settles on my face as she throws an elbow. When a ref warns her with a yellow card, she lifts her hands in the air like she doesn't understand what she got called for. Like she was just out there, minding her own business.

A smile curls around the edges of my lips.

That's my girl, all right.

Well...technically speaking, she's my girl, but not really.

From the moment the game begins until the buzzer sounds at the end of the second half, I find myself perched on the edge of my seat, gaze locked on the action. And there's plenty of it. I knew Sydney was an athlete, but I had no idea she was so talented. It's like she's got a motor tied to her ass. She never stops, gets gassed, or winded. Barely does she come out to guzzle down water before she's running back onto the turf. I'm exhausted just watching her.

Demi scores two goals. Each time the ball hits the net, Coach jumps to his feet and cheers, whistling like his life depends on it. I can't help but follow suit. It's almost a shock when two hours slip by with the Wildcats managing to pull off a win by the skin of their teeth. It's a hard-fought game. One they should be proud of.

What amazes me most is how much I actually enjoyed watching the match. Staring at Sydney while she makes moves on the field was certainly no hardship. I've always admired her spunk, but it's so much more than that. She's hard-core competitive, and as an athlete, I can totally respect that.

My gaze follows the blonde firecracker as she heads off the field and disappears inside the locker room with her teammates. I've always found Sydney to be smart and beautiful with a feisty personality to match. But there's so much more to her that I'm only now discovering. Her talent as an artist has blown me away and now watching her on the field...

What can't this girl do?

I have a newfound appreciation and respect for how relentlessly she must train to maintain that level of endurance. I work hard to stay in shape and make it through a three-and-a-half-hour game every week, but I suspect she could run circles around me. She has a ton of stamina. It's impressive.

And yeah, hot as hell.

It does the impossible and somehow makes me want her more than I already do.

I have no idea how this fake relationship will end. What I do know is that if Sydney is involved, it'll be interesting.

Chapter Seventeen

SYDNEY

Demi's arm is slung around my shoulders as we walk out of the locker room. As exhausted as I am, I'm flying high from that win. That was a tough game. There's nothing better than a victory on the field. Especially one that comes down to the wire and could go either way. With every second that ticked by, the crowd's cheers grew louder, pumping even more adrenaline through my body and giving me the extra boost I needed.

As a team, we worked like a well-oiled machine. Now we just need to keep performing at this level and we'll make it to the playoffs and, hopefully, championship. It'll be the perfect end to my soccer career. Unlike Demi, I won't be going on to play in the National Women's Soccer League.

"I'm starving." Now that the game is over and my nerves have dissolved, my appetite has rushed back to fill the void. Not wanting to be weighed down on the field, I never eat much before a game. Maybe a protein bar for energy. With the match behind us, my empty belly grumbles, searching for sustenance.

"Looks like Brayden stuck around," Demi says, knocking me from my thoughts of food.

My head snaps up and my surprised gaze locks on his dark one.

Awareness scuttles down my spine, making every nerve ending crackle with energy. "What's he doing here?"

"He was in the stands the entire time, watching with Rowan and Dad. I thought you realized it."

He was?

During a game, my world shrinks to the size of the field. I don't want any distractions. Especially when the other team's fans start chirping.

Why would Brayden bother?

There's no way he's interested in women's soccer.

The more distance that gets eaten up between us, the faster my heart thumps beneath my rib cage. The way Brayden's gaze stays pinned to mine makes everything inside me riot almost painfully. I draw in a deep breath, attempting to stomp out the attraction that has flared to life.

After our sketching session the other day, I've gone to great lengths to avoid being near him. It hasn't been easy. It feels like everywhere I go, there he is, bombarding my senses and attempting to scale my walls.

I have to remind myself that this is all a big façade. We might be trying to fool everyone else, but I can't allow myself to be tricked into believing this is anything more than a pretense. No matter how attracted I am to him.

As soon as we reach the guys, Coach pulls Demi into a hug and congratulates her for a hard-fought game. Then he does the same with me. I've known Nick Richards since freshman year. He's an amazing father and they have a close relationship. My guess is that he's somewhere in his mid-forties. And he's not bad looking for an older dude, either. That thought always brings a smile to my lips, because Demi hates when I talk about him being a hot, divorced daddy, which only makes me want to tease her more.

As soon as Coach releases me, Brayden wraps his arm around my shoulders and tugs me close before pressing a kiss against the crown of my head. "That was an awesome game. You killed it out there."

His praise shouldn't mean anything. Brayden doesn't know the first thing about soccer. In fact, it wouldn't surprise me to learn that this was the first game he's ever sat through. And yet, knowing all this, it doesn't stop the warmth from blooming in my chest before radiating outward.

I clear my throat and tamp down all of the unwanted sensations that are attempting to break through to the surface. "Thanks."

"I'm excited to check out the next one." There's a pause. "It's a week from today, right?"

Umm...what?

I tilt my head to meet his dark gaze before sifting through it carefully. I can't tell if the question is for show or if he actually means it.

"All right guys, I've got to head back to the office. I have a few recruiting calls to make before I wrap up for the night." Coach draws Demi in for one last quick hug before taking off with a wave.

"I bet you two are famished," Rowan says. "We should grab something to eat."

Spending more time with Brayden sounds like a disastrous idea. It's only been a week and already something unidentifiable has shifted in our relationship. I'm not entirely sure what it means, but it's enough to leave me rattled. Until I have a better handle on my emotions where he's concerned, it's probably best if I keep my distance.

"Does that sound like a plan?" Rowan asks when I remain silent.

I shake my head. "Sorry, I don't think—"

"Oh, come on, babe," Brayden wheedles, pressing me against his chest until I'm inundated with the spicy scent of his aftershave. It wraps slyly around me, cocooning my better judgment, making it impossible to think. "You worked hard out there. It's important to replenish and refuel."

With a frown, Demi cocks her head. "What happened to being famished? Isn't that what you said when we were walking out of the locker room?"

Damnit.

I should have kept my big mouth shut. But how was I supposed to know that Brayden would be waiting, or Rowan would suggest a late dinner?

"It's just that I have an assignment to finish up for tomorrow. I want to make sure there's enough time to get it done," I mumble, pulling the lie out of my ass like a magic trick.

"Don't worry, we'll make it quick," Brayden says easily. "I'll even help you with it afterward."

Hell, no.

That's the last thing I need.

The lines of our relationship have already blurred more than I'm comfortable with. I need to take a giant step back and get some perspective. Not that I'm in any danger of falling for Brayden, but still...

Stranger things have happened. The guy is to be avoided at all costs. He's nothing more than a heartbreaker. Take Kira, for example. Once upon a time, she probably had her head on straight. Now look at her. She's obsessed. There is no way I'd ever allow myself to become so crazy over a guy.

All right...I can admit that I'm physically attracted to him, but it's nothing more than that.

"Are we doing this or what?" Rowan asks, gaze bouncing curiously between us.

"Yup," my fake boyfriend cuts in, beating me to an answer and locking in this impromptu date, "let's meet up at the diner."

As soon as it's agreed upon, Demi and Rowan take off through the parking lot. Now that I've been left alone with Brayden, a burst of unwanted nerves explodes in my belly like a firework.

I stare after the couple with longing before muttering, "Is there a reason we can't all drive over together?"

He points to a shiny, black F-150 a few rows over. "My truck is right there. We'll just take that. It'll be easier."

For whom?

Whom, exactly, will this be easier for?

Not me.

I glance over my shoulder and realize with a sinking heart that my roommate and her boyfriend have already disappeared through the swirling darkness. I've been left to my own devices with Brayden. It's precisely where I didn't want to find myself. "We should all stick together."

With his arm wrapped around my body, he propels me toward the truck. "What's the matter? Are you afraid to be alone with me?"

I stiffen. "What? Of course not." One hundred percent. I am scared to death to be with him. He rouses feelings inside me that I'm not entirely comfortable with.

"Good, because I like spending time with you."

What?

I don't think I could be more shocked if he slammed me upside the head with a two-by-four.

Stunned by the admission, I slant a look in his direction. "You do?"

He unleashes a smile. It's one that has the potential to send panties dropping all over campus. "Yeah. You're smart and have a great sense of humor. You might find this difficult to believe, but I enjoy your wicked tongue. Not to mention, you're one hell of a soccer player. Even though this was my first game, I was pleasantly surprised to discover how fast paced and exciting it was." There's a pause before he tacks on, "You were pretty amazing out there."

For the second time in a matter of minutes, something warm fights to break free beneath my chest cavity. Only this time, I find it impossible to completely stomp out the unwelcome sensation.

"Thanks." My head spins with all these unsolicited compliments.

"Just stating facts," he says with an easy lift of his shoulder. "Rowan mentioned that Demi will probably try out for one of the professional soccer teams after graduation." He clicks the key fob before pulling open the passenger side door. "Is that something you're considering, too?" There's a beat of silence before he tacks on, "You didn't mention it the other day."

I shake my head. "No, I'm not good enough to play at that level."

Once I slide inside, his gaze stays pinned to mine as he loiters near the door. "You could have fooled me. It was difficult to take my eyes off you."

The heat he kindled to life is becoming more of a flame, radiating dangerously to other parts of my body. "I appreciate what you're saying, but you just admitted that you've never watched a game. You don't know anything about soccer," I mutter.

"True," he says easily in agreement. "But I watched you dominate and shut down their offense."

My mouth dries. When I fail to respond, he seals me inside his truck before walking around the front to the driver's side and settling beside me. A moment later, the engine roars to life and he's pulling out of the parking lot and into traffic. I shift, attempting to put as much distance between us as possible. Brayden is tall and muscular, easily taking up his side of the seat. I'm absurdly aware of him on every level. The more time we spend together, the more attuned I become to his presence. It's a strange sensation. It used to be so much easier to ignore and push to the outer recesses of my mind. That no longer feels possible. I find my thoughts turning to him even when we're not together. My stance is starting to soften when it comes to Brayden. Not only is that dangerous, it's unwise.

"There's such a serious expression on your face," he says, interrupting the whirl of my thoughts. "What are you thinking about?"

I blink away the disturbing realization and reluctantly glance at him. There's no way I can reveal the truth. Do you have any idea what he would do with that?

Even the thought is enough to scare the hell out of me.

"I'm, ah, just going over the game in my head. The mistakes I made. What I need to work on and correct." It doesn't escape me that the lie I'm forcing from my lips is exactly what I should be focused on. Instead, Brayden dominates all of my head space.

And that's a problem.

I need to do something about it before it spins any further out of control. This feels like a barely-contained fire. If I make one wrong move, I'll get burned alive.

By the time we reach the diner, I've given myself a stern talking to. I'm determined to reinforce the walls I've always kept in place when it comes to him. I can admit that Brayden isn't the asshole I originally suspected, but that doesn't mean he isn't a player. By his own admission, the guy doesn't date, he sleeps around.

A lot.

Chasing after the high-profile athletes on campus has never been my thing. Those are the guys I've made it a point to steer clear of. I know better than to fall for a player.

Especially when this is nothing more than a farce.

Can you imagine how pathetic that would make me?

I refuse to dwell on the answer.

Brayden holds open the door to the diner as we head inside. I give him a little side-eye in surprise. So far, he's held open both the car and restaurant doors for me.

He's laying it on a bit thick, isn't he?

In addition to playing the part of boyfriend, he's now also pretending to be the perfect gentleman?

A wide smile spreads across his face before he leans close and whispers, "You might find this difficult to believe, but I wasn't raised by wolves. My parents did attempt to instill a few manners in me."

I snort and say sweetly, "Let me guess, you always make sure to dispose of the condom afterward?"

His eyes spark with humor as his shoulders shake with silent laughter. "Yup, every time." Somehow, he manages to get close enough for his warm breath to drift across the delicate shell of my outer ear. It sends an unwanted flood of sensation skittering down my spine. "FYI, I'm extremely considerate in that department. I have a strict ladies-first rule in the bedroom. You should try it out. It comes with a hundred percent guarantee. If that's not enough to sway you, just check out my Yelp reviews. I'm extremely highly rated."

I roll my eyes with abandon. As much as I'm loath to admit it, our playful banter is one of the things I've come to enjoy. For obvious reasons, I won't be disclosing that to him. It would only encourage him, and that's the last thing I want to do.

Demi and Rowan are already waiting in a booth. My step stutters when I realize that they're sitting on the same side of the table.

Ugh.

These two.

It's beginning to feel as if everyone is conspiring against me, including my own roommate.

Brayden waves his hand with a flourish at the red vinyl seat. "Ladies first."

I narrow my eyes, knowing full well that he's not alluding to taking a seat. The guy means something else entirely.

A delighted grin simmers around the corners of his lips as I slide onto the vinyl. As soon as my ass hits the red cushioned material, he drops next to me, sitting so close that his thigh presses against mine. Since we're both wearing shorts, our bare flesh is forced together. If it were possible to scoot over further, I would, but there's nowhere for me to go. I'm stuck between a rock and a hard place.

Don't ask which one is which. At this point, not even I'm sure.

A waitress arrives, bringing us four glasses of water before writing down our order. Thankfully, it's not the one from Sunday morning. I don't think I could deal with her fangirling over Brayden for a second time. Once was more than enough.

Since I'm starving, I order a burger and fries. Normally, I try to eat healthily, but after all the energy I expended on the field, I'm treating myself. A burger and cheese fries will do the trick rather nicely. Both Rowan and Demi order the same.

For the next ten minutes, we rehash a couple of the plays and then discuss the other team. USC had a lot of good players, ones who will probably go on to play professionally. A couple of them have already signed contracts for the following season. It's pretty cool to play against and hold my own with women who will end up in the NWSL.

By the time the waitress returns with a tray loaded down with food, my stomach is in the process of consuming its own lining. After she finishes passing out the plates, I realize Brayden didn't order anything to eat.

"Aren't you hungry?" I grew up with four brothers who had big appetites. If it wasn't nailed down, they shoved it in their mouths. In our house, there was no saving something for later. You ate it now or accepted that it would most likely be gone in the not-so-distant future.

"Nah." One side of his mouth quirks. "I'll just share with you."

My brows skyrocket as I shake my head. "Yeah, sorry—that's not going to happen." I plan on devouring every last bite. Brayden is in for a rude awakening if he thinks I'm one of those dainty females who picks at her food and barely consumes anything. I can chow down with the best of them.

He angles his body toward mine, stretching his arm across the back of the seat in the process. When his fingers gently strum my shoulder, goose bumps rise in their wake. No matter how much I attempt to steel myself against the surge of excitement invading my body, it's a losing battle.

"Are you cold?" Concern flashes in his eyes. Before I can respond, he yanks off his sweatshirt and drags it over my head, grabbing my arms and thrusting them through the holes like I'm a small child. Then he pulls the soft, cottony material down until my head pops through the neck hole. "Is that better?"

"Yeah," I mumble, "it is. Thanks."

"No problem." The arm that had been resting against the back of the bench drops onto my shoulders, dragging me closer. "Anything for my girl."

Pleasure rushes through my veins. I suck in a deep breath, attempting to steady everything careening dangerously inside me. Instead, it has the opposite effect as I inhale a lungful of Brayden. His masculine scent surrounds me, inundating every fiber of my being until I'm dizzy with the sensation.

Unaware of my turbulent state, he picks up a fry and holds it to my lips. My gaze widens, locking helplessly on his.

When my lips remain pressed together, he whispers, "Open up."

I take a quick peek across the table only to find Demi and Rowan wrapped up in their own conversation. They're not paying the slightest bit of attention to us. Brayden's gaze drops to my mouth and combustible energy ignites within me. Any moment it's going to explode. As he holds the slim cut of potato to the seam of my lips, prodding it gently, I realize there's nothing I can do that won't cause a scene.

"Sydney," he growls. The low vibration of his voice does strange things to my insides and has me snapping to attention. Once my lips part, Brayden pushes the fry inside my mouth until it disappears. As I chew, my gaze never deviates from his. Glancing away isn't an option. He picks up another fry and pops it into his own mouth.

This continues for about five minutes. Nerves dance in the pit of my belly as he takes it upon himself to feed me. There's something surprisingly intimate about the process. As much as my mind is screaming for me to snap out of this strange paralysis, I can't. And I would be lying through my teeth if I didn't admit to enjoying the way his fingers stroke against my flesh with each piece of food that I take from him.

What's happening here is dangerous and yet I can't seem to put a stop to it.

"You two are so cute," Demi says. Her voice is what finally jerks me from my immobility. Instead of being thankful for the timely interruption, disappointment floods through me. "It's funny," she continues, "not in a million years did I ever see this coming."

I glance at Brayden to get a read on his reaction. There is no way I'm going to touch that comment with a ten-foot pole. His dark eyes seem near black as arousal engulfs his irises. "You know what they say—the line between love and hate is thin."

Demi's eyes widen before bouncing between us. "That's exactly what Sydney said."

He smirks, gaze latching onto mine. "I'm sure she did."

It takes effort to swallow down the rest of my fry before focusing my attention on the plate in front of me. My appetite has pulled a vanishing act, leaving behind a strange ache in its place. One that food won't be able to fill.

Chapter Eighteen

SYDNEY

By the time we leave the restaurant, I'm more than ready to go home. For my own sanity, I need to escape Brayden's overwhelming presence. I'm still cocooned in his comfy sweatshirt. It's tempting to pull it off and give it back, but the night has grown chilly. Since I wasn't expecting to go out after the game, I didn't dress with that in mind.

Brayden drapes an arm casually around my shoulders as we make our way to his truck. By this point, I'm practically speed walking in my haste to end this date.

What am I saying?

This isn't a date.

"That was fun," he says as if unaware of the thoughts swirling through my brain. "We should do it more often."

More often?

No way. That's definitely not a good idea. I don't think my body can stand it. I'm already vibrating with restless energy. And his nearness only makes it worse.

"Yeah, it was." I feign a yawn.

He glances at me, tugging me closer until all of his hard lines are pressed against my softer curves. "You must be exhausted."

"Yup. Long day."

He nods. "I can understand that. You really tore up the field. You should have finished your burger."

Yeah, that was impossible with him sitting so close. His proximity was much too distracting.

"Turns out I wasn't as hungry as I'd thought."

"Guess it was lucky that I didn't order a burger for myself."

When I was only able to choke down a few bites, Brayden easily polished off the rest.

"Yes," I mumble, not meaning a single word, "lucky."

"I'll get you home and then you can hit the sheets."

I expel the pent-up air from my lungs in relief. The quicker we part ways, the better off I'll be. I can untangle all these unsettling thoughts and get my head on straight.

Much like earlier this evening, Brayden hits the locks and holds open the passenger side door. Instead of immediately shuttering me inside, he leans down and grabs the seatbelt before stretching it across my torso and fastening it into place. My body stiffens at the innocuous contact. The clicking sound is like a gunshot in the silence of the truck as his gaze stays fastened on mine.

The moment stretches and lengthens between us, ratcheting up the thick tension that permeates the atmosphere. Everything in me stills. Just when I wonder if it's possible to pass out from lack of oxygen, he straightens to his full height and seals me inside. My heart hammers almost painfully against my chest as my muscles loosen and I collapse against the seat.

I don't understand what's going on here, and I'm afraid to push for too many answers. I'm scared of what I might uncover. What if we're only able to move forward instead of back to the way things have always been between us?

The drive to my apartment is made in oppressive silence. Brayden doesn't bother to turn on the radio in an attempt to break the growing pressure that fills the cabin. My fingers twist nervously in my lap. I need to get away from him and the stifling intensity that threatens to suffocate the life out of both of us.

By the time he pulls into the parking lot of my apartment, my fingers are curled around the door handle and I'm counting down the seconds until I can escape. A million butterflies have winged their way to life inside the confines of my belly. I don't remember the last time a guy provoked this kind of reaction from me.

It certainly wasn't Ethan.

Or Alex.

Or Daniel.

None of this makes sense. I don't even like Brayden.

What?

It's true, I don't!

So why is my body reacting to him like this?

As soon as he parks, I get ready to bolt. Before I'm able to do that, his hand slides into my hair, holding me in place. During the game, I'd had it up in a ponytail to keep it out of my face. When I showered afterward, I'd washed it and left it down to airdry naturally. The thick mass flows around my shoulders. His fingers slide through the golden strands until my temple rests against his wide palm.

"Don't go just yet."

"Oh, right. Your sweatshirt." My fingers flutter to the hem, ready to tear it from my body.

"No." The edges of his lips quirk. "I don't want the sweatshirt back."

"What then?" Barely am I able to force out the question.

Instead of responding, he closes the distance between us until his lips can ghost over mine. As soon as he makes contact, his hand slides from the side of my head to the back of my skull before tugging me closer.

There is nothing rushed about the way his mouth strokes over mine. It's lazy. As if we have all the time in the world to explore one another. His mouth caresses my upper lip before mimicking the movement on the lower one. When his tongue brushes against the seam of my lips, I open. It's not a conscious decision on my part. More like instinct. A deep-seated need to taste more of him.

And then he's delving in. Our tongues mingle until I lose myself in the taste and feel of him. Even though I realize this will only muddle the lines between us further, I can't stop myself from meeting every thrust of his velvety softness with a parry of my own. Worse than that, putting an end to this caress is the last thing on my mind. The feel of his mouth is like heaven.

"You taste so damn good," he murmurs against me before diving in for more.

An insistent voice inside my head continues to grow louder until it refuses to be ignored. My palms slide across the steely strength of his broad chest before pushing him away.

Brayden's eyelids are lowered to half-mast and there's a hungry look filling his dark gaze. It's one that sends my belly crashing to the bottom of my toes. His tongue darts out to lick at his lips as if he's intent on tasting me there.

"What are we doing?" It's almost impossible to fight my way out of the thick haze that has descended.

"We were kissing. I thought that would be obvious, but if you need further demonstration, I would be more than happy to provide it."

I huff out a shaky breath as some of the sexual fog clouding my better judgment dissipates. "That's not what I meant." There's a pause before pointing out, "We're alone. There's no need to put on a show."

His hand is still wrapped around the back of my skull. He drags me closer until his forehead is able to rest against mine. Only then do I realize how labored his breathing has become. "Is that what you think? That I've been putting on a show?" Before I can react, he says, "I assure you that any time I've kissed you, putting on a show was the least of my concerns. I kissed you because I wanted to." The fire that flares to life in his eyes nearly singes me alive. "It's the only thing I can think about."

With that, his lips slant over mine. First one way, then the other. They're as soft as a butterfly wing. I find myself anticipating the next angle and preparing for it until I'm once again a full participant in what's unfolding between us.

"I've spent months thinking about your mouth," he confesses in a rough tone. "Wondering what you would taste like. The way it would feel to explore it at my leisure. Don't you want that, too?"

Yes.

No.

I don't know. Everything feels so much more complicated than it did an hour ago.

When I fail to reply, he murmurs against my mouth, "Doesn't this feel good?"

Of course it does.

Although I'm of the mindset that just because something feels pleasurable, doesn't mean it's necessarily a great idea.

"Is there any reason this can't be more?" he whispers, continuing to stroke my lips.

More?

What kind of more?

"I want you, Sydney," he says as if to confirm the questions zipping around in my head. "And I'm pretty sure you want me, too."

It would be ridiculous for me to even attempt to deny it. Not after we've been making out for fifteen minutes in the front seat of his truck.

"Just because I want you, it doesn't make sleeping together a good idea."

"It certainly doesn't make it a bad one."

I blow out a steady breath. "It'll only complicate matters."

"It doesn't have to." His thumb rises to stroke over my lower lip. Back and forth it strums until I want to nip at it with my teeth.

Argh!

"It's just sex, Sydney. We can do whatever we want. We can make up the rules as we go. We're both adults here."

When he closes the distance between us, my palms land against the solid strength of his chest to hold him at bay. It becomes difficult to think when his mouth is gliding over mine. Even though it's so tempting to curl my fingers into the soft cotton of his T-shirt and drag him closer, I resist the urge.

"I should go." My body is clamoring for me to stay and make out with him, but I know *exactly* what that will lead to. Brayden isn't like the other guys I've been with. He rouses too much intensity within me to not tread lightly.

"Are you sure about that?" The hungry look in his eyes tells me exactly what he's thinking. And it would be so easy to give in and invite him upstairs. Somehow, I know that sex with Brayden would be good.

Oh, who am I kidding?

It would probably be mind blowing.

But I also realize that it'll mess with my head, and that's the last thing I need. I've got enough shit to figure out to invite further complications.

And Brayden is nothing if not a complication. Only recently have I managed to untangle myself from one relationship. The last thing I need to do is get sucked into whatever the hell this is. We're not involved.

It would be sex, pure and simple.

Unable to push the answer past my lips, I jerk my head into a tight nod and yank on the handle until the door flies open and I nearly tumble sideways. Brayden snaps forward, both hands wrapping around my shoulders to stop my descent.

We stare for a handful of heartbeats before I clear my throat. His fingers unlock from around me as I slide from the truck onto unsteady legs.

His gaze rakes over my body, nearly setting me to flame. "Have I mentioned how good you look wearing my sweatshirt?"

"Oh." I'd almost forgotten. I tug at the material. "Did you want it back?"

He shakes his head. "Nope. I'll get it from you another time. It's not like I don't know where you live."

"All right." I raise my hand in an awkward wave before hustling to the front entrance. When I glance over my shoulder, Brayden is still idling in the parking spot, watching me through the windshield. He might not be actively pursuing me, but that's exactly what it feels like.

Chapter Nineteen

BRAYDEN

Sydney and I are hunkered down at the library, putting the finishing touches on our accounting project. Every once in a while, my gaze will meander to hers. The other night, I oh-so-casually suggested that we should sleep together. I mean, why not? Even though she didn't immediately shut down the idea, she hasn't said a word about it. As tempted as I am to push for an answer, I won't. If she's not interested in having sex, then that's the way it is.

Which is too damn bad.

I'd like nothing more than to fuck this girl right out of my system. Then, when this is over with, I can relegate her to the back of my brain where she belongs. I've got enough on my plate with school and football to get caught up in a hot girl.

It's not like they aren't a dime a dozen around here.

But still…

There's something about the blonde soccer player that draws me to her. No matter how many times I've tried to move on, she continues to circle relentlessly at the back of my brain.

When my gaze cuts to hers again, I find Sydney's attention already locked on me. A little sizzle of awareness scuttles down my spine as she holds my stare, refusing to glance away. It's the stupidest thing. I have no idea why I react this way to her.

Every.

Damn.

Time.

When I raise a brow in silent inquiry, she shifts on her seat and breaks eye contact. Something inside me sits up a little straighter and takes notice. This girl is one of the most brazen chicks I know. She doesn't back down from anything. If there's something on her mind, she'll tell you about it. Whether you want to know or not. It's one of the things that attracts me. She doesn't take shit from anyone. Including me. And if that's not sexy as hell, I don't know what is.

My attention sharpens, only now noticing the slight flush that fills her cheeks. "What's going on?"

Her gaze flickers back to mine, momentarily touching it before flitting away. "I was thinking about what you said the other night."

That's all it takes for my muscles to tense and body to go on high alert. "Oh?"

She straightens on her chair before saying lightly, "You're right."

Of course I am.

Was there ever any doubt?

"About what?" I have a sneaking suspicion that I know what she's referring to, but I need her to confirm the information so there aren't any misunderstandings.

"We're both single." She gulps and forces out the rest. "We want each other and..." Her shoulders jerk as her voice trails off.

I press closer to the table until the thick wood bites into my rib cage. If I could leap across the damn thing, I would do it in a heartbeat. "We're both single, want each other, *and what?*" I repeat. My voice grows lower with each word I force out.

Do you have any idea how long I've waited to hear her say that?

This girl has spent years cutting me down with her sharp tongue. The thought of using it along with that sassy mouth for something all together different has my cock stirring in my athletic shorts.

Her gaze stays riveted to mine as a challenging light fills it. She reminds me of a warrior preparing for battle. That's exactly the way sex with Sydney would be. Like a battle. And I relish the thought of it.

"We should fuck," she says, head held high. Shoulders tensed. Gaze pinning me in place.

Damn.

She went there.

There's no coy skirting around the issue with this girl.

I bolt out of my seat so quickly that the chair scrapes back against the carpet, teetering precariously but not quite tipping over. I wouldn't give a crap if it did. We set up camp on the third floor where there's less student traffic. Plus, it's a Monday night. This place is like a ghost town.

Her eyes widen as I close the distance between us before reaching down and grabbing hold of her hand, hauling her to her feet.

"Brayden!" she squeaks.

Like I'm going to give her a chance to change her mind.

No fucking way.

When she doesn't put up a fight, I tow her through the stacks, winding my way to the very back row. It's doubtful anyone would stumble across us here. We're in a dusty section that doesn't get much action. All right...that's not true. If I have my way, it's going to see a little action tonight.

When I grind to a halt, Sydney stumbles against me. I shackle her other wrist so that both are locked in my tight grip before walking her backward until her spine hits the metal shelves. Her attention stays locked on mine as I press my chest against hers, dragging her hands upward until she's stretched out against the periodicals. Her chin tilts upward as my mouth ghosts over hers. The feel of her warm breath drifting against my parted lips as it comes out in short, sharp pants is nothing less than intoxicating.

I want more.

I want everything she's willing to give me.

Sydney has the look of a deer trapped in the bright glare of headlights. "What are you doing?"

Did this girl really think she could tell me that she wanted to fuck, and I wouldn't react like this? I'm so damn hard for her. It's been this way for a while. More than I'm willing to admit even to myself.

"What does it look like I'm doing?" Before she has a chance to respond, I answer the question. "I'm taking you up on your sweetly proposed offer."

She swallows thickly. The sound is like a gunshot in the stillness of the library that surrounds us.

"We can't do it here," she whispers, voice quivering.

A groan rumbles up from deep within me as her nipples pebble against my chest. "Why not?"

Her gaze jerks from mine as she glances around nervously. "Someone might see us."

"Isn't getting caught half the fun?" I lean forward and nip at her plump lower lip. The pressure is just enough to pull her attention back to me where it belongs.

Heat ignites in her eyes and her pupils dilate, eating up the green of her irises.

Actually, I have zero intention of screwing her here. But that doesn't mean I can't give her a little preview of what she can expect in the future. When I take Sydney, it won't be some rushed fuck against a bookshelf.

Hell, no.

It'll be in a bed, where I can take my sweet damn time. Where I can get my fill of her body. And if I'm lucky, it'll last for a couple of weeks, which will be more than enough time to purge her from my system.

It's the perfect solution.

Sydney isn't looking for long-term attachments, and neither am I.

It's nothing more than fucking.

"Should I stop?" I allow that question to hang in the air. "All you have to do is say the word and we'll return to the table and finish working on our project." I lower my mouth to her ear. "Or, if you prefer, I can take you back to your place, treat you like you're made of spun glass, and screw you nice and slow like some of the other guys you've been with. Maybe we can do it missionary style. I bet that's exactly what turns you on."

Not.

Her breath hitches as a delicate shiver slides through her body.

"Is that what you want? To be fucked carefully? Or maybe you want some selfish prick who won't bother to get you off?"

I wasn't joking about what I told her the other night. I always make sure the girls I'm with get off first. It's what keeps them coming back for more. Honestly, that's part of the fun. And it always feels amazing when their tight little pussies spasm around my cock, choking the life out of it. Their breathy moans of pleasure are ultimately what sends me careening over the edge.

Her teeth rake over her plump lower lip.

"Is that what you like, baby? To be left hanging? Unsatisfied? Because I know exactly what guys my age are like. They're horny little bastards who don't know the first thing about pleasing a woman." I tilt my head. "But you've already discovered that, haven't you? You want a man who can make you come. One who knows his way around your body." There's a pause. "Am I right?"

She jerks her head into a barely perceptible nod.

"Give me your words, Sydney. I'll be damned if I force you into something you don't want."

"I want it," she says breathlessly.

You're damn right she does. I could sense it in her from the very beginning. My guess is that no one else has ever given her what she needs. I'll be the one who changes that.

Those three words are all it takes for my lips to crash into hers. Unlike our previous kisses, I don't have to prod her into opening. My tongue sweeps inside her mouth, mingling and licking at hers. My fingers tighten around her slender wrists, forcing them into the book spines. Every hard line is pressed against her softer ones. Sydney's body isn't as lush as some of the other girls I've been with. She's toned and strong.

Athletic.

It's a major turn-on.

At this particular moment, I would be hard-pressed to offer up something I don't find attractive about this girl. As soon as that thought pops into my brain, I push it to the outer recesses, not wanting to dwell on it or what it means. This is nothing more than sex. We can enjoy each other without having to attach any significance to it. Hell, I do it all the time.

The whimper that escapes from her makes my cock throb. The strict control I've always prided myself on falters. Sydney doesn't realize how hard it's been to hold myself back where she's concerned. No other female has ever challenged me the way she does.

I nip at her plump lower lip before delving in for more. It's only when I've had my fill of her mouth that I kiss a fiery trail to her jawline before licking and sucking my way down the column of her neck. She tilts her head, baring more of the delicate skin for me to feast on.

I gorge myself until she's a quivering mess. The need to touch her thrums through me like that of a heavy drumbeat until it's all I can focus on. I transfer both wrists to one hand. They're thin enough for my fingers to wrap around. My other one drifts down her bare arm, before sliding around her sloped shoulder and settling over one breast. My palm is large enough to cover her entirely. She's the perfect handful. Anything more would be a waste.

Unable to resist, I squeeze the soft flesh. It's hard enough to elicit a gasp but not enough to cause pain. The last thing I would ever want to do is hurt Sydney. All I'm trying to do is nudge her out of her comfort zone and heighten the pleasure I'm capable of giving her.

When I tighten my fingers for a second time, I lean closer, nipping at her throat, biting down upon it. The thickness of my erection digs into her belly. I want to fuck this girl so badly. I want to drive myself deep inside her tight heat until we're both falling to pieces. I loosen my grip on her breast before my hand trails down to the button of her jeans where it hesitates for a beat. Her breathing picks up tempo.

With fear?

Or anticipation?

I'm willing to bet it's excitement rushing through her veins at the idea of me touching her in such a public space. If it were anything else, all she'd have to do is push me away. One word and I would stop. I wouldn't like it, but I'd respect her decision.

A long string of silent moments stretches between us. It only heightens the riotous intensity crackling in the air. Unable to wait another second, I flick the button of her jeans and drag down the fly. A shaky exhalation falls from her lips as I continue to kiss and lick her neck. Even if someone did happen to wander by and catch sight of us, my bigger body is pressed against hers, shielding her from prying eyes.

Hot shafts of need claw at me, attempting to find an escape. I've wanted to touch her like this for so long that it's difficult to believe it's actually coming to fruition. That Sydney now wants me in ways I've only dreamed about.

My fingers dip beneath the elastic band of her panties, grazing over her silky-smooth mound before sliding across her pussy. With my wrist, I press against her inner thighs in a silent command to widen her stance.

When she remains still, I lift my face from her neck and growl, "Open for me."

She snaps to attention before stepping further apart and giving me room to maneuver. As soon as she does, I part her lower lips. One finger dips inside her heat.

Holy fuck.

A groan escapes from me as I bury my face against her throat and close my eyes. Her body might be all angles and toned muscle, but here? She's so fucking plush. I can just imagine what it would feel like to drive myself deep inside her body and have her convulse around me.

It would be absolute heaven.

I thrust a few times before a second finger joins the first, widening her sheath. A whimper escapes from her mouth as she tilts her pelvis, silently begging for more. Perhaps she had been leery about making out behind the stacks, but that doesn't seem to be the case any longer. Whatever inhibitions Sydney had been clinging to are long gone.

"Your pussy is already wet," I whisper against the side of her face before pressing a kiss against it. "Is that all for me?"

She inhales an unsteady breath as our movements find a natural rhythm. Every time I drag my fingers from her body, her inner muscles clench, attempting to draw me back in again.

Is she even aware of it?

I wasn't joking about her being soaked. I'm so turned on that I'm about to go off like a shot. And just to be clear, that's never happened before.

When she remains silent, I prod her for an answer, needing her to admit the truth. "Is your pussy crying for me, Sydney?"

Instead of giving me a response, she bites her lip in an attempt to keep silent. If she thinks I'll allow her to evade the question, she couldn't be more wrong. I drag my fingers from her body and circle them around her clit before giving it a little pinch.

A gasp explodes from her.

"That's not an answer," I growl.

When I squeeze her for a second time, air rushes from her lungs. *"Yes!"*

My fingers slide through her slick heat to her opening. "Is all this cream for me?"

"Brayden..."

"Yeah, baby?" A beat of silence passes as I torment her flesh. She has no idea what I'm capable of, but she's damn well going to find out. "You don't like the dirty talk?"

I spear my fingers deep inside her until they're buried to the hilt.

"I do." Her forehead falls against my chest. "I like it a lot."

"Deep down," I whisper against her, "I knew you would." All it was ever going to take was the right guy to come along and open the door so she could walk through it.

And you better believe I'm that guy.

A garbled sound escapes from her. Her harsh exhalations are music to my ears. It won't take much more to push her over the edge.

"How badly do you want to get off?"

"Please..."

Instead of giving her what she wants, I tease her, pumping into her until she has no choice but to meet each thrust with the piston of her hips.

"I like the sound of my name when it's choked from your lips. And when you beg?" I drive inside her with a little more force. "It makes me fucking nuts."

She whimpers as her muscles clench around my fingers as if to keep them secured in place.

With her head bowed, I'm unable to see her face. I'm desperate to catch a glimpse of her expression. The need to watch her fall apart beneath my touch pounds through me, refusing to be denied. I don't think I've ever wanted anything more.

"Look at me," I growl.

She lifts her forehead until her gaze collides with mine. Even though she never answered my question, I pick up the pace before slipping my fingers from her slick heat to circle her clit.

The way her eyes darken, emotion crashing inside them like thunder, I know she's close to splintering apart.

And you know what?

So am I.

Even though this is the first time I've touched Sydney, I've catalogued every intake of breath, every flash of pleasure as it flickered across her face. All it will take is a little more pressure against her clit and—

Her head lolls back against the bookshelf as her eyelids flutter closed. Watching Sydney shatter is one of the most beautiful things I've ever seen. My heart clenches before hammering into overdrive. I have no idea what these strange sensations rampaging through me mean, and I can't be bothered to inspect them more closely.

All I know is that this experience has only whetted my appetite for more.

Chapter Twenty

SYDNEY

A week has slid by since the encounter at the library.

I almost snort.

Encounter.

That sounds so...I don't even know. I'm not sure what to call it. Him getting me off behind the stacks?

Sure, we'll just go with that for the time being.

I thought our relationship might take a turn for the awkward after what happened. Strangely enough, it hasn't. We're still playing the part of happy couple while out in public, which means a lot of hand holding while walking to class or hanging out at parties. He'll sling an arm casually around my shoulders and draw me close as if it's the most natural thing in the world.

Is it weird that it's beginning to feel that way?

Or that I miss his warmth when he's not holding me?

My breath will catch as his masculine scent wraps around me, teasing my senses. It's a cross between the ocean, citrusy sunshine, and something that is uniquely Brayden. There are times when I catch myself burrowing into the solid strength of him, almost forgetting this is an act we're putting on.

When I'm jarred back to reality, I force myself to step away. I can't allow myself to forget that this is nothing more than an exchange of services. I'm his pretend girlfriend. He's assisting with my art project. We're both getting something we need out of this arrangement. Although, I suspect that the modeling isn't a hardship for him. The guy seems to enjoy shedding his clothes and being full-on naked. He'd strut around in front of a crowd with no problem at all.

All right, I'll admit it. It's not exactly difficult to stare at that well-honed body for hours at a time. The guy is definitely built.

My gaze rises from the sketch pad to the man standing in front of me. Drawing him, shading in all his musculature is an absolute pleasure. I would never admit this to him, but I'll be sad when we wrap this up. The process has gone better than I expected. Since we're both in school and play a sport, our schedules mirror each other and it's easy to carve out time to get together.

I pick up a different charcoal pencil before filling in more detail. Then I flip over the thick sheet and start a new one. The more pieces I have to choose from for the final portfolio, the better off I'll be. My fingers move swiftly over the paper, forming the lines of his body before shading in the specifics. Bone structure. Muscles. Ligaments.

"Do you mind if I stretch for a minute?" he asks, breaking into my thoughts. "I'm getting a little stiff."

My attention drops to his cock.

"Not there," he says with a snort.

Color slams into my cheeks that I've been caught checking out his package. Normally, I'm able to remove myself from the situation and get into the frame of mind where I can stare at his body and not think of Brayden in a sexual manner. It's the same way you can stare at a piece of art or sculpture of a naked form and appreciate it solely for its beauty without getting turned on.

He chuckles when I avert my gaze to the sketch pad and pretend to examine the drawing. It's a low sound that strums something deep inside.

Brayden has the rare ability to make me feel like a stupid schoolgirl, and that's not who I am.

Like, at all.

I was sixteen years old and a junior in high school when I had sex for the first time. That was five years and many boyfriends ago. He shouldn't be able to affect me so easily.

Maybe it's because I've always been the aggressor in relationships. I've taken control and set the pace, deciding what happened. That, however, isn't the way my pseudo-relationship with Brayden has unfolded. Since the beginning, he's the one who's assumed control and called all the shots.

Maybe that's the issue. Maybe I need to wrestle a bit of power away from him and then everything else will fall into place. Instead of feeling at a disadvantage, I'll have leveled the playing field.

The idea churns in my head as my gaze lifts to his, watching as he stretches his arms overhead. The long, lean lines of his muscles lengthen. The image he makes hits me like a punch to the gut before settling like a heavy stone in my core. I've never felt this kind of intense physical attraction to someone before.

Making a snap decision, I toss the sketch pad aside. Enough work has been accomplished for the day. With my gaze locked on Brayden, I rise from the chair I'm perched on. As soon as I do, his gaze sharpens. Other than his arms falling back to his sides, he doesn't move, only continues to watch me through hooded lids.

When I'm no more than a foot away, I raise both hands before settling my palms against the warm flesh of his chest and the sinewy muscle that lies beneath. Even though I have yet to explore his body physically, I feel intimately acquainted with it. I could describe every ridge and contour in glorious detail. Every dip and swell. I've spent so many hours staring at him that my fingertips itch to discover the firm flesh for themselves. I want to feel every hard line instead of simply capturing them on paper.

My gaze falls, needing to study him up close and personal. It no longer matters if he's watching me from beneath the thick fringe of his dark lashes. He stands perfectly still as my palms drift upward, gliding across hard pectorals and over sculpted shoulders. I move from his tightly corded neck to his powerful arms before smoothing them over the bulge of his biceps.

Unwilling to end my perusal, I reverse the motion until my palms once again arrive at his broad chest. Even though he remains immobile, his heart picks up its tempo, thumping faster.

Is it my touch that causes this reaction?

The thought is a heady sensation.

My gaze lifts, flickering to his. The heat that fills his eyes is enough to scald me alive.

Instead of moving upward again, my palms descend, floating over washboard abdominals. They are so damn tight. Hard as a rock. I can almost imagine how many hours Brayden must put in at the gym. This isn't the kind of physique you get just showing up for practice every day. Hours' worth of work have sculpted every tightly honed muscle. My body is trim, but I don't have this kind of impressive definition. I have neither the time nor commitment to achieve it.

As my fingers slide downward, my gaze follows their path. Just like he accused earlier, I'm eating him up with my eyes. I can't help myself. On each side of his lower abdomen are the chiseled lines of a V that look as if they've been carved from marble. They're like a brightly lit Vegas Strip sign, arrowing toward his thick erection.

Another punch of arousal slams into me, nearly knocking the breath from my lungs. Everything about this man is beautiful. Even his cock. That's not something I've ever thought before, but it's true where Brayden is concerned.

My hands gravitate lower until my fingers can wrap around his hard shaft. Carefully, I stroke him from the root to the very tip before repeating the movement. His cock is steel encased in silk. I'm captivated by the sight of it.

"Fuck," he groans.

I tip my chin until my gaze can capture his. There's a heavy-lidded look to him. His eyelids are lowered to half-mast as he watches me from beneath them.

Now that I've spent time learning the feel of Brayden, the need to taste him thrums through me until it's all I can think about. I close the little bit of distance that separates us until my lips are pressed against his sternum. A deep groan rumbles up from his chest. I feel the low vibration of it as my lips hover over his flesh. My tongue darts out to lick him. He tastes fresh and clean as if he showered right before arriving on my doorstep.

Following the same path my fingers took moments ago, I caress him with my mouth, nipping at his skin and the taut muscle that lies beneath. Every inch of him is sculpted perfection. When I reach his navel, I drop to my knees and sit back on my heels before surveying him from this angle. His powerfully built legs are braced apart as if he's attempting to steady himself on a roiling ship. I've witnessed him on the football field and watched how explosive his movements can be when he bursts into action.

At twenty-one years of age, Brayden is all man. There is nothing boyish about him. Desire ignites in my core and dampens my panties. My fingers trail over the crinkly hair that is sprinkled across both his thick thighs and chiseled calves. Every part of him is rock solid.

My gaze fastens on the rigid length standing proudly to attention. A bead of moisture has gathered at the tip. Unable to resist, I lean forward and swipe my tongue across it. Another rumble escapes from him.

Earlier, I had been embarrassed to be caught staring at his dick. Now, I want to look my fill and commit it to memory. My fingers trace over the thickened length, circling over the blunt tip before sliding back to the root. As fascinated as I am by his erection, I can't resist brushing my fingertips over the heaviness of his balls and learning their texture.

It's strange to realize that I was wrong in my assessment of his body. Brayden isn't hard everywhere. His scrotum is soft. I palm one side and then the other. And just like the rest of him, this is big as well. I rise onto my knees to close the distance between us. My tongue flicks over one ball, circling it with the tip of my tongue before sliding over to give the same attention to the other.

"That feels so damn good," he groans.

I dance beneath the soft flesh of his sac before licking a path to the root of his cock. Only then do I flatten my tongue against him, running it to the crown and circling around the bulbous head before finally sucking him inside my mouth. A hissed breath escapes from his lips. Even though I've only just taken him inside me, already I feel the tension that radiates off him in thick waves. It won't take much for him to lose all semblance of control.

His pelvis tilts forward as his fingers tunnel through my hair, locking around the sides of my skull to hold me in place. I flick my gaze upward, only to find his attention riveted to me. There's something incredibly intimate about maintaining eye contact while performing this act. It's not something I always do, but, in this moment, it feels strangely right. I want to savor every expression as it flashes across his face. He stares at me as if my mouth alone could bring him to his knees.

Every time I draw him in deeper, the crown of his cock nudges the back of my throat. With each repetition, I swirl my tongue around the tip. His jaw locks, the muscles ticking. If he clenches it any harder, it'll shatter into a million jagged pieces.

"Fuck, baby," he groans, "that's going to make me come."

When he attempts to push me away, I give my head a little shake.

"Sydney," he growls.

"It's fine," I say around his length.

"Are you sure?" His voice dances precariously close to the edge, just like he is. And I love it. Love that I have this power over him. That I can so easily make him lose control.

The look in my eyes must say it all. The edges of his lips quirk just a bit as his fingers tighten around my scalp as if to guide me along his length. His gaze stays locked on mine as his muscles stiffen.

A long, guttural groan explodes from him as a burst of saltiness hits the back of my throat. My mouth turns voracious as I keep up a constant pressure until he finally softens. Only then do I pull away and kiss the tip. Before I can catch my breath, Brayden reaches down, lifting me from my knees and pressing me against the broad expanse of his naked chest. His lips crash onto mine, kissing me as he thrusts his tongue inside my mouth.

He pulls away enough to growl, "You taste just like me. Do you have any idea how sexy that is?"

And then he's back to devouring me. It's enough to make my head spin. There's a heated look in his eyes as he places me on the bed. His fingers go to my shirt, peeling it away from my body before he makes quick work of removing the jeans.

"Turnabout is only fair play, don't you think?"

Actually, I couldn't agree more.

Before I can blink, every stitch of clothing has disappeared. His movements still as his gaze roves greedily over me, touching upon every dip and rise. It's strange to think that this is the first time Brayden has seen me naked when I've studied him on multiple occasions for hours at a stretch. I've scrutinized every slab of muscle and contour of his form. I could close my eyes and sketch every single inch of him.

"How are you this gorgeous?"

The tightly muttered compliment sends a thrill of pleasure through me. His words should be meaningless, but it's obvious they're not.

We both agreed that this is just sex.

Nothing more.

A perk of our fake relationship.

As he moves between my spread thighs, his warm breath drifts across my core. A shiver of anticipation slides down my spine as his tongue dances over me before spearing inside.

Pleasure gathers inside me as a whimper escapes. It won't take much to push me over the edge. I'm already so turned on by taking him in my mouth.

That's a first for me.

His hands fasten on my inner thighs, pushing them further apart before worshipping every delicate inch. He licks from the bottom of my slit to my clit, lavishing me with so much attention that holding back the orgasm becomes impossible, and, within seconds, I find myself coming undone beneath his talented mouth.

Before I can blink, he's crawling up my body and settling on top of me. His mouth crashes against mine, his tongue thrusting inside to tangle with my own. The taste of my arousal floods my senses and heightens my desire.

My breath catches at the back of my throat when his thick cock settles at my entrance. Even though I came just moments ago, another wave of need crashes over me, threatening to drag me to the bottom of the ocean.

Just as he's about to thrust inside me, he pauses.

"I need a condom." His voice is strung so impossibly tight, it could snap at any moment.

Oh my god. How could I forget about protection? I'm a safety girl. At least, I usually am. This just goes to show how crazy this guy makes me.

When I nod, he rolls away. His feet hit the floor before he hastily searches through his pile of clothing for his wallet and grabs a small packet. With deft fingers, he rips into the square before sheathing himself in latex. And then he's back, taking up his position between my spread legs.

It only takes one sharp thrust before he's filling me to the brim. Less than a dozen strokes later and his muscles tighten. The moment he arches, a growl leaves his lips as I follow him over the precipice. My body convulses, milking every last drop from him until he collapses on top of me.

No matter what I thought sex with Brayden would be like, I could never have imagined how spectacular it would feel.

Unwilling to dwell on those thoughts, I squeeze my eyes tightly shut. No matter what this is between us, I'll enjoy it for as long as it lasts. And when it's over, I'll walk away with my emotions firmly intact.

Shouldn't be a problem, right?

Chapter Twenty-One

BRAYDEN

I'm cruising through the Union, mentally going over the list of bullshit that needs to get checked off before the end of the day. I'll tell you what, the grind never ends. After an early morning lift, I hit the showers and got dressed before hauling ass to two classes. One of my business professors was considerate enough to surprise us with a pop quiz.

Dick.

It took every bit of brain power to dredge up the answers and get them onto paper.

With the first part of my day finished, the plan is to grab lunch and head over to the library for an hour of studying. After that, I have one last class before I need to hustle back to the stadium for a two-hour practice. I'll shower again, cram in a little more studying, and hit the sack. Then I'll get up tomorrow and do it all over again.

Anyone who thinks it's easy to be a student athlete doesn't know what the hell they're talking about. Sometimes, it sucks major ass. When we're in season, my day is scheduled down to the last minute.

That being said, have I ever thought about quitting to be a regular student on campus without all the responsibility that comes along with being an athlete?

Nope.

The endgame is the NFL. For the foreseeable future, I'll work my ass off to attain my goals. No matter how much time it takes or how little sleep I get. If I have to burn the candle at both ends to make it through graduation, I'll do it.

My father played football at Western before getting drafted to the pros. I want to follow in his footsteps. Memories of throwing around the ball in the backyard are some of the most cherished ones I have. And I hold them the closest. He played in the pros for fifteen years before sustaining an injury he couldn't come back from.

He was there for every game I played from elementary up through high school until he was taken away from us. He spent years coaching me. I enjoyed how both the kids and parents would crowd around him, wanting to listen to the stories of his glory days. My chest would puff up with pride as I hung onto every word, even though they were tales I'd heard so many times I could recite them myself.

What I'm trying to achieve is not only for me. It's a tribute to him.

So far, I'm on track to make it happen. It's bittersweet to know that the man who was my hero is no longer here to see me accomplish my goals. To take pleasure in his son turning his dreams into a reality. The ones we set together when I was just a skinny-ass kid who could barely catch a football.

I glance at the different restaurants that line the inside of the building and try to decide what would be the easiest to grab and eat on the go. There's a smoothie shop that sells pitas and wraps, another with burgers and chicken sandwiches, and then pizza. The pizza gets instantly nixed. All the grease and cheese will end up settling like a rock at the bottom of my gut. That leaves a grilled chicken sandwich or a wrap.

Since I had a sandwich yesterday, we'll go for a wrap today.

I can wolf it down on my way to the library and it won't ruin my girlish figure. I'm doing my best to stay in top form. The NFL Combine is coming up and I need to impress the scouts. Rowan is lucky. There's already a buzz surrounding him. And there's talk about me as well, but a lot of sportscasters will bring up my father and rehash the highpoints of his career. I want them focused solely on me. On my accomplishments and abilities.

As I step in line, my hand automatically reaches for my phone. I hate how tempting it is to shoot Sydney a text and see what she's up to. As soon as I conjure up a mental image, memories of what it feels like to slide deep inside her crash over me like a tidal wave, flooding me with pleasure. We've had sex a few times and it just keeps getting better and better. There's something about her and the way our bodies fit together perfectly. It's almost as if she were made for me.

The moment that thought pops into my head, I stuff the phone back into my pocket, resisting the urge to touch base. I had assumed we would knock boots once or twice and then I'd get bored or lose interest. Most of the time, that's what happens. But it's turned out to be the complete opposite. The more I have, the hungrier I am. Where that girl is concerned, I'm insatiable. This is a first for me, and I'm not quite sure what to make of it. Fucking Sydney out of my system hasn't turned out to be as clear-cut as I'd originally assumed. Maybe I need to chill out on the whole sex thing for a few days until I get a firm handle on the situation.

That's probably a good plan moving forward. It's not like I don't have enough to occupy my time.

I almost snort.

Although, a jam-packed schedule certainly hasn't prevented me from dropping by her place for a little naked time.

Someone calls out my name as they saunter past. Just as I raise my hand in response, I catch sight of a familiar blonde head on the other side of the open space. I shift my stance and crane my neck, attempting to get a better look.

Yup, that's definitely Sydney. It seems like everywhere I go, there she is. I'm about to force myself to turn away when I realize that she isn't alone.

My brows snap together.

Wait just a minute...

Is that a guy sitting across from her?

All thoughts of the wrap I'd been about to grab disappear as I stalk through the Union to the table where Sydney and the interloper are parked. As I get closer, I realize there's a tray with crumpled wrappers pushed off to the side, which means they must have grabbed a meal together.

What the hell is she doing, eating lunch with another guy when she's fake dating me?

A genuine smile lights up her face as she laughs. Even from this distance, I hear the husky sound of her amusement. When was the last time she looked at me that way?

Happy and totally carefree.

Oh, right—it was never.

Sydney is more guarded in her responses when we're together, as if she's holding bits and pieces of herself back from me. Sure, she'll laugh, but it's never carefree and relaxed.

Who the hell is this douche?

My narrowed gaze lands on him. There's something about the guy that has me suspecting he might be older. Most college students go for more casual, comfortable clothing. Instead of a T-shirt and jeans or athletic shorts, he's wearing khaki pants and a crisp, blue button-down. His dark, wavy hair is styled instead of looking like he rolled out of bed in the morning and ran his hand absently through it.

Is this what she's into?

Older dudes?

Something white hot bursts to life inside me before blazing its way through my body like molten lava. My feet almost stutter to a halt when I realize what this unknown emotion is.

Jealousy.

I'm fucking jealous.

Guess there really is a first time for everything. I've never liked a girl enough to feel this kind of all-consuming sensation take root inside me. I want to grab that guy by his perfectly pressed shirtfront and haul him to his feet. Maybe punch him in his pretty boy face a few times before tossing him to the side. How much would Sydney be smiling at him if I were to do that?

She wouldn't be. Although, it's doubtful she'd be showering me with happiness either.

I drag a hand through my hair as I consider how to play this.

Unfortunately, there isn't any more time for decisions. I've arrived at the table, and Sydney's head is turning in slow motion. Her green eyes widen when she catches sight of me. Or maybe it's my pissed-off expression that has her muscles tensing and her face freezing.

Not bothering with a greeting, I grab a chair from a nearby table and drag it next to hers before dropping down and slinging my arm around her shoulders. My gaze stays pinned to the guy across from her.

If this dude thinks he can just waltz in and steal my girl, he's seriously mistaken.

Wait a minute...*my girl?*

Fuck.

This situation is much worse than I suspected. But there isn't time to dwell on that now. I'll deal with the ramifications later. First, I've got a douchebag to set straight.

"Hey, babe." My other hand slides across her jaw, rotating it until she has no other choice but to meet my gaze. When she opens her mouth—most likely to ask what the hell I'm doing—I press my lips to hers. The kiss might be brief, but I've proven my point as to who this girl belongs to.

Me.

She belongs to me.

The asswipe seated across from us raises his brows as I give him a chin lift in silent greeting.

He settles back against his chair before crossing his arms over his chest, looking none too pleased that I've swooped in on his action. "Who are you?" he asks in a clipped tone.

Who am I?

Who am I?

That's rich.

"Brayden Kendricks." There's a pause before I drop the bomb that should put an end to this. "Sydney's boyfriend."

"Huh. Well, that's certainly interesting," he muses, nodding in her direction. "My sister failed to mention that she recently acquired one of those."

I'm sorry, come again?

Did he just say *sister?*

I give Sydney a bit of side-eye to get a read on the situation. By the tight slash of her lips, I'm fairly sure that I made a massive tactical error. One I can't come back from.

Well, shit.

Everything inside me loosens as I hold out my hand. "Nice to meet you."

Now that he's pressing his lips together in the same way the girl bristling next to me is, I'm able to see the family resemblance. Although, it's doubtful Sydney would appreciate me commenting on it.

"Brayden, this is my brother, Court," she grumbles, sounding none too pleased about being forced to make introductions.

The other guy tips his head toward me as his gaze pins Sydney in place. "So how long has this been going on for? I just saw you last week and you didn't say a word."

If it's possible, Sydney's lips flatten even further. They're barely perceptible. My guess is that she's about to blurt out the truth, and I don't want her to do that.

"It's a relatively new development," I cut in smoothly before she can blow our cover to smithereens. "Just a couple of weeks."

His eyes narrow as he ignores me. "Last I heard, you were taking a break from dating."

Sydney draws in a deep breath before steadily releasing it back into the world. I can't claim to know her well, but I'm fairly certain she's on the verge of losing it.

"If you have to know," I pipe up, "I swept her off her feet and didn't give her much choice in the matter." It's not a total lie.

The choice part, anyway.

"Huh. I suppose you'll be bringing him to the party on Sunday?" Court asks.

I can practically hear Sydney groan. "No, I don't—"

"I bet Mom would love to meet him," he interrupts as a slow smirk curls around the edges of his lips. "In fact, *everyone* would enjoy meeting him."

"What?" Her eyes bulge from their sockets before she shakes her head. "No, it's much too early for something like that. Give it a month or two."

"Nonsense." There's a pause as his gaze lands on me. "What do you say, Brayden? Any interest in meeting the fam?"

"As much as he would love to," Sydney cuts in, "he's busy this weekend. You might not realize this, but Brayden plays football, and his schedule is packed tight."

"Yeah, I'm aware of who he is." The challenge is there in his eyes. It's like he just threw down a gauntlet and is waiting for me to pick it up.

And I'll be damned if I don't rise to the occasion.

"Luckily for me, I just so happen to be free on Sunday, and I'd love to meet your family, babe."

"Great." Even though he smiles, there's nothing friendly about it. "I'll share the good news with everyone."

"Looking forward to it," I add so that he doesn't think I'm the least bit intimidated.

It's only when Sydney makes a garbled sound before burying her face in her hands that I wonder if I've made a mistake.

Chapter Twenty-Two

SYDNEY

Through narrowed eyes, I watch the girl rushing toward me as she dribbles the ball easily between her feet. The moment she crosses the midfield line, I'm on her, pushing into her space, attempting to steal the ball away. Unlike the adversaries we face on a weekly basis, I know Marina. She's my teammate, and this is nothing more than a scrimmage. Since I understand all of her weaknesses, it's almost too easy to swoop in and knock her off balance. The few seconds it takes for her to right herself is all the time I need to kick the ball away. I push myself a little harder before racing ahead and passing it to another player who runs with it down to the opposite side of the field before shooting it into the goal.

"Bitch," Marina huffs, sucking wind. She's a sophomore attacker. By the time she's a senior, she'll be unstoppable. I kind of wish I'd be around to see it, but this is my last season playing with the Wildcats before graduating in the spring.

I chuckle, not taking offense before knocking my shoulder into hers. "Your footwork was sloppy," I say with a shrug. "Work on it and you won't have to worry about me."

She grumbles before returning to her side of the field.

Fifteen minutes later, Coach Adams blows his whistle and ends practice. After two hours of drills and scrimmaging, everyone is out of breath. Although, some of the older girls are able to hide it better. I'll be damned if I double over in front of anyone, especially Coach.

Demi throws her arm around my shoulders as we kick a few of the balls toward the bag for clean-up before heading to the locker room.

"Sydney," Coach calls out, "can you stick around for a few minutes?"

"Yup," I raise my voice in order to be heard across the field.

Demi's hands go to her hips as she nods toward the sideline where Coach waits. "What's that about?"

I jerk my shoulders. "Not sure. Probably the game on Thursday. I think he's actually concerned about Florida State."

Her expression sobers. "That makes two of us. I'm kind of worried as well."

"Don't be. Every practice, the younger girls are picking up the slack. We're not going to crush them, but I think we'll hold our own." Jogging backward, I say, "I'll catch you in the locker room." With that, I turn around and take off toward Coach.

I almost groan when he pulls out his grease board and goes through a couple of plays from the scrimmage. There's a lot of head nodding on my part and drawing, wiping away, and then redrawing on his. Luke Adams might be young, but he's a rising star in Division I women's soccer. We're lucky to have him at Western. It wouldn't surprise me in the least if he makes a move to coach professionally in the next five years. Even though I won't be jumping up to the next level, he's helped me improve my game.

By the time Coach releases me, fifteen minutes have slid by. A lot of the girls have already showered, changed, and taken off. Western is an academically rigorous school, and it won't be long before we're headed into midterms. Everyone has tests to cram for. Before we know it, December will be here, and the semester will be drawing to a close. The women's soccer team has one of the highest collective GPAs at the university. And that's the way we like to keep it.

How else can we rub it in the men's faces?

Demi is already throwing her freshly washed hair up into a ponytail when I make it to the locker room.

"That took forever," she says.

Tell me about it. "He wanted to go over a few mistakes I made."

She snorts. "The guy is really wound tight about this one."

"Yup, he is. I have to stop in tomorrow afternoon to review game film. He wants me to cover number sixteen. Apparently, she's a real dynamo."

Demi nods. "I meet with him tomorrow morning between classes."

I strip off my practice jersey before tossing it into the laundry bin. Everything Coach went over on the field circles through my brain. I might have just played down how competitive this team will be, but that doesn't mean my nerves aren't jacked. I don't want to lose this game, and I sure as hell don't want number sixteen to show me up.

A few of the girls call out goodbyes as they grab their athletic bags and head out of the locker room. As the silence settles around us, echoing off the cement walls, I realize we're the last stragglers.

"Rowan and I are heading over to Dad's for dinner tonight. Any interest in coming with us?"

"I appreciate the offer, but go without me. I'll probably be at least ten minutes." More like fifteen. "I don't want to hold you guys up." Plus, I'm not interested in third wheeling it tonight. Been there, done that. I'd rather head home and study by myself.

"Are you sure?" She glances around the now empty locker room. "It's kind of creepy now that everyone has cleared out."

I snort. "I'm pretty sure you meant to say serene. Without all those noisy bitches yapping away, it's actually quite peaceful in here. I can hear myself think and don't have to put up with a bunch of useless gossip."

"Please girl, you live for all the dirt," she says as I strip off my shorts and toss them in the bin.

I grin. She's right. I do. Especially when that chatter has to do with Annica. I'm relieved for Demi's sake that the red-headed viper is no longer part of the team. Most of the injured players still show up for practices and games, but Annica hasn't bothered. One of the girls mentioned that she's upset and doesn't want to be around soccer right now.

Oh well.

My bestie pulls out her phone when a text message rolls in.

"Let me guess," I snicker, "it's lover boy." It's not even a question. We both know it is. Those two are inseparable. And their relationship is a drama-free zone. Maybe one day, I'll have something like that.

A girl can dream, right?

A light blush fills her cheeks as a smile spreads across her lips. On Demi, this is what happy coupledom looks like. Instead of being jealous or resentful, I'm thrilled for her. For both of them. They are the perfect match.

Before she can open her mouth, I wave her away. "Go on and get out of here. I'll be fine."

"Are you sure? We can wait around for you to finish up. It's not a big deal."

I shake my head. "It's all good. I'll catch you back at the apartment later on. My plan is to heat up something from the fridge and delve straight into work."

When I stopped home last night, Mom had packaged up a few dinners for me to take back to school. One was vegetable lasagna made with eggplant instead of noodles, and the other was broiled chicken with a lemon artichoke dressing.

Yum!

After that grueling practice, I could mow both of them.

"Only if you're sure," Demi says, cutting into my thoughts.

"I am. Now get moving before your man comes in here looking for you."

With a quick wave, she takes off and then I'm all alone.

Now that the locker room has emptied, the only sound that can be heard is the steady drip of the water from the showers. It echoes off the cement block walls and throughout the rectangular-shaped room. Contrary to what Demi claimed, I find it more soothing than creepy. I grew up in a loud, noisy family. It made me appreciate the quiet moments.

I strip out of my socks and shin pads before reaching around my back to unsnap my bra. Once it's peeled away, I remove my underwear. The socks get tossed in the laundry bin, the sports bra and panties shoved in my locker to be taken home and washed.

With careful fingers, I pull the elastic band from my sweat-soaked hair and shake it out before scooping up my shower gel, shampoo, and conditioner. Then I pad into the tiled shower area. I grab the silver handle and turn it until the water is hot and steam is rising around me. Only then do I step under the spray, allowing it to rush over my body. After lathering up my hair, I scrub my fingers over my scalp. It's a rosemary mint shampoo that makes my skin tingle. I close my eyes and inhale the calming scent. Every sore muscle loosens under the hot water. It feels so damn good. Conditioner is the next step in the process. While that sets, I lather up my body, washing away the dirt, sweat, and turf from the two-hour practice.

My eyelids feather closed as my mind wanders, going over the mental list that needs to be finished up this evening. I'm jerked out of those thoughts when strong hands reach around to cup my breasts. A scream builds in my throat as a hard body presses against me from behind.

Just as I'm about to release a deafening cry, a deep voice murmurs near the outer shell of my ear, "Don't worry, sweetheart. I plan to make you scream, but we haven't reached that portion of the evening quite yet."

Brayden.

Air rushes from my lungs as he tweaks my nipples, pulling and elongating them with skillful fingertips. That's all it takes for relief to morph into arousal.

"How did you get in here?" I ask breathlessly.

Not that it's difficult. We're not the men's football team, surrounded by security. Every once in a while, a girl—or plural—will attempt to slip into the guys' locker room after a game or practice. They're usually caught within minutes and tossed out on their asses.

"I was waiting around with Rowan outside when Demi mentioned that you were in here all by your lonesome." The low timbre of his voice grows deeper. "How could I resist sneaking in to help clean you up?"

His words send my belly into freefall as he grabs the liquid soap and drizzles it over my breasts before stroking his hands across them, lathering them up again. What he's doing feels so damn good that my head lolls back, resting against the solid strength of his chest.

"Have I mentioned what a fan I am of your breasts?"

Gahhh.

Barely am I able to focus on the question. Just when I don't think I can take another moment of the pleasure he's stoking to life inside me, his fingers drift down my rib cage, spreading soap suds over my skin, turning it slippery in the process. He doesn't leave one inch of my flesh untouched. Hot licks of desire burn through me as I squirm against his bigger body. By the time his fingers reach the lips of my pussy, I'm ready to come undone. Already I know that it won't take much to push me over the edge. One dip inside and I'll shatter into a million pieces.

A whimper escapes from me as his fingers skate over my soaked flesh.

"You like that, baby?" he growls against my ear.

My bones feel as if they're melting as one thick digit teases my heat. If he weren't propping me up, I would sink to the floor. His movements are leisurely, as if we have all the time in the world. As if my body hasn't been set on fire and I'm not already teetering on the precipice. He promised to make me scream and already I'm on the verge of doing it. But still, he doesn't quicken his pace. It remains measured and controlled. Brayden is always in command of the situation. Breathy little sounds continue to escape from me as we fall into a natural rhythm.

Oh god.

How does he do it?

How does he know exactly what touch will elicit the most pleasure?

Each time we're together, the sex feels explosive. And it only continues to ratchet up in intensity. He's constantly changing things up and pushing me higher than I've flown before. No one has ever made me feel like this. His touch has become an addiction.

Instead of finishing me off, he flips me around, forcing me back a couple of steps until my spine hits the tiled wall. Barely am I able to suck in a breath before his lips collide with mine. I open as his tongue forces its way inside my mouth before tangling with my own. Another bolt of anticipation crashes through me. I tilt my head, allowing him better access.

One of his hands glides down my body before wrapping around his cock. He gives it a few slow pumps before aligning the blunt tip with my entrance. In one smooth movement, he thrusts deep inside my sheath. It feels as if I'm being impaled before I'm pinned against the steamy wall. And nothing has ever felt so amazing.

"I fucking love your pussy," he growls before pulling almost all the way out and plunging back inside again. He's embedded so deep within my body that I have no idea where he ends and I begin. Even though I bite down on my lower lip to keep all the pleasure trapped inside, containment becomes impossible.

There isn't a gradual build up to climax. It all happens so fast. We go from zero to a hundred in two seconds flat. Just as an orgasm explodes within me like a firework, Brayden groans, finding his own release. My inner muscles spasm around him as hot jets of cum spurt inside my womb. Intensity crashes over me, threatening to drag me under as I scream out my pleasure.

Stars burst behind my eyelids as Brayden continues to stroke his length deep inside me. My knees weaken as he buries his face in the hollow of my neck. His warm breath rushes out in sharp, short pants. We stand pressed together, his softening cock nestled inside me before he drops a kiss against the delicate skin below my ear.

That was...

Like nothing I've ever experienced before.

If I'm not careful—

No.

As soon as the thought pops into my brain, I shut it down and shove it far away where I can't inspect it. Sex does not equate to feelings. That's exactly what I need to remember. Otherwise, I'll get hurt, and I don't want that to happen.

Brayden pulls away to search my face as if it's possible for him to sift through my innermost thoughts. I force a pleasant smile to my lips.

His eyes narrow in response.

"Is everything all right?" There's a hesitancy to his voice, as if he realizes that an invisible wall has just slid into place to keep him firmly at bay.

"Of course." My lips quirk. "Thanks for the stress relief. I really needed that."

With a grunt, he pulls out of my body. His large hands go to my cheeks, cupping them tenderly. "Any time."

The way his gaze stays pinned to mine makes me squirm. This certainly isn't the first time I've been naked with a guy, but it's the only one that I can recall a feeling of vulnerability stealing over me. It's as if Brayden is able to see more than I'm comfortable with. More than I want him to.

It takes everything inside me to break eye contact and glance away. "About this weekend—"

"What about it?" His voice sharpens, commanding my attention.

My gaze jerks to his in surprise. "You really don't have to—"

"It's already a done deal." His jaw clenches. It's almost as if he's daring me to argue.

My mouth tumbles open, and for a moment, I'm unsure what to say.

His hands tighten around my face as he angles it toward him. "I was invited to your house and I'm going. End of discussion."

Sure, maybe he feels that way now, but Brayden has no idea what he's getting himself into. It only feels right to warn him. Plus, there's little point to introducing him to my family. It'll only complicate matters in the long run. And the situation is already chock-full of difficulties. We don't need to add more to the mix.

"My relatives..." My tongue darts out to smudge my lips. "They're a lot to deal with." If he thinks Court was the most obnoxious brother in the Daniels clan, he's sadly mistaken. Dealing with them individually is one thing; taking on the pack is quite another. They're like jackals.

Instead of taking my comments seriously, his attention shifts to my mouth, which is still swollen from his kisses. He swallows up the distance between us before nipping at my lower lip. "You don't need to worry about me. I'm more than capable of taking care of myself."

Yeah, I know, but...

As he sucks the plump flesh into his mouth, another burst of arousal sparks to life in the pit of my belly. It seems almost crazy that he's able to turn me on so quickly after I came a handful of minutes ago. And I'm not the only one getting excited either. His cock has thickened and is now pressing insistently against my lower abdomen.

Brayden releases my lip before backing away enough to stare down at his full-fledged erection. A sly smile lifts the corners of his lips. "Can I interest you in a second round?"

My gaze drops to his gorgeous length. The conversation we'd been engaged in falls to the wayside as more urgent matters take precedence. "I'd really hate to see a perfectly good boner go to waste."

He flashes me a knowing grin. "You're my kind of girl, Sydney."

And then he's sliding inside me and filling me to the brim. He doesn't fuck me hard and fast. He takes it slow, driving me over the edge one thrust at a time.

Chapter Twenty-Three

SYDNEY

I glance at my phone as a text from Brayden pops up on the screen. He's here and waiting in the parking lot. My belly hollows out as a burst of nerves explodes inside me. There's no longer a way to stop the wheels that have been set in motion. For better or worse, this is happening.

I tried several times to talk him out of attending this party and he was having none of it. The more I broached the subject, the more adamant he became in his stance. The guy is seriously stubborn. Doesn't he understand that I'm trying to save him from an afternoon of hardcore interrogation?

If we were the real deal, I could understand his desire to go through with this, but we're not. So why put himself through the wringer?

I grab my small, black purse off the desk and walk into the living room. Demi glances up from where she's sitting on the couch.

"Wow, you look nice!" Her lips quirk. "Not that you don't always."

I roll my eyes. I'm wearing a pale pink skirt that hits mid-thigh and a loosely knit, white sweater that I've paired with ankle boots. My hair is long and loose around my shoulders. I spend so much time with it pulled up into a ponytail or messy bun that it feels good to leave it down every once in a while.

"Big day! Introducing Brayden to the fam, huh? That's a huge step."

More like a nightmare. I keep telling myself that we only have to stay for an hour or two and then we can take off. I'm sure Brayden will be traumatized on the drive home. He'll be in desperate need of therapy afterward.

"Yeah," I force myself to say, "let's hope they don't eat him alive." Then again, maybe that would be for the best. I need to nip this faux relationship in the bud before it can spiral any further out of control.

She waves a hand. "Please, if anyone can hold their own with your family, it would be Brayden. He'll have them eating out of the palm of his hand within thirty minutes. Maybe less."

Hmmm. Demi might be right about that. The guy can be a real charmer when he turns up the wattage. Although, I don't think my brother, Court, was too impressed. I'm sure the first thing he did after meeting Brayden was call my oldest brother, Ryan, to fill him in on all the gory details. When I phoned my mom a few hours later, she'd already been brought up to speed on the situation and was overjoyed that I was bringing Brayden home to meet them. People like to talk about women being the biggest gossips, but they're way off target. Some of these guys are like old ladies standing around in a church parking lot, trading stories like baseball cards.

"All right," I finally say, "I should go." As I walk to the front door, it feels like I'm marching to a slow, tortuous death.

"Have fun!" Demi calls out, oblivious to my inner turmoil.

There's no chance of that happening.

As I take the stairwell to the lobby, I run into Ryder, a Western Wildcats hockey player I've known since freshman year.

"Hey, Syd," he says, eyeing me up and down. "Must have a hot date. You look amazing."

"Thanks. No date. Just a family party."

He holds open the door. As soon as I exit into the spacious entryway, he pulls up alongside me, asking questions about how soccer is going. I tell him about tying Florida State on Thursday and how the game went into overtime. I'm still kicking myself for giving number sixteen a little too much breathing room. The sneaky little bitch actually made it past me and scored.

Once.

Just once.

We push out into the bright sunshine. The day looks like it will be a nice one for Mom. I'm sure everyone will be outside, enjoying one of the last seasonable afternoons before the weather turns cold.

As Ryder and I say our goodbyes, I spot Brayden's shiny, black Ford F-150 parked a couple of rows over. Even though I'm unable to see him behind the tinted glass, I feel his attention locked on me as if it's a physical caress. My skin pebbles as a horde of butterflies wing their way to life inside the confines of my belly.

I'm not sure if it's the thought of spending the day with Brayden that fills me with so much anxiety or if it's the idea of taking him home and introducing him to my family. What I can't deny is that the more time that slides by, the more genuine our relationship begins to feel. My breath catches, getting clogged in my throat as those thoughts echo throughout my brain. That's *exactly* what I can't permit to happen. We might be attempting to fool everyone around us, but I can't allow myself to get caught up in the charade.

I almost have to force myself to grab the door handle of his truck and yank it open. As I do, my gaze lands on Brayden. The air gets wedged in my throat as I take him in.

He looks...

Hot.

He's outfitted in a pale pink polo that hugs both biceps along with his chest before being tucked into jeans that do amazing things to his thighs. My mouth turns cottony. At this very moment, I'm probably eating him up with my eyes.

"Hi." I clear my throat and force my voice to be nonchalant. The last thing I want is for Brayden to suspect the thoughts that are crashing through my head at lightning speed.

"Hey yourself." His gaze flicks to the sidewalk before he nods. "Was that Ryder McAdams you were talking with?"

My brows draw together as I glance at the hockey player's retreating form.

"Yeah."

"Were you two hanging out or something?" His expression darkens.

"No, we just walked out together." I shrug before asking with a snort, "Why? Are you jealous?" That's a joke, obviously. Feelings would have to be involved in order for that to happen, and there aren't any between us.

"Maybe."

What?

That's not the answer I was expecting. I still, surprised by his blunt response. "I've known him since freshman year. He was friends with Ethan."

His muscles loosen. "Good to know."

It's a surprise when he reaches over and wraps his hand around the back of my head before drawing me in for a kiss that makes me forget every single qualm.

How does he do it?

How does he scramble my senses so completely?

The more he lays his hands—not to mention his lips—on me, the quicker it happens.

By the time we finally break apart, I'm breathing harshly. It's as if I've just run a marathon. His gaze slides down my body, taking in every minute detail, before he flicks his gaze to mine again. "You're looking good enough to eat, Sydney."

An arrow of lust detonates in my belly before settling in my core.

"Thanks." It doesn't escape me that his compliments have come to mean more than anyone else's. Both Ryder and Demi commented on how nice I looked, and yet it's only Brayden's words that fill me with pleasure.

If I hadn't already realized that I was knee-deep in shit, it's now been slammed home with the force of a two-by-four. I need to figure out an extrication plan before this sticky situation becomes more problematic.

"Would you look at us," he says, humor simmering in his deep voice. "It's almost like we planned to be all matchy-matchy."

I rack my brain, trying to remember if I mentioned what I might wear to the party. Since I picked out the outfit a few hours ago, and we haven't spoken since last night, that's impossible.

When I remain silent, he adds, "We're the perfect couple."

What?

No way. We would have to be the real deal in order for that to be true. This is nothing more than a coincidence.

My heart crashes into my chest. "Please," I mumble, slamming the door closed and sealing myself inside the truck. "we're hardly that."

Brayden's gaze trails over me for a second time before he reaches out and twirls a thick lock around his finger. For a moment, he seems enamored by the blonde strands. "I like it when you wear your hair down."

I ruthlessly stomp out any pleasure attempting to bloom inside me. Even though I know it won't do a damn bit of good, I can't resist making one last ditch effort to stop this from happening. "You know, it's not too late to bail on this party. I could tell them you got food poisoning and are busy vomiting your brains out."

"No way." He throws the truck into reverse. "I'm excited to meet the rest of your family." His gaze flickers to mine. "There are so many questions I'm dying to ask that have stumped me for years. Adorable baby pics I want to ooh and aah over." He waggles his brows in a comical manner. "Maybe you can take me to your childhood room, and we can pour through your old yearbooks."

I really hope he's joking. The look in his eyes tells me that he's not. His lips tremble at the corners when I slump in my seat and release a defeated groan.

"Come on, Brayden," I whine. "Is that really necessary?"

"Sure is. You're my girl. I want to find out everything there is to know about you."

"I'm your fake girl," I snap, in case he's in need of a reality check. The words serve as a reminder for not only him but myself as well. "Emphasis on the *fake*. There's no reason to delve any deeper than you already have."

Instead of continuing in the same vein, he changes the subject. "Would you mind putting your address into my phone?"

He rattles off the password. Left with no other choice, I plug in my parents' address. A few minutes later, we're turning onto the highway and heading north. Since the drive should only take roughly half an hour, it'll be a quick trip.

All through high school, I'd imagined going far away for college. After Peter died, all that changed. There was no way I could move halfway around the country. So, I threw my application in at Western and spoke with Coach Adams about playing soccer. All in all, it's been a good experience. If I hadn't attended Western, I wouldn't have met Demi.

"You're not very far from school. Do you get home often?" he asks.

I blink back to the present. "Umm, yeah. Usually about once a week."

With his gaze focused on the ribbon of road beyond the windshield, he nods. "You must be close to your family."

My voice softens. "Yeah, I am."

We were always a tight knit group, but the death of my brother made us even more so. Once you experience that kind of gut-wrenching loss, it makes you hold onto the people you love with both hands and never let go. Every time I say goodbye and walk out the door, a lump settles in the pit of my belly, knowing that it could be the last time I see one of them. It sucks. Worse than that, there's no way to banish the internal thoughts or ignore them. They've taken root deep in my psyche.

"How about you?" I ask.

Although, given that Brayden went through a similar experience, my guess is that he is. It's a shit thing to have in common. And yet, I feel inexplicably closer to him because of it. He's one of the few people that I didn't meet in a support group who understands how that kind of grief can break you.

"Yup. Unlike you, I only have one sister. Elle. You met her at the party."

"Ahh, yes," I say lightly, "the infamous party where I discovered I was in a committed relationship. Who could forget that?"

He chuckles. "Certainly not me. You must thank your lucky stars every night that we found our way to one another. Fake boyfriend or not, I'm a real catch."

I snort. Could this guy be more full of himself?

"All you've done, believe it or not, is complicate my life." I shake my head and mutter, "Thank my lucky stars...Give me a break."

He flashes me a charming smile that has undoubtedly dropped hundreds of panties on this campus alone. "Aww, sugar-booger, don't be that way."

Oh no, he didn't.

My eyes widen as I swing toward him in horror. "Don't ever call me that again."

My reaction has his smile morphing into a full-on grin. "What's wrong?" There's a beat of silence. "You don't like my pet name for you?"

"God, no." I shudder for good measure.

He presses his lips together for a contemplative moment. "How about snookums?"

Is he seriously demented? "Forget it."

"Muffin?" he asks with raised brows.

"No," I snap.

"Sexy pants?"

"Really?" I twist in the seat until I can face him.

"Sure." He shrugs. "Why not?"

"I can think of about twenty reasons off the top of my head. How about we just forget the cutesy names for the time being?" And when I say *the time being*, I mean forever.

"Come on, that's part of the fun of being a couple." There's a pause before he tacks on, "Sugar lips."

"You're seriously killing me right now."

His shoulders shake with mirth. "All right, pudding, I'll stop. Turns out my girl doesn't like pet names. Who knew?"

It's almost a relief when we pull up in front of my house. Since I'm dreading this party, that's really saying something.

Brayden looks past me to the two-story brick residence with its white columns and matching red brick walkway that cuts through the front lawn. Leafy green hedges hug the front of the structure, giving it an idyllic look. There's always a sense of peace that fills me when I return home.

Except for this time.

I glance at him as he continues to quietly stare. "Having second thoughts?" Because it's much too late to do anything about it now. We've probably been spotted from the windows and the alarms have been sounded.

"Nope," he says, sounding strangely like he means it. "I'm looking forward to meeting everyone."

A puff of air escapes from me. "It's doubtful you'll feel that way in twenty minutes," I mutter. "If they're in rare form, fifteen."

"Bring it on."

We exit the truck and meet on the sidewalk before heading to the front door. I don't get more than two steps when Brayden slips my hand into his larger one. For a heartbeat, I stare at the place we're now connected. As nervous as I am, his strong fingers wrapped securely around mine settle something deep inside me.

When I reach out with my other hand for the door handle, Brayden clears his throat.

I pause when he says, "You know that I'll be on my best behavior, right?"

Surprise floods through me. Before I can come up with a response, he continues. "I won't do anything to embarrass you."

The earnestness of both his words and expression has my muscles loosening.

I jerk my head into a tight nod. "Thank you."

He gives me a wink and I throw the door open.

Chapter Twenty-Four

SYDNEY

Brayden is a step behind me as we enter the foyer. There isn't one moment when I'm not intensely aware of his male presence. As soon as the door closes, boisterous voices greet my ears. We are not, nor have we ever been, a quiet family. We're loud and energetic—sometimes even a little unruly—with a proud Italian heritage. When my grandparents were alive, both my Nonna and Nonno were always here, adding to the commotion.

My mother peeks around the corner of the kitchen at the back of the hallway. As soon as our gazes fasten, the edges of her lips bow up into a delighted smile. "Sydney! You're here!"

Her excitement has the last of my nerves draining away. You would think by her enthusiastic reaction that she hasn't laid eyes on me in years, which couldn't be further from the truth. I was just here last Tuesday to pick up Lucus and take him out for ice cream. It's a tradition we started when I was sixteen years old after passing my driver's test, and we've been doing it ever since. If my twenty-three-year-old brother has one weakness, it's for triple chocolate fudge brownie ice cream. It's the only time we spend together where it's just the two of us. It's his chance to tell me everything that's going on in his life.

"Hi, Mom," I say in greeting.

Her gaze immediately slides to the guy towering over me. The heat of his large body burns into my backside, making me even more cognizant of his overwhelming presence.

"And this must be Brayden." Mom steps more fully into the doorway before wiping her hands on a dish towel. "We've heard all about you."

Oh, lord.

I'm going to throttle Court when I get my hands on him.

My father fills the space behind Mom along with two of my brothers. Court beams a wide smile in my direction as if he knows the thoughts currently circulating through my head. When I narrow my eyes, silently promising retribution, his shoulders shake with barely suppressed laughter.

Juliette, my oldest brother's wife, joins the throng. My nephew, Caden, is held in her arms. He's two years old and into everything. I've babysat for him on several occasions and at the end, I go home more exhausted than if I'd played every minute of a soccer match. I would never say this to my brother or his wife because I love them more than anything, but Caden could be a posterchild for birth control. As adorable as the little demon appears, he's hell on wheels. That kid is the reason I won't be having offspring any time soon.

My oldest brother, Ryan, emerges behind his wife.

"Still looking forward to this?" I whisper between gritted teeth so only he can hear. It'll be a miracle if he makes it out of here in one piece.

"Absolutely."

The only reason Brayden sounds so confident is because he has no idea what he's gotten himself into. Just wait a couple of hours—he'll be curled up in the fetal position, sucking his thumb in a corner. These people don't care if he's Brayden Kendricks, Wildcats football stud who will go on to play in the pros. They'll eat him alive for dinner and ask what's for dessert.

"Sydney!" Lucus shouts in excitement, drawing my attention back to the growing crowd of family members as he barrels through them before closing the distance that separates us and throwing his arms around me. "I missed you!"

"I missed you, too, bud." I hold him close for a moment before releasing him and stepping away. I point to the tall guy beside me. "This is my friend, Brayden. He's here to help us celebrate Mom's birthday."

Even though Lucus is only a few inches shorter than Brayden, he tilts his head and sizes up the dark-haired football player silently.

Air gets wedged in my throat. There have been a handful of times when my brother has taken an instant dislike to someone and nothing anyone says or does is able to change his mind. It's an awkward situation for all involved. I really hope my family prepared him for this.

Only now does it occur to me that I should have mentioned to Brayden that my brother has Angelman Syndrome. It's not often that I bring guys home, and when I do, the way they handle themselves in his presence gives me a true glimpse into the kind of people they are. Call it a litmus test of sorts.

Brayden raises a hand in greeting. "Hey. It's nice to meet you. Thanks for letting me drop by."

A hushed stillness falls over the group that stretches just to the point of discomfort. I'm about to jump in and save us from impending doom when Lucus tilts his head. "You play football?"

"Yup," Brayden replies easily, "I'm a wide receiver for the Wildcats." There's a beat of silence. "Do you like football?"

My brother's eyes light up and some of his earlier reserve falls away. "I love football! I watch all the games on television. Sometimes Dad takes me to the stadium."

A smile curves Brayden's lips. "It's pretty cool to sit in the stands and watch, isn't it?"

Lucus nods as his voice ratchets up in intensity. "I get to have popcorn and a hot dog and sometimes," his gaze flickers to our mother as he drops his voice, "if Mom isn't there, Dad lets me have an orange soda, but that's only for special occasions."

"I heard that," Mom says over the babble of voices. She shoots my father a mock glare. Even though she pretends otherwise, she's well aware of what happens when she's not around. "We'll be having a little chat about that after the party."

Dad shrugs before pulling her close and pressing a kiss against the side of her face. "Let's focus on your birthday and save that unpleasant conversation for another day."

"Uh-huh," she says, the edges of her lips curling upward.

"That sounds like a good time," Brayden says, focusing on my brother.

"It's a lot of fun."

"If you're interested," Brayden shifts his weight before offering, "I can probably get a couple tickets at the fifty-yard line."

My brother's eyes widen, and his mouth drops open. "*Really?* That would be awesome!" He glances at our father. "Right, Dad?"

"Sure would," he replies, looking pleasantly surprised at how well the conversation is going.

Emotion wells in my throat, making it difficult to swallow past the thick lump that has become lodged there. I glance at Brayden, only to find him smiling at my brother.

Who is this guy?

And why is he being so nice to Lucus?

Confusion swirls through me like a thick fog, throwing me out of whack. It's not the first time it's happened where he's concerned. Just when I start to feel like I have Brayden figured out, he does something that makes me question everything I assumed I knew. It takes a moment to grasp that I'm reluctant to alter my perception of him. I don't want to feel any differently about Brayden or like him more than I already do. That realization is enough to constrict my heart, making it impossible to suck a full breath into my lungs.

Thankfully, I'm saved from further introspection when Caden lets loose a scream so loud it could wake the dead. Conversation and movement erupt all at once, filling the hallway with commotion. It's almost as if now that Lucus' seal of approval has been earned, my family is free to descend on Brayden, shaking his hand and introducing themselves as I stand by helplessly and watch.

To have the handsome, six-foot football player in my home, meeting my family feels surreal. The way he easily interacts with them is equally strange. He's like a chameleon, fitting in effortlessly wherever he goes.

Three hours later and I'm polishing off a slice of chocolate birthday cake. If there's one thing I can't resist, it's chocolaty cake with buttercream frosting.

Yum.

"Well, I must say that he seems nice," Mom says, sidling up to me near the basketball court in the driveway where Lucus has roped Brayden into a game of horse. I've lost track of how many times they've played. It has to be somewhere around a dozen.

My gaze flickers to the dark-haired guy.

Oh, who am I kidding?

My attention has been laser-focused on him for the last hour. Instead of mingling with my family, I'm watching Brayden shoot hoops and goof around with my brother.

I shrug, torn between blurting out the truth regarding our relationship and allowing her to believe that we're a legit couple without an expiration date in sight. Lying to my family has never sat well with me.

When she arches a brow, I clear my throat and decide to keep the truth buried deep inside, "Yeah, he is." Maybe more than I originally gave him credit for.

Trust me, it's not an easy admittance. Even privately to myself.

She nods toward the boys. "Lucus certainly has taken to him. My guess is that he's found a new best friend."

It does appear that way. Lucus hasn't left Brayden's side since we arrived earlier this afternoon. And Brayden...he doesn't seem to mind in the least. If I didn't know better, I might even say that he was actually enjoying himself. Emotion settles in the middle of my throat, making it feel as if there's a clump of wet sawdust sitting there.

None of the other guys I've brought home have spent so much time with Lucus. They'll usually engage him in a little conversation, and, when it turns awkward, they look at me to throw them a life preserver. Brayden doesn't need rescuing.

"I can see why you like him," she continues.

Woah. Woah. Woah.

Who said anything about *liking* Brayden?

I don't like him. Not in that way. The guy is a complete pain in my ass. Except...that's changed over the last couple of weeks. Our relationship isn't what it once was. It's morphed into something new, and I'm not sure what to make of it.

Uncertain how to respond, I press my lips together and remain stoically silent.

That doesn't stop her from slipping an arm around my waist and adding, "Your father likes him as well."

This conversation is spiraling out of control. Not in a million years did I expect my family to like Brayden enough to champion this relationship.

This fake relationship.

Argh.

I need to do something to put a damper on her hopes. I rip my gaze away from the guy we're talking about. "Look, Mom. Don't get ahead of yourself here. What we have is really new." I pause before tacking on, "Who knows how long it'll last."

Probably not more than another week, if that.

"For what it's worth, I can tell he really likes you."

I almost snort. Shows how much Mom knows. We're not even a real couple. Somehow, we've managed to snow Jane Daniels, who usually isn't fooled by anything or anyone. She prides herself on being able to ferret out the truth in a matter of minutes. The woman is like a pig sniffing out truffles. And she's good at it. I've been on the receiving end of her weird mom radar for years.

"And the way you look at him..." she adds lightly. "It's nice to see."

Excuse me?

Exactly how do I look at him?

My eyes flare as I do a quick mental rewind. "What do you mean?"

Before she can respond, Lucus lets out a loud whoop, drawing our attention to the driveway. It looks like another game of horse has come to an end. Now they're playing a little one on one. I'll tell you this, Brayden has a ton of energy to be able to keep up with Lucus. My brother can bounce off the walls, much like Caden. Or maybe it's the other way around.

Mom nudges my shoulder when I become mired in my own thoughts. "Maybe you should bring the boys a couple bottles of water. I'm sure they're thirsty after all this activity."

"Sure." Added bonus, I can get away from Mom before she's able to make any more unhelpful observations about my pseudo-relationship.

Even though this afternoon has gone much better than expected, all it's done is open up another can of worms. Once we part ways in a week or two, I'll have to make up a story for my family as to why it didn't work out with Brayden. Honestly, I've gone through my fair share of breakups, so no one should be overly surprised when this one crashes and burns like the others.

As I walk through the backdoor into the kitchen, I find my other two brothers with their heads bent together. Their voices come to an abrupt halt as soon as they catch sight of me.

"Hey, Syd. Why don't you come over here?" Court calls out, attempting to suck me into their conversation. "We want to ask you a few questions."

I can just imagine what they want to discuss. More than likely, it's to give me the third degree about Brayden.

No, thanks. I'm fresh out of lies.

"Sorry," I say, pulling open the fridge and grabbing two bottles of water before slamming it shut again. "I just popped in to grab a few drinks."

"It'll just take a couple of minutes," Ryan wheedles. "We want to talk."

Please...was I born yesterday?

I don't think so.

These two will tag team me with questions regarding the seriousness of my relationship, and I'm not up to defending something that isn't legit. Neither of them has ever liked any of my past boyfriends. In fact, they usually rip them to shreds. With their teeth. They are the epitome of overprotective assholes.

I mean brothers.

Sometimes those two words are interchangeable.

The last thing I need is one of them sniffing out the truth. I shake my head and beeline for the backdoor.

"All we wanted to tell you was that we really like him," Court calls after me as I slip outside.

Yeah, right. Unlikely story.

Air rushes from my lungs when I manage to escape the house unscathed. I glance at the sports watch adorning my wrist. If we're lucky, we can take off and head back to school in about an hour.

The only problem will be finding a way to break it to Lucus that his new hero wasn't serious about the football tickets. Ugh. I really wish he hadn't thrown out the offer. Brayden has no idea that this will be all my brother talks about for the next couple of weeks. When he ends up forgetting and ultimately not delivering on his promise, Lucus will be devastated.

That's the thing about my brother. If you tell him you're going to do something, you damn well better follow through with it. Don't dole out empty promises just to shut him up or impress him, because it'll only cause more damage in the long run.

I glance around the basketball court, relieved to find that Mom is holding Caden and is now embroiled in a conversation with Juliette.

When Brayden's gaze catches mine, I hold up both bottles. He says something to Lucus before patting him on the shoulder, and then they're both heading in my direction. My brother is pink-cheeked as his chest rises and falls with labored breaths. There's a happy light filling his eyes. No matter how I try to steel myself against it, everything inside me softens.

If there's a quick way to my heart, it's through Lucus.

Even though I'm eighteen months younger than my brother, I've taken on the role of protective sister. I've spent years watching out and sticking up for him. What I learned at an early age is that kids can be real assholes. Especially in middle and high school. There were at least a dozen times when I ended up in the principal's office for getting into a fight. If some jerks were going to pick on Lucus, then they could expect to get their asses kicked.

The first couple of times it happened, my parents tried to convince me that I shouldn't let my classmates make me so angry. But what did they expect me to do? Stand idly by and listen to these assholes spew crap? With four older brothers and one with a genetic disorder, you learn to stand up for yourself and not take shit from anyone. It's the *not taking shit* part that gets me into trouble to this very day.

Regardless of how old I am, I'll always stick up for my family. Especially when they aren't strong enough to do it for themselves. That kind of loyalty extends to my friends. Once a person burrows beneath my skin and into my heart, I'll defend them to the death. That's just how I roll. Demi can attest to that.

Brayden points toward a bottle. "I hope one of those is for me."

Knocked from my thoughts, I blink back to the present before thrusting a plastic container at him. That familiar zip of energy buzzes through me as our fingertips brush. I quickly draw away and shift my attention toward my brother before holding out the second one.

"Are you thirsty?" I ask.

He nods before wiping the sweat from his brow with the back of his hand. Then he twists off the cap and guzzles down every last drop. Brayden and I stand by and watch with amused expressions.

"I need another water," he says, sounding winded.

"Sure. There's more in the fridge."

Lucus nods before taking off without another word, leaving me to stand alone with Brayden in the driveway. It doesn't take long for awkwardness to descend, and I find myself shifting my stance, racking my brain for something to fill the growing void.

Brayden's gaze stays locked on mine as he takes another drink. Once he finishes, he says, "If I had realized I'd be playing basketball all afternoon, I would have worn athletic shorts and a T-shirt. Or at least brought a change of clothes."

Whatever tension had been swirling through the air, ratcheting up in intensity, thankfully dissipates.

My teeth sink into my lower lip as I survey his appearance. I almost feel bad—the guy really is a sweaty mess. Albeit a handsome, sweaty mess. Even with the slight wind that wafts over us, his hair is damp. Bits and pieces of it stick to his forehead. The urge to run my fingers through it and push the dark strands away from his eyes thrums through me.

Instead of giving in to the impulse, I tighten my fingers and force my gaze away. "Thanks for playing with my brother. I can tell that he's having fun."

He steps toward me, swallowing up some of the distance between us. My attention skitters back to him only to realize that I have to crane my neck to meet his steady gaze.

"There's no reason to thank me. Today's been a blast."

I think that's the first time those words have been spoken by one of my boyfriends.

Fake or not.

A burst of nerves explodes in my belly as his gaze burns into mine. I jerk my shoulders, unsure how to respond. For some reason, it feels like we're talking about so much more than just the games he's played with Lucus. That's all it takes for the noisy party around us to fade away. And then it's just the two of us. His face looms closer, and for a moment, I wonder if he'll kiss me.

But why would he do that?

There's no one that we need to put on a show for.

Instead of ending this farce, I tilt my face upward until our lips can align.

Just as his mouth ghosts over mine, a voice calls out, "Hey, Brayden, I found a football in the garage. Wanna throw it around?"

I jerk away and blink up at him before shaking off the strange sensations that have fallen over me. I mumble something under my breath before swinging around and heading to the relative safety of the house. Even if my brothers pounce, it's easier to deal with them than what almost happened in the driveway.

Chapter Twenty-Five

BRAYDEN

I lift the bottle of beer to my lips and take a long swig. As I do, my gaze cruises over the thick crowd that has gathered. It might be Thursday, but our house is packed to the gills. Everyone knows that the weekend officially begins tonight and runs through Sunday, ramping up in intensity. Tomorrow evening, most of my teammates will lay low. At least, that's what they're supposed to do. We'll have a walk-through practice, eat a carb-loaded dinner, and hit the sheets early. Some of these guys are superstitious and, much to their girlfriends' annoyance, will refrain from sex in an effort not to sap their energy for game day.

Even though I tell myself that I'm not on the lookout for Sydney, that's exactly what I'm doing. I almost shake my head before taking another sip. If fucking that girl was supposed to get her out of my system, that plan has backfired spectacularly. It seems like the more sex we have, the more I want. It's becoming a problem.

So far this evening, Sydney has remained elusive. But then again, Demi hasn't made an appearance either. And those two are usually attached at the hip. Unless Demi is with Rowan, which has been happening more and more lately. They're so lovey-dovey that it's almost enough to induce vomiting.

And no, that's not jealousy talking.

All right...maybe a little bit.

As soon as that thought pops into my brain, I shove it away. I really need to get my head on straight, which is exactly why I've been keeping my distance from a certain blonde soccer player this week.

When Sydney told me that I could bail on her mother's birthday party after we screwed in the locker room, I probably should have jumped at the chance to bow out gracefully. Instead, I'd doubled down on my stance to attend the family gathering.

Big mistake.

I'd expected to be bored off my ass. Instead, I'd had a surprisingly good time. Her family is pretty awesome. And yeah, she's right—there's a lot of them. My guess is that the normal decibel level at their house is somewhere around chaos. I ended up spending most of the afternoon playing basketball with her brother before tossing around the football. I also talked with her father and one of her brothers about our accounting class.

The most interesting part of the day had been watching Sydney lower her guard and reveal a totally different side than I've been treated to in the past. Her two older brothers enjoy giving her shit for just about everything. Instead of getting upset or pissed off, she dishes it right back at them. It had been a real pleasure to watch her rip both of them to shreds.

It goes without saying that I now have a better understanding of why she's so damn feisty. Can't say I blame her for it either. It must have been hell to grow up with the two of them picking on her nonstop. Teasing aside, they all seem thick as thieves. My guess is that they might enjoy giving their sister shit, but they won't allow anyone else to get in on the action. It's also obvious from her interactions with Lucus that she's extremely protective of him. She softens when he's in the vicinity, becoming almost—dare I say—nurturing? It was a strangely touching revelation.

Now that I realize Sydney has a totally different facet to her personality, I'd be lying through my teeth if I didn't admit to wanting to tease it out of her.

What would it be like to have that Sydney more often?

It's those thoughts that had me mentally pumping the brakes and deciding that a little time and distance to clear my head would be the shrewdest move to make. The only reason we're in this situation is because of Kira. The tawny-haired girl might have been skeptical at first, but she seems to have fallen for the fabrication.

Even though a couple of weeks have already slipped by, I think we need to give it a little more time. A solid month, maybe even six weeks, should be enough for her to move on to her next victim.

I mean, guy.

I'm sure by then, I'll have gotten my fill of Sydney and won't give a crap about parting ways.

Thankfully, Carson rounds the corner at that precise moment and I'm able to shove these pesky thoughts from my head before I'm forced to inspect them more thoroughly. He pushes his way through the thick mass of bodies until he reaches my side.

"Hey, man," I say, "what's up?"

He jerks his head toward the jam-packed dining room. "Did you notice that Kira has turned up tonight?"

It's almost like my thoughts have conjured her up like a specter. I shake my head. Before I can decide what to do, the crowd parts like the Red Sea and I'm given a direct sightline. I'm tempted to duck out of the way so that she doesn't notice me. The last thing I want to deal with tonight is her crazy ass. Kira needs to let go of the idea that we'll ever get together and move on with her life. Find a twelve-step program if that's what's necessary.

Strangely enough, her gaze stays pinned to whomever she's talking with as she flashes the person a smile before twirling a lock of hair around her finger. I straighten to my full height, knowing exactly what a smile like that implies. She's flashed it at me hundreds of times. Interest piqued, I crane my neck, attempting to get a better look at the person she's talking to.

It's one of the junior players.

"Yeah," Carson says, slapping me on the back, "I've seen them together a few times this week on campus. And get this—they've been holding hands. Crazy as it sounds, I think your plan actually worked."

Well, I'll be damned.

Carson just might be right about that. Air escapes from my lungs as the thick tension that had taken up residence in my shoulders gradually dissolves. It feels like a huge weight has been lifted from me. That girl was really starting to venture into scary stalker territory. It's a relief that I no longer have to worry about her climbing into my bed or tailing me around campus.

He taps his glass bottle against mine. "Congrats, dude. Thanks to your fake girlfriend, you pulled it off."

Sydney.

Right. I'll have to let her know that we can put an end to this charade and go back to—

Not talking.

My brows pinch together at that unwelcome realization. At this point, I'm not interested in our relationship reverting back to the way it's always been. I'd like to think that we've become friends over the past month.

Shocker—I actually enjoy hanging out and spending time with the girl.

And the sex is fan-fucking-tastic.

My gaze bounces to Kira and the guy she's set her sights on. If Sydney caught them together, she'd pull the plug on our fake relationship faster than I could blink. Maybe it's a good thing she's been a no-show tonight. But still...I'll have to tell her about it sooner rather than later. If those two are walking around campus holding hands, Sydney could stumble across them at any time. And then I would have some explaining to do.

"Now you can cut Sydney loose," Carson adds.

The thought of actually doing that feels like a fist closing slowly around my heart, squeezing it until it becomes painful. I drag a hand over my face as understanding dawns. Somehow, when I hadn't been looking, I developed real feelings for her.

Fuck.

Now what the hell am I going to do?

Sydney has made it perfectly clear that she doesn't feel the same way. Hell, if she'd gotten her way, I wouldn't have met her family. She attempted to talk me out of attending the party half a dozen times.

Oblivious to my inner turmoil, Carson glances around. "Speaking of Sydney, where is she? I haven't seen her in a while."

Yeah, me neither. Although, that had been by design on my part.

I jerk my shoulders. Since we aren't dating for real, it's not like we check in with each other every moment of the day. It's one of the things I like about her. She lets me do me and I give her the same courtesy. We don't need to be in constant contact every second of the day.

Instead of shooting her a text, I decide to be stealthy and do a little social media recon. She doesn't need to know that I'm curious about her whereabouts. Even though I don't post a lot of shit on Insta, that doesn't mean the app isn't on my phone. I bring up her profile and check to see if she's been posting. Chicks are so like that. They need to take a selfie and update the world on what they're up to every other minute.

Earlier this evening, there'd been a soccer game. I showed up for half of it and then took off. The girls probably went to grab something to eat afterward or are hanging out at their apartment, chilling and watching a movie. Maybe even cracking the books. I know Sydney has been loaded down with schoolwork.

Instead, I find something all together different. My lips tug down at the corners as I drag the phone closer to my face to get a better look at the screen. And the freshly posted photos that have popped up. In the first one, there's a group of girls all smashed together in the frame. They're all wearing sparkly, lowcut dresses.

Are they at a party?

I scroll through a few more shots and realize they're at one of the clubs downtown.

The last pic has me seeing red. It's one of Sydney. That hockey playing douche, Ryder McAdams, has his arms wrapped around her while he pretends to bite her neck, and she's laughing.

What the actual fuck?

Fake girlfriend or not, there's no way in hell I'll allow *that* to happen when she belongs to me. Does Sydney think that it's okay for some random dude to get handsy with her when I'm in the picture? I thought we had an understanding. What exactly that understanding is, I'm not sure. All I know is that I'm fucking furious.

"Hey," Carson yells as I stalk toward the entryway, "where are you going?"

Not bothering with a response, I slam through the front door.

Chapter Twenty-Six

SYDNEY

"Happy birthday, Sasha!" a dozen girls shout before clinking their glasses together and tossing back their shots.

The club is dark with colorful strobe lights that flicker and techno music that pulses in my ears. Not only is this our goalie's twenty-first birthday, but we won our game earlier this evening. Everyone is in a celebratory mood. They're cutting loose and getting a little wild. All right, maybe more than a little. What the hell—they deserve it. *We* deserve it. Without Annica here, we're like one, big happy family. This is exactly how a team should be.

We've been drinking, dancing, and flirting with some of the cute boys that have shown up to party. I'm having a great time. The very last person I should be dwelling on is Brayden. It's like he's taken up permanent residence inside my brain and there's nothing I can do to evict him. Had I suspected it would turn out this way, I never would have agreed to our arrangement in the first place. He was never supposed to burrow beneath my skin. Kind of like an itch I can't quite scratch.

More frustrating than that, my feelings were actually bruised when he didn't stick around and wait for me after the game with Rowan and Coach Richards. The reality of the situation is that I shouldn't have any expectations when it comes to Brayden. But somewhere over the course of the past few weeks, this fictitious relationship has begun to feel like the real deal.

My first mistake was allowing myself to get caught up in playing pretend. The second one was in thinking I could sleep with the guy and not develop feelings for him. Not fall into...

Something with him.

In hindsight, it's better that this happened before I could become any more entrenched. At this point, I can still pull back. With any luck, we can put an end to this farce sooner rather than later.

Because I'm over it.

It's the light tap on my shoulder that knocks me from those troubling thoughts. And for that, I'm grateful. Brayden Kendricks is the last person I want to dwell on. Especially when I'm out celebrating with my teammates. I should be carefree and living it up. I swing around, only to find Ethan standing in front of me.

"Hey," he says, raising his voice in order to be heard over the loud pulse of music.

"Hi." I'm a little surprised to find him here. He was never one for the clubs, preferring to party near campus or at one of the local dive bars where the beer is cheap.

He leans toward me, swallowing up the distance between us. "Congratulations on your win tonight."

"Thanks, they were a tough team." There were definitely a few times when I was afraid the outcome could have gone the other way.

"You were all over number five. You had her locked down tight. She couldn't make a move without you on top of her."

I blink, thrown off by the comment. "You were there?"

He nods before sucking the corner of his lower lip into his mouth. "Yeah, I thought I'd show up and support."

When we were dating, Ethan always made a point of attending my games. It was one of the things I loved about him. He plays baseball and his schedule is just as crammed as mine, so I always appreciated him carving out time for me. I'm a little surprised that he would do that after everything that happened between us.

Without me giving voice to the words, he seems to understand the questions swirling through my eyes. Instead of addressing them, he asks, "Do you think we could go somewhere and talk?"

Umm...

"If now isn't a good time, maybe tomorrow?" He jerks his hand toward the group of girls I arrived with who are showing no sign of slowing down. More shots have been ordered and are currently being passed around. "I know you're out with friends. It's just," there's a pause, "I'd really like to talk to you."

I shift from one foot to the other and cut right to the chase. "Aren't you dating someone?"

"It didn't work out." With a jerk of his shoulders, he shakes his head. "It would seem like I'm not completely over my ex."

Oh.

Oh.

My eyes widen at the curveball he's just thrown me. Ethan and I were together for about six months, and I really liked him. There was a time when the sight of him sent my pulse skyrocketing. That's no longer the case. As painful as it is to admit—even silently to myself—there's only one guy capable of producing that kind of reaction within me, and it happens to be the one I'm fake dating.

The one I should most definitely *not* have feelings for.

Before I have a chance to collect my scattered thoughts and come up with a response, Ethan takes hold of my hand. "I know our relationship wasn't perfect, but it could be different this time. I still lo—"

"Hey, babe." The connection is broken between us when a thickly corded arm snakes around my waist and hauls me close. Before his masculine scent has a chance to wrap around me and tease my senses, I already know who's taken hold of me. "I've been looking everywhere for you."

The awareness exploding inside me like a firework only reinforces the fact that whatever I once felt for the baseball player now pales in comparison to the feelings I've developed for Brayden. It takes effort to bite back the disheartened groan attempting to escape from my lips.

How did I manage to fall so hard for him when I was trying my damnedest not to?

Ethan glares at Brayden before his gaze cuts to mine. "Are you two still together?"

I open my mouth to respond, but Brayden beats me to the punch.

"Yup," he says, "we are." His arm tightens around my waist, pressing me closer as if he's afraid I might try to escape.

Honestly, I'm not sure how I was going to tackle the barked-out question. The truth of the matter is that Brayden and I aren't *really* together. We're playing make believe. It's only during the last fifteen minutes that I've come to realize how disastrous an idea this has turned out to be. We need to end this charade before someone gets hurt.

Someone like me.

Instead of taking Brayden's word for it, Ethan's gaze burns into mine. It's like he's waiting for me to contradict him.

Even though it would probably be best for everyone if I did, I find myself agreeing with Brayden. "Yes, we've been seeing each other for the past couple of weeks."

Ethan's shoulders slump before he nods. "Then I guess there isn't much of a reason for us to talk, is there?"

I release a steady breath and shake my head. "Probably not."

Even if Brayden weren't involved in the picture, I still wouldn't get back together with Ethan. We were way too volatile. We're much better off as friends.

"All right. I guess I'll see you around, Syd." His gaze hardens as it flickers to Brayden, whose muscles are coiled tight. "Let me know if anything changes."

A low growl emanates from deep within his chest. When he steps forward, I grab his arm to hold him back. "Brayden!"

Ethan melts into the crowd before anything further can happen, which is probably for the best.

When he glances at me, I'm shocked by the possessiveness that has flared to life in his eyes. I don't understand why he's acting like this. It's not like we're actually together. There's no reason for him to be jealous or angry.

"We need to talk," he bites out in a surprisingly gruff tone. If I'd thought he would drop the pretense now that Ethan has disappeared, it doesn't happen.

Considering how he almost went off the rails, that's probably a good idea. The sooner we straighten out this mess, the better off we'll be.

"Yeah, we do." The response is barely out of my mouth before his fingers lock around my wrist and he's dragging me through the crowded nightclub. I stumble on my heels in an attempt to keep pace with him.

I've never seen Brayden behave like this before. He's usually so laid back.

We make our way through the main part of the club before turning down a long corridor that is less crowded. A heartbeat later, he's shoving through an exit into the darkened alley. Cool night air slaps at my heated cheeks. Before I have a chance to catch my breath, Brayden wheels around, forcing me up against the rough brick of the building. I find myself caged in by his muscular body. His forearms rest on either side of my head as I stare in wide-eyed surprise.

"What was that with Ethan?" he bites out. Sparks of anger fly from his eyes. Any moment and I'll be singed alive.

If he were any other guy, I'd assume he was jealous. But that can't be.

I blink, attempting to find my bearings. My heart pounds a painful staccato beneath my rib cage. Any second and it'll burst out of my chest. "He wanted to talk." It's only when the words escape from my lips that I question why I'm even telling him this. The last thing I owe Brayden is an explanation. That certainly wasn't part of our deal.

"Do you still have feelings for him?" He presses closer until his lips can hover over mine.

The feel of his warm breath drifting across me is nothing short of intoxicating. I want to squeeze my eyes closed and inhale a big breath of him.

Oh god, this is such a disaster. Lines have been crossed and all it's done is blur our relationship.

When I remain silent, uncertain how to respond, he growls, "*Sydney!*"

"No," I snap.

"And what about Ryder?"

I shake my head. Where is all this coming from? "I already told you, we're just friends. Nothing more."

My answer has the thick tension that had been wafting off him in suffocating waves gradually dissipating. The muscles that had been whipcord tight loosen one by one as he presses closer. Close enough for me to feel the thickness of his erection jutting into my lower abdomen. Arousal explodes in my core.

This is exactly what I didn't want.

If I'm smart, I'll stop this in its tracks. My palms land on his chest in a feeble attempt to keep him at a safe distance. If I don't push him away now, I won't be able to do so later. This entire situation has spiraled too far out of control. I'm able to see that, even if Brayden can't.

"We need to end this," I force myself to say. "It's gone on long enough."

Brayden jerks away as if my touch has scalded him. "Is that what you want?"

No.

"Yes." It takes effort to swallow down the unexpected lump of emotion that has become wedged in the middle of my throat. "The lines have become too blurred."

"Really?" He cocks his head as his eyes sharpen. "I don't think they're blurred at all. I know what I want, and I think you do, too."

My throat grows parched, making it difficult to swallow. When I say nothing in response, he lowers his face until his lips can drift over mine.

Slowly.

So slowly that the movement becomes almost tortuous.

As much as I try to keep the sound buried deep inside where it can't see the light of day, a whimper manages to escape.

"You want me, don't you?" His voice is thick. *Knowing*. I hate that he's able to see right through me. That somehow, in the short amount of time we've been together, he's come to understand my wants and needs. It was never supposed to be this way.

Brayden nips at my lower lip, sucking the fullness into his mouth and holding it captive until my knees turn weak and it feels like I'm in danger of falling to the pavement.

Once the plump flesh has been released, he growls, "Answer me, Syd. I'm done playing games with you."

That's almost laughable. This entire relationship has been one giant farce from the beginning. The only reason we're involved with one another is to fake another girl out. Doesn't he understand that our very foundation has been built on lies and subterfuge?

Brayden's mouth slides lower as he peppers hot kisses along the curve of my jawline. "Tell me."

My brain clicks off as I bare my throat, giving him unrestricted access to my flesh. "Yes," I groan, unable to hold back the truth any longer, "I want you."

He pulls away enough to meet my gaze with a dark look. "Good. Because that's exactly what I want, too. This might have started out as a fake relationship, but that's not how it's going to end. Whatever this is between us, I want it to be real. I want *us* to be real."

Is Brayden saying what I think he is?

"You...want to actually go out with me?" My head is spinning so hard that latching onto one coherent thought feels impossible. I don't know if it's because of his kisses or what he's telling me. Maybe a potent combination of both. "You want us to date?"

"That's *exactly* what I want." There's a pause before he adds in a softer voice, "I like you, Sydney. I have for a while. I've never been one for relationships, but I want to give this a shot. I want you to belong to me."

I can't believe I'm hearing this from him. Brayden can have his pick of females on this campus, and yet, *I'm* the one he wants to spend time with?

The Brayden I've known for the past three years has always been so full of confidence. It's strange to catch a glimpse of the uncertainty lurking within his dark eyes. "What do you say, Sydney? Are you going to give this a chance?"

His hesitant question has the breath catching at the back of my throat. How can I possibly say no when he's staring at me with such a hopeful expression?

My lips lift into a smile before I jerk my head into a nod.

A relieved grin flashes across his face before his mouth crashes onto mine. And then I'm lost. Swept away on a rising tide of sensation.

Chapter Twenty-Seven

SYDNEY

"I'll tell you what, girl. I can't remember the last time you were this happy," Demi says, bumping her shoulder into mine in an attempt to reclaim my attention.

My gaze slides from the Wildcats stadium field where my brother is tossing around a football with Brayden to the girl who has been my best friend since freshman year of college.

Pent-up air rushes from my lungs in a burst as I turn her comment over in my head. I'm almost afraid to admit the truth out loud, because she's right. I *am* happy. Happier than I've been in a long time.

I never expected to feel this way about Brayden.

I mean, come on...*Brayden Kendricks?*

That just seems plain crazy.

But there's no denying the truth.

I'd been so sure that I had Brayden pegged as a handsome, football playing jock who enjoyed all the perks of being an athlete on this campus. Now that we've scratched beneath the surface, I've discovered that there is so much more to him. He's smart, caring, and protective of his younger sister, Elle. He talks to his mother on the phone every couple of days. Family means everything to him. It's just another thing we have in common.

I've come to enjoy the quiet times that we work together. Sketching him for my art project has been an absolute dream. I could stare at the thick length of his cock for hours. Actually, I *have* stared for hours.

And the way he touches my body...

A shiver of awareness slides through me before pooling like warmed honey in my core. I shift uncomfortably on the bench and attempt to tamp down my arousal.

Know what I find even more attractive than all of that?

The way he is with my brother. It makes my heart swell with thick emotion. Brayden doesn't talk down to Lucus or treat him like he's slow on the uptake.

There have been a few guys that I've brought home and introduced to my family. Right from the moment they meet Lucus, it's obvious that some aren't comfortable around an individual who also happens to have a disability. They're unsure how to treat or talk to him so they end up ignoring him and that pisses me off. It doesn't take a genius to realize that you treat everyone the same way you want to be treated. Or the way you'd want people to treat your loved one.

Is that really such a difficult concept to grasp?

Apparently so.

There's no reason to talk to him like he's in pre-school and can't understand basic concepts. He understands them just fine, thank you very much. If those people can't act like normal human beings around Lucus, then I cut them loose and move on. I refuse to waste my time with someone who isn't capable of common courtesy.

Last week, Brayden tagged along with us to get ice cream. True to his word, he secured tickets to a Saturday afternoon home game. I let him share the good news with my brother while we were enjoying our frozen treats. I thought Lucus was going to burst out of his skin with excitement. The sheer happiness Brayden was able to give Lucus actually brought a sting of tears to my eyes. I had to blink them away before either of them noticed.

When Demi nudges my arm for a second time, I say without hesitation, "I am happy."

Her gaze slices to where the team is warming up before the game.

The three of us arrived at the stadium two hours early. We have the best seats in the house. They're two rows up from the field on the fifty-yard line. We're so close to the bright green turf that it feels like I could reach out and touch it. Most fans are only now filtering in. There were a ton of students outfitted in black and red tailgating in the parking lot earlier.

As soon as we found our seats, I texted Brayden and he jogged out of the tunnel to retrieve my brother before taking Lucus back to the locker room. They were gone for about thirty minutes before returning to the field with the team for warm-ups.

My attention settles on Lucus. He has a black Wildcats ballcap pulled over his head and is now wearing a red and white Kendricks jersey with Brayden's number stamped across the back.

Instead of running through his own set of drills, Brayden is tossing a ball around with my brother. There's a wide smile on Lucus' face. I can't remember the last time I saw him this ecstatic. It's like he's walking on clouds.

Demi's father also took a moment to speak with him. I could see Coach pointing to the field. Even from where I'm seated, it's impossible not to notice the way Lucus is vibrating with excitement. Every once in a while, my gaze will catch Brayden's. He'll give me a wink or flash me a smile. That's all it takes for everything inside me to melt into a puddle of goo.

What I now realize is that this Brayden—the one I've gotten to know over the past several weeks—is someone I could definitely fall for.

If I haven't already.

Chapter Twenty-Eight

SYDNEY

"I'll take a large caramel macchiato, please."

The girl behind the counter taps a few buttons on the cash register. "That'll be five dollars even."

I dig through my purse, attempting to locate the money. I'm notorious for dumping bills and loose change into my bag. This is usually when that bit of laziness will bite me in the ass. Now I have to sift through all the contents to find it.

"Here," a deep voice says from behind me, "I've got it covered."

My head whips up only to lock gazes with Brayden. Before I can tell him that I'm more than capable of paying for my own drink, he's handing the barista a couple of bills.

"Keep the change," he tells her with a smile before his attention returns to me.

"Thanks," I say.

"No problem." A sly expression settles on his face. "You can pay me back later."

I snort before raising my brows. "For some reason, I don't think you want to be paid back in cash."

"Nope." He wraps his arms around me and tugs me close before pressing his lips against mine. "We haven't even been together that long, and look how well you already know me."

The girl behind the counter sighs, drawing our attention. Her face goes up in flames before she spins away to prepare my drink.

"I missed you last night," he whispers. "I really hate sleeping alone."

A bubble of giddiness rises up inside me.

"Me, too." Which is strange. In the past, when I've been in a relationship, I've always needed my space. We'll spend a few nights together and then I need an evening to myself. Or I want to go out with the girls.

That hasn't turned out to be the case with Brayden. Maybe I shouldn't be so surprised. Everything with him is different. Even though we haven't been together long, I like him more than anyone else I've been with. It's kind of scary how perfectly we fit together. There are times when I'm tempted to pump the brakes and slow things down, but then I look at him and all of those thoughts disappear in the blink of an eye. Whatever this is between us, it's happening fast, and I don't think there's a way to curtail it. Most of the time I don't think I want to.

When the girl behind the counter calls out my drink, Brayden grabs it. Her face fills with bright color when their fingers brush. I almost shake my head and roll my eyes. This is exactly how the female population at Western reacts to him. One dark look speared in their direction and they lose all sense of rational thought. It should probably drive me crazy. But how can it when Brayden continually goes out of his way to prove that I'm the only one he's thinking about?

He grabs the door and holds it open. The moment we hit the sidewalk, a burst of cool autumn air wafts over me. The leaves have already fallen from the trees and the temperatures are beginning to dip into cooler digits. The only saving grace is that the sun is bright and shining, cutting through the chilliness of the breeze.

As we take a few steps away from the coffee shop, Brayden grabs hold of my hand, loosely interlocking our fingers. "I love the fall. It's my favorite time of year."

I glance at him in surprise. "Me, too." Even though it's small, it's yet another thing we have in common.

"So, I was kind of thinking that after the game on Saturday, I could take you to our family cabin. It's not far from here. Only about an hour. We could spend Saturday afternoon, all of Sunday, and then head back in time for class Monday morning." There's a pause. "What do you think? Any interest in tromping around the woods? Or we can just sit inside and chill out."

I mentally sift through my school and soccer schedule for the upcoming week and think about what can be shifted around. The idea of getting away for even a few days sounds amazing. "Yeah, that could work."

A smile lifts the corners of his lips. "Cool. It'll be fun." He tugs me close, sliding his arm around my waist before adding softly, "It's been a while since I've been there."

I glance up, trying to decipher the emotion that weaves its way through his deep voice. Most people wouldn't pick up on the difference, but I've been spending so much time with Brayden that it's more noticeable. What I've discovered is that we're similar in how we deal with our emotions. We both tend to lock away the painful ones where we can't inspect them too closely. It takes us a while to share our inner thoughts and feelings with other people. It makes me feel special that he's gradually opening up, revealing the guy buried beneath all the hype.

And I like the guy he's proving to be. That's not something I expected to happen.

"How come?"

Brayden jerks his shoulders as his expression clouds. Gone is the lighthearted, easygoing guy from moments ago. A heavy silence descends as we continue walking. It feels strangely at odds with the bright sunshine that slants down on our heads. I'm almost tempted to change the subject or fill in the sudden stillness with idle chatter.

"When I was a kid, we used to spend a ton of time at the cabin. Sometimes the entire summer. Since my father's death, I've only been there once or twice. It hurt too much to be there without him, so I stopped going."

His earnest response has my heart cracking wide open. Even though we're in the middle of campus and there are people rushing past on the way to class, I grind to a halt. His footsteps falter as he turns and stares at me in question. My hand rises to drift over his shadowed jaw as I hold his gaze. Only now that I'm staring at him do I see the pain and grief swirling through his dark eyes.

"If you're not up to it, we don't have to go," I say softly.

The thick tension filling his muscles loosens as he sinks into my touch. "I know, but I want to take you there and share how special the place is with you. I want to have you all to myself." He glances around the crowded path overrun with students. "We can't do that here."

Brayden lives in a house with four other guys, and I share an apartment with Demi. It's almost impossible for us to grab more than a handful of hours alone together. Plus, we're both in the middle of our seasons. Our schedules are packed tight. It's not often that we can carve out a large chunk of time to spend with one another.

As much as I would love to get away from campus, even for a few days, it's obvious that the cabin holds a lot of bittersweet memories for him. I know exactly what that's like. It's not easy to deal with.

"Are you sure? We could always drive somewhere else for the day."

It takes a few seconds for Brayden to blink away the heavy emotion in his eyes as he jerks his head into a nod. Before I can dig any deeper, he presses his lips to mine and murmurs, "Yeah. I want to share the cabin with you. Who knows, maybe it'll help. We had a lot of good times there, and I want to make new memories with you."

The edges of my lips curl upward, liking the idea. "I want that, too."

He squeezes my fingers. "Good, now let's get moving before we're late."

Chapter Twenty-Nine

SYDNEY

Demi stretches out on my bed as I grab a few shirts from my drawer and toss them in the duffle bag I'm packing. Brayden and I are leaving tomorrow after the game. Even though we'll be gone for less than forty-eight hours, I'm excited to get away from school.

"I can't believe you two are taking off for the weekend."

Yeah, that makes two of us.

"I almost have whiplash from how fast this relationship is moving," she muses before adding, "It doesn't seem like all that long ago that you were ready to punch his lights out if he looked at you sideways."

I snort.

She's not mistaken about that. Anytime I was forced into close proximity with Brayden, I would bare my teeth like a rabid dog, ready to bite his head off at the slightest offense. A flicker of guilt slides through me at my treatment of him. Had I understood what was going on at the time, I would have shrugged it off and moved on. Instead, I took his behavior personally and let it fester inside.

I guess that old saying is true—you never know what's going on in someone else's life. Just because they project a happy façade to the world, doesn't mean they aren't splintering apart on the inside, barely able to hold it together. My heart constricts, thinking about how much pain Brayden must have been in freshman year. Instead of dealing with his grief in a productive manner, he chose alcohol and girls to drown himself in. As close as we've grown in the past few weeks, we haven't spent a lot of time talking about the people we've lost. Right now, it's simply enough to know that we've had similar experiences and understand what that kind of heartache feels like. It's a bond that no one wants to have.

I glance at my best friend.

Demi would be shocked to learn that my relationship with Brayden has progressed at even more of a rapid pace than she realizes. I still haven't disclosed that we were pretending to go out in the beginning. Now that we're actually a couple, there doesn't seem to be much point in revealing the truth.

"You're right," I agree, "that's exactly the way I felt. What I've discovered is that Brayden isn't the guy I'd assumed he was. And now that I've taken the time to get to know him, I realize how wrong I was."

She nods. "He's a really good guy. I've always had a soft spot for him. And you know what?" Before I can respond, she continues, "I like that you two are drama free. I no longer have to worry about walking into the middle of World War III when I walk through the door."

Demi's joking.

Kind of.

So many of my relationships were like riding a roller coaster with the ups and downs. This one couldn't be more different. Brayden and I are so in sync with one another. That's not something I've experienced with other guys. Even though it hasn't been long, I can appreciate that what we have is special. That knowledge makes me want to hang on tightly to it with both hands and never let go.

None of my past relationships were on this level. Even the one with Ethan. The highs and lows were exhausting. And it never truly allowed us to drill beneath the surface and get to know one another on a deeper, more meaningful level. It's only now that I'm with Brayden—and have experienced something more even keeled—that I can understand and appreciate the difference.

"Now all I have to worry about is walking in on the two of you getting it on," she adds, cutting into my thoughts.

Ugh.

Demi has yet to let me live that down.

"Technically," I point out, "that's your fault for not knocking on the door. And at least I was in my own bedroom when it happened. If I recall correctly, I walked in on you and Rowan making out on the couch." Unlike me, she'd been topless.

Color slams into her cheeks. "Yeah…that was definitely not one of my finer moments."

Maybe not, but it had been hilarious.

For me, anyway.

Demi, not so much.

When the corners of my lips tremble, hers do the same. Pretty soon, we're both laughing. It takes a few moments before our humor subsides.

"You know what's funny? I'd always suspected that Brayden had feelings for you."

Ironically, I hadn't been able to see if for myself. I had thrown up enough walls to make my heart an impenetrable fortress where he was concerned. And yet, somehow, he managed to smash through all of them.

"You two make a really great couple," she continues. "I hope it lasts."

As much as I've tried to hold myself back and take things slow, the truth is that I've fallen hard and fast. I'm in deeper than I ever thought possible. And it scares the shit out of me.

I glance up from the bathing suit I'm shoving in the bag. Brayden mentioned there was a hot tub, and I want to be prepared for whatever this weekend has in store.

"Me, too," I admit softly.

This is the first time I've acknowledged my feelings out loud. And doing so makes them all the more real.

"Who would have ever thought that Brayden Kendricks would turn out to be your boo-thing?"

I snort.

No one. That's who.

Do we really need more proof that miracles can happen?

Chapter Thirty

BRAYDEN

I turn the truck onto a narrow, country road that's flanked on both sides by tall trees spearing up into the bright blue sky. The closer we get to the cabin, the more nausea churns at the bottom of my gut. Why the hell did I think bringing Sydney here was a good idea?

At the moment, it seems like a pretty shit one. This place holds way too many memories. And the closer I get to the property, the more the nerves sitting at the bottom of my gut feel like they'll revolt. The hardest part is that all of my recollections are happy ones. I don't have a single bad one of this place. Except they all revolve around my father. Thinking about him always feels like ripping open an old wound.

Other than the football field, this was Dad's happy place. After he and Mom got married, they purchased a couple hundred acres of wooded property with a spring fed, five-acre lake in the middle. After each NFL season ended, we would spend time here, tromping around in the forest, riding ATV's, hiking, fishing, and camping. It was the only time that we had Dad all to ourselves. Here, he wasn't a famous NFL player. He was simply a loving father and husband.

Summers were always the best. Even though the cabin is massive, Dad and I would pitch a tent in the yard near the lake and sleep outside under the stars. A small campfire would burn all night. In the morning, we'd wake up bright and early. He would cook eggs and bacon over an open fire and then we would fish for the day.

Those are some of the best memories I have of my childhood. It's painful to acknowledge that we will never make more.

Dad is gone.

This is the one place on the face of the Earth where there's no avoiding the past. My father *was* this place. He and the land are deeply entwined. You can't have one without the other. Every year I fail to return makes it more difficult to consider the possibility of coming back in the future. The cabin used to fill me with so much happiness. I can't imagine that ever being the case again.

I wouldn't be making this trip without Sydney by my side. If there's anyone capable of soothing the anguish that lurks deep within me, it's this girl. She understands what loss feels like on this kind of gut-wrenching level because she's experienced it, too. She's quickly becoming my everything. These feelings snuck up on me when I was least expecting them.

Know what the real kicker is?

That I have Kira to thank for it.

Yeah...*Kira.*

It's doubtful the two of us would have gotten together if not for her. For obvious reasons, I won't be sharing that information with the tawny-haired girl anytime soon. Even though she seems to be going strong with her new boyfriend, I think that news would go down like a lead balloon.

I'm jostled from those thoughts when Sydney reaches over and wraps her fingers around mine. "Are you doing all right?" The question is hesitantly asked.

She's worried.

One flick of my gaze in her direction confirms the concern brimming in her vivid, green eyes. I probably should have kept my reservations about returning to myself. But that's the thing, I don't want to hold back the truth from Sydney. After all the lies that were told in the beginning of our relationship, I can't tolerate anything less than raw honesty between us. And being candid with her feels a little bit like vanquishing the ghosts of my past. Afterward, they don't seem quite so formidable.

"I'm fine. Maybe a little nervous," I admit, twisting my fingers so that I can encompass hers. The last thing I want to do is freak her out.

With a nod, she nibbles at her lower lip. "We don't have to do this, Bray. We could easily rent a hotel room for the night and stay there. Maybe explore the area tomorrow before heading back to school."

Yup. We could. But I don't want to do that. It's been years since I stepped foot on this property, and with Sydney by my side, I feel strong enough to finally come face to face with the past. I don't question that she's become so important to me in such a short span of time. When something feels right, there's no need to overthink it.

And Sydney feels *right*. Our relationship feels *right*. It's as if something fundamental has finally clicked into place that I never realized was missing. It's not something that can be explained away with logic.

It just is.

"I promise I'm good."

I turn the truck onto a narrower road. The woods grow thick and dense, hugging the sides of the lane until it feels like the branches could scrape against the door panels. If it were summer, the leaves would form a canopy and block out the bright shafts of sunlight that pour down.

A frown settles on her face as Sydney straightens and stares out the passenger side window. "Are you sure we're going the right way?" A nervous edge has crept into her tone. It takes a lot to rattle Sydney. The girl has nerves of steel.

My lips lift into a smile as I shoot her a quick glance. This isn't a place where I want to take my eyes off the road for long. I'm liable to wrap the front end of the truck around a tree. "Yup." It's a little more overgrown than I remember, but it's still the same.

"I'm going to keep it real with you. It feels like this road is going to dead end and we'll be stuck out here in the woods." There's a pause before she adds, "And then we'll get murdered by a roving band of psycho killers."

I snort out a laugh. "It's highly doubtful that psycho killers even know this place exists. Plus, you're much more likely to get mauled by a bear than a crazy with a chainsaw."

Color drains from her face as her eyes widen. "You better be joking."

"Of course I am."

Sort of.

Every rut we hit in the road makes Sydney yelp and grab the oh shit bar. Three minutes later, the lane finally opens up to a wider driveway. Both the log cabin and lake come into view.

Sydney leans forward in her seat as her eyes widen for the second time in a matter of minutes. "Wow," she breathes.

Yeah.

The view is spectacular. No matter how many times I've been here, it always hits me the same way as we come over the hill and the road opens up, surveying the land and water. The truck rolls toward the embankment that overlooks the lake before I shift the gear into park and cut the engine.

For a long, silent moment, we sit and take in the landscape beyond the windshield. The water is surrounded by dense forest with cattails on the sides. Both deciduous and pine trees make up the jagged landscape. Even though all the leaves have fallen, carpeting the earth in reds, browns, and golden hues, it's still a majestic sight. The land looks pristine and untouched by the hand of man. There are a few puffy, white clouds marring the cornflower blue sky. Their reflection is echoed in the glassy surface of the water.

"This is really beautiful, Brayden." Her gaze stays fastened on the view.

"Yeah, it is." And I've missed it. My dad loved this land, and just being here, seeing it again, smelling the crisp fall air, makes me feel like he's here with me. Maybe I can't see or speak with him, but his presence is all around me and somehow, that eases the ache in my heart. It only reconfirms that bringing Sydney here was the right decision to make.

My fingers settle over hers. "Are you ready to see the cabin?"

Her attention flickers to mine as she nods. We exit the truck and grab our bags from the backseat before heading toward the house. Our shoes crunch the gravel that lines the drive beneath them.

"You know, when you told me we would be staying in a cabin, I'd prepared myself for something...smaller. Maybe even a little dilapidated."

My lips quirk as a chuckle bursts free. My family has always referred to this place as a *cabin* because that's exactly what it is. A log cabin made from the poplar trees harvested from this very property. The structure itself is three thousand square feet and two stories high. There's a wide front porch that wraps around the entire first floor. A white swing has been hung near the front door and other seating arrangements are spaced out to enjoy the differing views. In the mornings, I'd always find my parents lounging on the couch with steaming mugs of coffee. There were even a few times when I stumbled upon them kissing. Back then, it had embarrassed the hell out of me, but now it brings me comfort to know that they had a happy marriage. They rarely fought and always enjoyed being in each other's company. Dad has been gone for four years and not once has Mom mentioned dating. As difficult as it would be to see her move on with someone else, I want her to be happy.

It takes effort to shake myself out of the sly memories attempting to wrap around me. "No, there's nothing dilapidated about it."

I pull out the key and slide it in the lock. We have a neighbor about twenty minutes away who stops by every other week to check on the mechanicals and make sure everything is in working order. Mom and Elle try to make it up here a few times a year. Whenever they plan a weekend, they invite me along. I always have a handy excuse ready. Neither of them has pushed the issue. I think all three of us realize what I'm doing. Mom was thrilled when I told her I wanted to bring Sydney here for a few days. I haven't introduced them yet, but that's next on the agenda.

When I open the door, she steps inside with her bag hoisted over one shoulder. Her gaze bounces around the double story family room. Beyond the expansive area is a kitchen. My parents designed the space to be open and airy. They wanted to create a place where we could all gather comfortably and spend time together as a family.

At the far end of the room is a massive field stone fireplace that takes up the entire wall. A chandelier made of antlers hangs from the ceiling. A white, oversized sectional curves around one of the walls. Opposite that is a long stretch of windows that overlook the lake. It would be a challenge to not find a gorgeous view from anywhere in this house. But the one from here is especially breathtaking.

"This place is amazing," Sydney says quietly, soaking up all the details. She looks slightly overwhelmed. I probably should have mentioned that my family has money. It's just not something that usually comes up in conversation.

When she remains motionless, I wrap my arm around her waist and tug her close. "I've really missed this place." Now that I'm standing inside the cabin, taking in my surroundings, I realize just how true the sentiment is. I stayed away because I thought it would be too painful to return without my father. It's only now that I wonder if I didn't inflict more damage by not digging deep and finding the courage to return sooner.

Dad's presence is everywhere. In every detail of the craftsmanship. I never expected it to feel like balm for the soul. In fact, I had prepared myself for the opposite.

"Are you ready for the grand tour?"

"Yup, I want to see it all," she says lightly.

After spending the last few days worried that I'd made a mistake, everything now feels buoyant. There's a lightness that fills the atmosphere. The smile Sydney showers me with says that she feels the shift in energy as well.

With my fingers clasped around hers, I tug her through the first floor. The kitchen, with its stainless-steel appliances and massive granite island, is our first stop. Mom mentioned that the refrigerator would be fully stocked for the weekend. I open the door and find enough food to feed a small army. I'm sure the neighbors brought over groceries so we wouldn't have to run to the store. There's a large dining room on the other side of the kitchen with views of the forest. We peek in the master suite before jogging up the staircase to the second floor and arriving at a loft that overlooks the family room. There's an overstuffed couch that we used to hang out on and watch movies. I have so many fond memories of my sister and me sprawled out on the carpeted floor, playing board games while Mom puttered around in the kitchen, making dinner or baking chocolate chip cookies.

Down the wide stretch of hallway are four spacious bedrooms, each with their own en suite. Mine is the first door on the right. I pull Sydney inside and glance around the space. The walls are painted a dark blue and there's a thick, plaid comforter covering the queen-sized bed. The decor is outdoorsy and fits with the theme of the cabin. A heavy wave of nostalgia crashes over me as I stare at what I've always considered my second bedroom. It all looks and feels the same as it did when I was a kid. In the summers, my parents allowed us to bring friends for a week or so. Carson has been here dozens of times, but inviting a girl is a new experience. I've never liked anyone enough to want to share this place with them.

As I drop my bag on the bed, Sydney does the same. I step closer and take her into my arms before pressing a kiss against the crown of her head.

"I'm glad you're here." Honestly, I don't think I've ever meant anything more.

She tilts her chin until our gazes can lock and hold. "Me, too."

For the remainder of the afternoon, we hold hands and tromp through the woods, spotting a couple of deer before they disappear through the underbrush. The forest is teeming with life. Birds chirp overhead, squirrels chatter in the trees, and larger animals crunch leaves beneath their feet in the distance. I've missed the property so much, and it feels good to share it all with Sydney. Everything my dad taught me about the forest as well as the memories. Instead of being filled with sorrow and grief, I actually feel lighter talking about him. I haven't done that in a long time. Once the floodgates open, it's almost impossible to close them. Sydney listens attentively, only asking questions every once in a while. It's like she understands that I need to get the words out and she quietly allows me to do that.

Our hands remain clasped as we walk along the water's edge. Even though the weather has turned cooler, there are still swarms of fish at the end of the dock where the sun warms the water.

Now that I've ripped off the Band-Aid and it hasn't turned out to be as painful as I anticipated, I can imagine returning here more often. I like getting Sydney away from campus. She's more relaxed and easy-going in this environment.

When seven o'clock rolls around, we're both famished from our explorations. We search through the fridge and cabinets and find everything we need to make spaghetti. It's something simple yet filling. She boils the water and takes charge of the noodles and garlic bread. I man the sauce and make the salads.

The relaxed way we move around the kitchen feels like we've done this hundreds of times before. There's a natural camaraderie between us that I've never experienced with anyone else.

By the time we eat dinner and clean up the kitchen, it's after nine o'clock. With her fingers enclosed in mine, I pull her out to the back porch. There's a wide swath of lawn that makes up the yard. One side is flanked by the lake and the other by dense foliage. In the middle of the space is a firepit with brightly painted Adirondack chairs scattered around it. Steps away from the back door is a small hot tub. I pull back the cover and check the temperature. It's set to one hundred degrees, which, in this weather, is perfect.

A smile simmers around my lips as I yank off my T-shirt and drop it to my feet.

Sydney jerks her thumb toward the house. "I need to go inside and change into my suit."

"That's not necessary," I say with a smirk.

She shakes her head before peering into the darkness that surrounds us with narrowed eyes.

"There's not a neighbor around for miles," I remind.

"What about the psycho killers?"

"I'm pretty sure they've got the night off."

She snorts out a laugh before dragging her shirt over her head. Then she shoves the denim material down her legs before stepping out of it until she's standing before me in nothing more than a black sports bra and thong.

Holy shit. Sydney has proven that a sports bra can be just as sexy as one made out of lace. The sight of her is enough to bring me to my knees. My mouth dries as I shove my jeans down and kick them away so that I'm left standing in my boxer briefs.

With her attention fastened on me, she reaches around her back and flicks open the clasp of her bra. The straps slide down her arms, revealing slightly rounded breasts with small, dusky-colored nipples.

My gaze travels over her greedily, touching upon every single inch of her naked flesh. The lights from the house cast her in a mixture of soft light and shadow. Does Sydney have any idea how fucking beautiful she is? Or how much I want her? How much I've always wanted her? Even when I was trying to fool myself into believing that I didn't.

Her fingers hover at the elastic band around her hips.

Before she can slip them beneath the stretchy material, I break the heavy silence that has fallen over us. "Let me do that."

It only takes three steps to close the distance. I sink to my knees, tilting my head and staring up at her until our gazes catch and hold. Anticipation thrums through me as I slip my fingers beneath the band and slowly slide the tiny scrap down her hips until her perfectly shaved pussy is revealed. Once the thong has been removed, I press a kiss against the top of her slit.

Sydney's fingers tangle in my hair as I slip my tongue between her lower lips. A sigh of contentment erupts from her, and she tightens her hold. Doesn't this girl realize that the grip is unnecessary? There's no way in hell I'm going anywhere. For the first time in my life, I'm exactly where I want to be, and that's with her.

I spread her lips before running the flat of my tongue over her softness. Another whimper escapes as she arches her pelvis. I focus my attention on her clit, licking and sucking the tiny bundle of nerves into my mouth until she explodes. I work her delicate flesh until her muscles finally loosen. Only then do I rise to my feet and shove the boxers down my legs before picking her up and carrying her to the hot tub. She rests her head against my chest as we sink into the warm water.

With her tucked close, I realize this is the happiest I've been since my father died.

And that has everything to do with this girl.

The one who has changed everything for me.

Chapter Thirty-One

SYDNEY

I wake to the steady rhythm of raindrops hitting the windows. I have no idea what time it is, but the skies are a dark, leaden gray. It only makes me want to snuggle against Brayden and stay in bed, cocooned in his blankets for the entire day. And since we don't have any plans, we can do exactly that.

Yesterday turned out to be one of the most enjoyable afternoons I've ever experienced. My parents never took us camping, so this is the closest I've come to it. In no way am I saying that I'd like to pitch a tent and sleep outdoors, but this is a good compromise. I'm not going to lie, the idea that we're so far from civilization is a little disconcerting. If I opened my window at home and yelled, half a dozen people would come running. Here, I could probably scream my head off and not a soul would hear me.

What I like most is that I have Brayden all to myself. We're free to do what we want, even if that means lounging around and being lazy. That's not something either of us gets to indulge in very often. It's a real treat to not have a schedule for the day.

If the skies don't clear, we can make popcorn, curl up on the couch, and watch movies. If the sun comes out, we can explore the forest and lake. Maybe relax in the hot tub again. Arousal stirs in my core as I remember the way he tongued me, getting me off before scooping me up and carrying me into the water where we had sex.

The guy is insatiable, and I absolutely love it.

Since he's still stretched out beside me, snoring soundly, I slip quietly from the bed before grabbing a sweatshirt and yoga pants and padding to the kitchen to make breakfast. I'm starving, and I'd bet money that Brayden is, too.

I pull out everything I need to make pancakes and bacon before getting to work. There's something relaxing about the sound of the rain plinking against the vast expanse of windows. It doesn't take long before I'm humming to myself.

This kitchen is like a chef's dream. Everything looks to be top of the line. The stove is massive and has an industrial appearance to it. Once the griddle is heated, I pour batter onto the non-stick surface and wait for it to bubble.

It's funny—since I'll be graduating in the spring, I've spent a lot of time thinking about my future. Those thoughts have always centered on my career and the accounting job waiting for me at my father's company. Boys have come and gone from my life with such regularity that I never considered someone might actually stick around after graduation. Brayden is the first person I could imagine being with long term, which seems crazy and yet...there's something about him. Something about the way we are together. It makes me think that we could be going strong years down the road.

I shake my head; I'm getting way ahead of myself. This must be what relationship happiness feels like.

Brayden chooses that moment to stumble into the kitchen. His eyes are barely cracked open, and his hair is mussed. I'm tempted to run my fingers through the short strands. He didn't bother putting on anything other than boxers that hug his lean hips and thighs.

"What are you doing up so early?" he grumbles, voice all low and sexy. It strums something deep inside, nearly making me forget about the pancakes I'm in the process of flipping.

I glance at the clock. "It's after nine. I thought you might be hungry."

"I woke up craving something, but it's not food," he says, padding over and wrapping his arms around me before pressing a kiss against the column of my neck.

His words make my belly hollow out as need throbs to life in my core. "How about we eat pancakes and then talk about the other." My voice comes out sounding breathless, even to my own ears.

"I'm not interested in talking," he growls against my neck. "I'm interested in fucking."

Oh god...

The way Brayden talks is enough to start a veritable inferno in my panties. As he nibbles his way from my throat to my mouth, I realize that I need to push him away or breakfast will end up a burnt disaster, and I've put in way too much effort for that to happen. Plus, I get the feeling we'll need our sustenance for the rest of the day. Whether or not the skies clear.

Once I've piled the pancakes on the plate and pulled the perfectly crisped bacon from the oven, we sit down and eat. Or, I should say that Brayden tugs me onto his lap, and we share one plate until both our bellies are full. Only after every bite has been consumed does he push the dish away before wrapping both hands around the small of my waist and hoisting me onto the long stretch of table as if I weigh nothing at all.

His fingers trail from my hips to my thighs before nudging them open. The heated look he shoots me is enough to send my belly into freefall. "Why are you wearing so much clothing?"

My mouth turns cottony. "It was cold when I got out of bed."

"Don't worry, I'll keep you warm." With that, he pulls the sweatshirt over my head and tugs the stretchy yoga pants down my hips and thighs until I'm completely naked.

His hands stroke over my inner thighs, spreading my legs impossibly wide as his gaze stays locked on my core. I've never been embarrassed or shy about my body. I've been an athlete my entire life. I'm focused on how strong and fast I am rather than the physical attributes men find appealing. I'm well aware that my breasts are small, and my thighs are more muscular than most girls. To have Brayden stare so blatantly sets my nerves on edge. No one has ever studied me with such intensity. Especially while stretched out on the dining room table like I'm a main course to be feasted on.

As tempting as it is to close my legs or pull him up so that he'll kiss me and stop staring at the most intimate part of my body, I remain still, allowing him to look his fill. The only reason I'm able to do so is because of the reverence shining in his eyes. He makes me feel beautiful. His fingers drift over my core, rubbing but never lingering in one place for long. It doesn't take much before I'm growing restless beneath his expert touch.

"You're so fucking pretty," he whispers, gaze pinned to my center. "I can't get enough of you. I love everything about your pussy," he muses, almost as if he's talking to himself rather than me. "So soft and tight. I love when my cock is buried deep inside you. The way your muscles clench around me right before you come. The little moans that escape from your lips when I lick you." His gaze flickers to mine. "You love it, don't you?"

It's not a question. We both know that I do. Brayden has a very talented tongue. I can't get enough of it. When I remain silent, his fingers brush over me before circling around my clit, giving it a little pinch. The pressure isn't enough to cause pain. It does, however, send a bolt of need spiraling through me.

"Tell me you love it," he growls.

"I do," I say in a heady rush, "you know I do."

His lips lift into a smug smile. "Yeah, but I like to hear you say it." There's a pause before he adds, "I don't want anyone else to ever touch you this way."

At this moment, it's impossible to imagine anyone other than Brayden running his hands and mouth over me like this. There's a level of intimacy we've managed to achieve that feels rare, and I don't ever want to lose it. Just when I can't take another second of his caresses, he rises to his feet and yanks down the front of his boxers until his thick cock is able to spring free. He pumps his erection a few times as I spread my legs further. I'm mesmerized by the movements. I've never seen anything as hot in my life as Brayden stroking himself.

With his hand still wrapped around his girth, he positions the crown at my entrance, sliding in only an inch or two. It feels so damn good, but it's not nearly enough to get me off. The wicked smile that curves his lips tells me that his movements are purposeful. A little flex of dominance to let me know who is in charge.

At least for the moment.

I arch off the table, attempting to coax him further inside me.

"I decide how much you get, not you," he growls, slapping my clit with the tips of his fingers.

A gasp escapes as a thousand little shockwaves explode inside me. Even though the strike isn't hard, it's certainly enough to capture my attention. Brayden slides in another inch and my body shudders with pleasure. This little game he's intent on playing only intensifies my arousal until it turns unbearable. Until climax is all I can focus on.

"Brayden, please," I whimper, unable to stay still, "I need more."

Almost stingily, he gives me a bit of length. As ecstasy ripples through my being, he withdraws, leaving me feeling bereft once again. "I know you do, baby." His voice is tightly strung as if he's just as pained and full of need as I am.

And then it starts all over again.

Each time he teases me, the pleasure ratchets up to unprecedented heights. The smooth slide of his cock fuels my senses until they reach a fever pitch. Until I don't think I can take any more of this torment before breaking out into frustrated sobs. Just as I'm about to beg him to fuck me, Brayden drives deep inside my sheath, and a scream explodes from my lungs. The orgasm slams into me like a tidal wave, crashing over me, threatening to drag me to the very bottom of the ocean.

The intensity of my reaction seems to spur him on as Brayden finds his own release and we come together. He chants my name before collapsing on top of me and burying his face in the crook of my neck. We lay there for a long time, our hearts beating like the wings of a hummingbird before eventually settling.

When he finally lifts his head, there's a cocky smirk curving his lips. "Now that's more what I had in mind for breakfast."

A chuckle slips free as I tunnel my fingers through his thick hair.

The pancakes were definitely good, but Brayden is right.

This was much better.

Chapter Thirty-Two

SYDNEY

The soft patter of rain continues to fall for the rest of the afternoon. It would have been nice to go outside and explore the area, but I can't say that I mind curling up on the couch and having a movie marathon. With flames dancing in the grate, we lay entwined on the sectional, covered in a blanket. For lunch, Brayden whips up a few grilled cheese sandwiches and tomato soup. It's the perfect meal that hits the spot. While he cleans up the dishes, I wander around the cabin.

That thought makes me snort. In no way does this place resemble a dark, dank cottage. This could legit be someone's home. It's outfitted with all the amenities and creature comforts a person could need. Other than being situated in the middle of nowhere, it's perfect. My thoughts meander back to this morning as I stroll through the family room, taking in all the knickknacks on display.

Maybe I'm wrong about the privacy thing.

Maybe it *is* kind of nice.

I gravitate to the massive stone fireplace with its jagged rocks in rich hues of gray and blue. Warmth emanates from the fireplace, and I hold out my hands to warm them. Even though the cabin's temperature is toasty, the heat feels good as it seeps into my bones.

I study the framed photographs propped on the mantle. There are numerous ones of Brayden and his sister, Elle, at various stages of their childhood. I pick up one silver frame and examine the picture. My guess is that Brayden must be somewhere around ten years old. A huge grin lights up his youthful face and his dark eyes dance with excitement. His chest is bare as he holds up a fish with one hand.

There's another of him and Elle at Christmas. In the background is a beautifully decorated tree that stretches toward the two-story ceiling. Both siblings are busy ripping into gifts with excited expressions painted across their faces. I run my finger slowly over his image. It's not a surprise that he was such a cutie.

The third picture is one of a woman and man. They look to be in their mid-thirties. He's tall and muscular, built much like Brayden, and she's more petite, coming only to his shoulder. Their arms are wrapped around each other as they beam at the camera. I study the photograph as something pings in the back of my brain. His face looks vaguely familiar. Although there's no reason to suspect that I would have met Brayden's father. I pull it closer and examine the image more carefully.

I'm shaken out of my scrutiny when Brayden comes up behind me and slides his arms around my waist before tugging me close and nuzzling my neck.

"That's Mom and Dad."

"It's a beautiful picture." They look happy.

He nods. When he says nothing more, I twist around and find sadness flickering in his eyes as he stares at the photograph. I can almost see him getting lost in the memories. I'm intimately acquainted with that feeling, and all I want to do in this moment is banish it for him. Carefully, I set the framed photograph back where I found it before turning and looping my arms around his neck.

"If it's too painful, we don't have to talk about your father," I say softly. "The fact that you've come here is a big step. It's enough."

"No, I want to tell you about him. I want you to know the kind of guy he was and how much he meant to me." There's a pause. "To all of us."

Brayden shifts our bodies so that we're facing the mantle before pointing to a large, silver framed photograph of the four of them.

"That's the last family picture that was taken of us. I was a junior in high school."

Again, I study his mother. She's beautiful with shining, dark hair and eyes. It's obvious who Elle takes after as she stands in front of her. Even though she has braces, she flashes a bright smile toward the camera. My gaze moves to Brayden. He's not as tall as he is now and certainly not as broad in the shoulders or chest. His hair is a little longer than I'm used to seeing, but he's still ridiculously handsome. And then my attention settles on the man who was ripped from their lives.

"He and my mom met when they were in high school and fell in love. They got married when they were still in college before Dad was drafted to the NFL."

I glance at him, brows drawing together. "He played professional football?"

Brayden nods. "Yup, for fifteen years, and then he injured his shoulder. That's when he decided it was time to retire."

I study the picture more intensely as something continues to niggle the back of my brain. I didn't realize Brayden's father played in the NFL. I guess it makes sense that he would want to follow in his footsteps. "What was his name?"

"Jake."

And just like that, a trapdoor opens and I'm in free fall.

"Jake Winchester," I murmur. My voice comes out sounding strangled. It's as if someone has their hands wrapped around my throat and is slowly squeezing the life out of me.

Brayden's gaze flickers to me in surprise. "Yeah, that's right. The last team he played for was the Chicago Bears before retiring. We got to spend about five years with him before a dumbass kid who was drunk took him out."

Oh, god.

Oh, god.

Oh, god.

I can't believe this is happening. My head spins until I'm dizzy with the sensation, and I can't catch my breath.

"You don't have the same last name," I wheeze.

"No. My mother never changed her maiden name. So, I'm stuck with both. Mine is hyphenated, but I just use Kendricks. It's easier that way." A small smile quirks the corners of his lips. "Kendricks-Winchester is kind of a mouthful. Plus, can you see that on the back of a jersey?"

I can only stare as my mind cartwheels.

Brayden is the son of Jake Winchester. Not once did it occur to me that his father could be the same man Peter killed in the accident.

"Hey," he says, interrupting the whirl of my thoughts, "is something wrong? You've gone pale. Do you need to sit down?"

It isn't until he lifts his thumb to wipe away the moisture gathered beneath my eyes that I realize I'm crying. It's almost impossible to blink back the hot tears. "No, I'm fine." I gulp down the thick emotion before forcing out the rest. "I'm just really sorry." In no way does that adequately describe what's crashing around inside me. The grief that is crushing the very life out of me, making it impossible to breathe.

He pulls me closer until the side of my face is pressed against his chest before dropping a kiss against the crown of my head. "There's absolutely nothing for you to be sorry about. It's not like you had anything to do with the accident."

I squeeze my eyes tightly closed, wishing that were the truth but knowing it isn't.

And sooner or later, Brayden will arrive at the same conclusion.

Chapter Thirty-Three

SYDNEY

I tip my face toward the warm spray of water and pray that it washes away the guilt that's eating me alive.

I have no idea what to do.

Should I tell Brayden what I've only now discovered? Do I confess that it was my brother who hit and killed his father? That Peter was the stupid kid who'd had too many drinks before sliding behind the wheel of his car?

The thought of pushing out those words makes me sick to my stomach. There have been so many times throughout the afternoon and then evening when I turned to him, fully prepared to vomit out the truth. Each time I opened my mouth, prepared to come clean, I couldn't do it. The sound refuses to be summoned. It's only a matter of time before Brayden makes the connection. I'm a little shocked that neither of us pieced it together before this very moment.

Even with different surnames, I should have realized it.

For so long, I've done everything in my power *not* to think about the man Peter killed. Or his family. I'd relegated the information to the back of my brain and locked it safely away. The guilt and sorrow were too heavy to carry around on a daily basis.

Only now do I realize why the photographs had seemed so eerily familiar. After the accident, there had been a slew of articles splashed across the front page of the paper and stories reported on the local news. Every time I'd caught sight of the pictures, it had been like a sucker punch to the gut. There had been one of him in his football uniform the last year he played in the NFL, and then one of his family. It's the same image displayed on Brayden's mantle.

Nausea churns at the bottom of my belly until it feels like I'm going to heave everything I've recently ingested. I don't know how much longer I can withstand this. I can't even look at Brayden without wanting to cry.

When fresh tears sting my eyes, I tilt my face toward the hot spray and allow the water to wash them away. It's only when my emotions are wrestled under control that I twist the handle and turn off the steady stream of water before stepping out and grabbing a towel. After drying off, I wrap the plush cotton material around my body and stand in front of the mirror. I swipe my hand over the fogged-up glass and glance at the haunted reflection that stares back at me.

You have to tell him.

It's only right that he knows the truth.

Fresh bile rises in my throat.

Once he understands how our pasts are entwined, he'll despise me. And I can't blame him for that. *I* would despise me, too.

My shoulders collapse under the crushing weight of that knowledge before I swing away from the mirror, unable to look at myself any longer. I grab a second towel from the sleek, silver rack and dry my hair before running a brush through the long strands.

The time we've spent at the cabin has been amazing. I feel so much closer to Brayden than I did two short days ago. But now there's this huge secret weighing me down, pinning me to the Earth. There's no way this information won't blow our entire relationship to smithereens. Shrapnel will be everywhere. There's no doubt in my mind that this will alter the path we've been on and send us careening through the atmosphere, never to be the same again.

You have to tell him.

The backs of my eyes burn as I grab the door handle and open it before stepping inside Brayden's room. As soon as I do, his head swivels, gaze coasting over my towel-clad body. A smile curves the edges of his lips as heat ignites in his dark eyes.

He wouldn't look at you like that if he knew the truth.

In fact, he wouldn't look at you at all.

You would cease to exist.

Those thoughts are like a knife to my heart.

He holds out his hand. "Come here, baby."

The words are perched on the tip of my tongue. All I have to do is force them out. And I have to do it now. If he touches me, I'll lose my nerve and won't be able to tell him.

My tongue darts out to moisten my lips. "Brayden."

"Come here," he repeats, voice dipping lower, strumming something deep inside me.

"We need to talk." Even as I push out the words, I gravitate toward him. It's like there's an invisible string connecting us.

"We can talk later. I need you now."

His fingers lock around mine as he tugs me closer to the bed until I'm tumbling into his arms. My towel unravels before floating to the floor. And then I find myself sprawled out on top of his hard body.

My strength wavers as I open my mouth to make one final attempt. Instead of giving me a chance to clear my conscience, his other hand slides into my hair and cups the back of my skull, forcing my lips to his. Once his tongue delves inside my mouth, I'm lost on a rising sea of sensation. Before I can fully grasp what's happening, I'm flipped onto my back as Brayden looms over me. He's propped up on his elbows so the full weight of his body doesn't rest on me as his mouth roves hungrily over mine.

Every last thought of doing what's right vanishes as arousal bursts to life in my core. It licks like fire over every misgiving that has taken up residence inside me. If I'm being completely honest, there's a tiny part that's grateful for his hunger. For his forcefulness. It allows me to ignore everything that has been gnawing at me for the last couple of hours. And really...is there any harm to giving in?

What I need more than anything is to feel Brayden's touch one last time before I reveal the truth and our relationship is forever changed.

I find myself capitulating as my mouth meets his greedy one. My arms rise until my fingers can tangle in his thick hair and hold him close. There's a desperateness to my movements. I want to hang on to Brayden forever, even though I realize that it's impossible. It's doubtful that we'll make it through the weekend intact.

I understand this, even if he does not.

Instead of fucking me furiously, which is how our sex can be, Brayden slows things down. His kisses become more languid, as if we have all the time in the world to explore. He angles his head one way before tilting it the other. He licks at my mouth, peppering caresses along my chin and throat before sinking lower to my breast. One crested nipple gets drawn into the warmth of his mouth before he showers the same amount of attention on the other. I arch my back, wanting to be as physically close to him as possible.

I can't help but already mourn this relationship.

No matter how this plays out, nothing will be the same between us. Brayden will never look at me as he does now, and that realization floods me with bitterness. Unaware of the thoughts that are circling through my head, he caresses his way from my rib cage to my belly before settling between my thighs. He presses a kiss against the top of my slit before tonguing my pussy. A whimper escapes from me as I widen my legs. Nothing feels as amazing as his face buried between my thighs.

I wish it were possible to live in this moment, this space, forever. But it's not. At some point, reality will crash down on both of our heads. As soon as those thoughts attempt to take root inside my brain, I shove them away. If this is the last time we'll be together, I want to enjoy it to the fullest.

He licks at me, teasing my flesh until I'm arching against his mouth. It doesn't take much before I'm splintering apart beneath his clever tongue. As I fall back to Earth, he presses a tender kiss against me before crawling up my limp form. With one swift movement, he yanks the boxers down his hips and thighs before kicking off the material until he's as naked as I am.

Our gazes lock and hold as he slides deep inside my heat. Unlike this morning, there's no teasing or games. He cages me in with his arms as my legs wrap around his waist, securing his body to mine until we are one. There is an intensity that fills his dark eyes as they stay trained on mine. So much emotion is conveyed in that one look.

Even though I came only moments ago, I feel the stirrings of an orgasm deep in my core. Except this time, there's something different about it. It's almost as if our connection has been strengthened. A powerful emotion that refuses to be denied.

As Brayden thrusts inside me, our bodies fall into a natural rhythm. His fingers find mine before lacing them together. It would be impossible for us to be more attuned with each other. Physically. Mentally. Emotionally. I've never felt this kind of bond with anyone else. It's as if we are truly one. When my body convulses again, Brayden dives headfirst over the edge with me, holding my gaze the entire time before collapsing. His harsh and labored breath echoes in my ear until it's the only sound I'm cognizant of. That and the heavy weight pinning me to the mattress are what ground me in the moment. Otherwise, I would float away into the atmosphere.

"Sydney?"

It takes effort to blink back to awareness.

His gaze searches mine before he whispers, "I love you."

My heart twists painfully beneath my breast. Instead of echoing the sentiment, I keep the words trapped deep inside where they can't inflict further damage. How can I share what I truly feel when I haven't been honest with him?

Sorrow and regret churn through me, threating to swallow me whole as I bury my face against his chest and wish for what feels like the hundredth time that everything could be different between us.

Chapter Thirty-Four

BRAYDEN

I scoop up a pair of boxers from the floor and toss them into my bag before glancing around the bedroom to make sure I've got everything. Even though it's still early, we're packing up and getting ready to head back to Western. The past thirty-six hours sped by way too quickly. It's like I blinked and it was time to go. I wish we could stay at the cabin for a couple more days, but that's not possible. We both have school and athletic commitments that can't be missed.

My gaze flits to Sydney. She's standing on the other side of the bed, gathering up her belongings. She's been unusually quiet since we woke up this morning. I'm not sure if it's because, like me, she wishes it were possible to keep the real world at bay for a bit longer, or if there's something else going on.

Uncertainty mushrooms up inside me as I draw one side of my lip between my teeth and chew on it. Is she quiet because I blurted out my feelings last night? Did the declaration make her uncomfortable? It's just that the moment had felt so right. And the words had been circling in the back of my mind, clawing at me, fighting to break free. Maybe I should have beaten back the urge and given it more time.

But that hadn't been possible. The sex had been different last night. Instead of a means for physical release, it felt deeper and more profound. The funny thing is that I'd thought Sydney had been with me every step of the way and experienced it, too.

Afterward, she'd clung to me before falling asleep wrapped up in my arms. I'd woken up this morning with the urge to make love to her one last time before we hit the road, but the sheets beside me had been empty. Already cool from her absence. I'd found her sitting in the kitchen, staring out the window. Her aloof behavior takes me back to how it was before we decided there was nothing fake about this relationship. Something has shifted, and I'm not sure what it is, but I'm going to damn well find out.

After the closeness we shared last night, this conversation feels awkward. "Is everything all right?" When Sydney glances up, skewering me with her bright green gaze, I tack on, "You seem...*off*." That's a major understatement, but I'm not sure what else to say.

She shifts her weight from one foot to the other before breaking eye contact, dropping it to the bed. If I needed further confirmation that something isn't right, I have it. What's strange is that Sydney has always been a straight shooter. It's one of her personality traits that I admire most. If there's something going on in her head, she'll tell you about it. Whether you want to know or not.

So why isn't she doing that now?

Why is she holding back?

A long silence ensues, and the muscles in my gut twist into a series of complicated knots. Emotion flickers across her face and everything inside me sinks. "Sydney?"

If I hadn't realized it before, I do now—blurting out my feelings last night had been an epic mistake. She wasn't ready to hear them. All I've done is push her away when I only wanted to hold her close.

Uncertain how to rectify the situation, I plow my fingers through my hair. "I'm sorry about springing my feelings on you," I mumble, feeling like an ass. "I know we haven't been together that long." I jerk my shoulders, unsure how to explain without fucking things up any further than they already are. How do I convey that nothing feels more right in my life than she does? Then *we* do? "Maybe it was too much too soon."

Here's a bit of irony—I've never told anyone except for my parents that I loved them. I've never dated anyone long enough to develop strong emotions. Or maybe I didn't allow myself to go there for whatever reason.

And now that I have...

She wasn't ready to hear it. Hell, if a girl told me that she loved me, I'd run for the hills.

That's exactly what Kira did, and it freaked me out. I mean, come on, we weren't even going out. That girl didn't love me. How could she possibly when she didn't even know the real me?

But Sydney does. She understands me better than anyone else. I've shared stuff with her that I've always held deep inside.

Her fingers freeze on the shirt she's holding. Her eyes stay lowered, pinned to the duffle she's in the process of packing. Is this really what it's come to? She can't meet my gaze or give me a straight-up answer?

"What's going on?" My fingers flex with the need to wrap around her. The scary part is that I can feel her slipping away and I have no idea how to stop it. Before I realize it, I'm on the move, stalking around the queen-sized bed and pulling her into my arms. "You need to tell me what the problem is. How else can we fix it?"

When she refuses to look me in the eyes, I grab hold of her chin and lift it so that she has no other choice but to meet the intensity of my gaze. A strange mixture of guilt and grief flash across her face. Nothing about this conversation—if that's what you want to call it—makes sense. All I know is that my insides are being eaten alive by nerves.

"Talk to me," I plead.

Why won't she tell me what's going on?

What the hell could be so wrong?

Sydney sucks in a long, shuddering breath, holding it captive inside her lungs before forcing it back into the atmosphere. "This isn't working."

I blink. *"What?"*

Her tongue darts out nervously to moisten her lips before she whispers, "This isn't working, Brayden."

Those four words are enough to make my heart skip a painful beat before jackhammering into overdrive against my rib cage.

What's not working?

Wait a minute...

My mouth drops open. "Are you saying that the two of us together isn't going to work?" I can only stare in shock. "You want to break up?"

When her gaze darts away and she remains silent, I growl, *"Sydney!"*

Her eyes widen before snapping back to mine. "Yes, I do."

I shake my head as if to clear it, but it doesn't help. No matter what I was expecting her to say, this wasn't it. Not by a long shot. "I don't understand. Why?"

"It's just..."

When her voice dies a slow death, I'm left hanging. Or maybe I'm in free fall. I have no idea. This conversation doesn't feel real.

"It's just *what*, Syd? Tell me what the hell is going on here, because I don't understand any of it. I'd thought everything was good. I'd thought *we* were good."

Tears spring to her eyes, making them appear even more vibrant than usual as she presses her lips together until they drain of color.

Why won't she give me an answer?

Tension fills my shoulders. "Is this because of what I said last night? Is our relationship moving too fast for you?" I gulp down the growing desperation that clogs my throat, making it impossible to breathe. When Sydney remains silent, I start to babble. I can't stop myself. "If that's the case, then we can slow track it. I'm sorry, I thought we were both on the same page." It had sure felt like it last night. Hell, this entire weekend.

You know what?

This entire damn relationship. Even when we were fake dating, it still felt like we were moving at the same pace, in the same direction even when we didn't understand what direction that was. It's a real kick in the ass to realize that I couldn't be further off base. Her continued silence is killing me. "You've got to give me some answers here, Syd. I don't want to keep playing this guessing game with you."

There's a long pause before she murmurs, "I...I don't feel the same way."

The acidic taste of bile rises up in my throat. The pounding of my heartbeat fills my ears until it sounds like the roar of the ocean, making it impossible to think straight. "You don't think you'll ever feel that way?" It takes effort to force out the rest. "Is that what you're trying to tell me?"

Her fingers tighten, biting into the fabric clutched in her hands. "Please, Brayden," she whispers. "Do we have to do this now?"

Is she fucking serious?

"Yeah, we're doing it," I grit between clenched teeth. "I deserve answers." I need something concrete that I can wrap my brain around that will make sense, because right now...absolutely nothing does.

She breaks free of my hold before taking a step in retreat. The distance isn't just physical, it's emotional as well. "I wish I could give you more, but I can't. This relationship isn't going to work out in the long run. I'm really sorry. I can't force feelings that aren't there to begin with."

It takes everything I have inside to remain upright when all I want to do is double over from the excruciating pain licking its way through my body. It's like I've been kicked in the balls and can't catch my breath. Actually, it's much worse than that.

Force feelings?

She's been *forcing feelings* the entire time?

What the fuck?

Anger crashes through me. I don't know what's going on here or why Sydney is acting like this, but that's total bullshit. The emotions unfolding between us weren't in my imagination. And it sure as shit wasn't one-sided, either. She felt it.

It's on the tip of my tongue to argue, but I can already tell that I won't get anywhere with her. She's shut down and closed off. As much as I hate to leave the conversation—not to mention our relationship—in this uncomfortable limbo, there's no other choice for the time being.

I jerk my head into a tight nod. "All right."

The relief that floods into her face is yet another kick in the ass.

Chapter Thirty-Five

SYDNEY

As soon as I pull my bag from the backseat of Brayden's truck, he says goodbye in a clipped tone and pulls away. I can't blame him for being angry. I totally blindsided him. The look in his eyes when I told him that I didn't feel the same way was so much more brutal than I anticipated. As soon as I forced out the words, I wanted to fall to the floor and beg his forgiveness. To confess the real reason for the unexpected shift in my behavior.

But how could I do that?

After we made love—because that's exactly what it had been—I'd laid awake for hours, trying to figure out what to do. How could I possibly tell him that it was my brother who killed his father in the accident? I slipped out of bed at dawn, padded into the living room, and stared out at the lake, trying to figure out a way to word my explanation so he wouldn't end up despising me. In none of the scenarios did it end with us being friends, much less staying together and carrying on with our relationship.

How could he forgive me?

How could he *not* look at me differently after discovering the truth?

No.

Even if Brayden somehow attempted to make peace with the situation, he would still end up resenting me. If the scenario were reversed, wouldn't I feel the same?

It's much better to cut things off now and keep the truth buried where it can't hurt either one of us. Maybe Brayden will hate me for a little while, but he'll eventually get over it. Come on, this is Brayden Kendricks we're talking about. I've never seen him lose sleep over a female, and my guess is that I won't be the exception that breaks the rule. In a few weeks, he'll be back to his old ways, screwing groupies and soaking up all the fan adoration. I'll end up being nothing more than a blip on his radar.

Me, on the other hand?

It's going to take time to get over the loss of him. I never expected Brayden to claw his way inside my heart, but that's exactly what he's managed to do in the short amount of time we've been together. I might have been with Ethan for six months, but my feelings for Brayden are infinitely deeper. It doesn't necessarily make sense, but that doesn't change the way I feel.

With a sinking heart, I watch his black truck disappear from the parking lot and down the road before I turn toward the building. The entire way up the elevator, uncertainty claws at me. Did I make the right decision in setting him free?

I try to imagine the hatred that would grow in his eyes if he ever discovered the truth. This morning was bad enough. I don't think I could bear for that to happen. With a heavy heart, I shove my key in the lock before pushing open the door to our apartment. Demi's head pops up from the back of the couch.

"Hey girl, you're back early. Did you have a nice mini vacay?" Before I can answer, she chirps, "Tell me all about it! I've got about ten minutes before I have to take off for my first class."

As much as I want to keep this all to myself, there's no point in prolonging the inevitable. Demi will hear about it eventually. Better to get it over with now and move on.

I clear my throat and attempt to keep my voice devoid of emotion. "Actually, we broke up."

She jerks to attention and stares at me for a long heartbeat before searching my face as if she expects me to burst out with a *just kidding*!

When I remain silent, she whispers, "Are you serious?"

I inhale a deep breath and battle back a heavy wave of emotion as it crashes over me, threatening to suck me under. "Yep." It's a struggle to keep the thin waver from invading my voice.

"I..." Brows furrowed, she shakes her head as if she's at a total loss for words. Demi might not be as outspoken as I am, but she's rarely shocked into silence.

I press my lips together before forcing myself to repeat the lie I'd told Brayden. "In the end, it just wasn't going to work out."

"Oh." Confusion flickers across her expression. "I thought you really liked him. You seemed so happy and got along so well."

"Yeah...well." I shrug. When the backs of my eyes begin to burn, I realize that I'm precariously close to falling apart. That's the last thing I want to happen. Demi is my best friend, and I can tell her anything. Even if she doesn't necessarily agree with my decision, she'll stand by my side because that's the kind of ride or die she is, but I don't want to reveal the truth about Peter. She understands that he died in a car accident but doesn't know the entire story. Only the bits and pieces I've chosen to share.

Even though I didn't go far away to college, it was a relief to leave the claustrophobic halls of high school behind and start over with people who didn't know who I was or the tragedy that had occurred. After the accident, there had been a lot of pitying looks mingled with accusatory ones aimed in my direction. Kids I'd known since grade school whispered behind my back, gossiping about how my older brother had been out drinking with friends and had gotten behind the wheel of his car. He'd killed himself and taken an innocent man with him.

Not only did we have to work our way through the grief and loss, but we had to reconcile ourselves with the disastrous decision he'd made. One that not only altered our family but someone else's as well. There is no way to wrap that up with a pretty bow.

"Do you want to talk about it?" Demi asks gently, cutting into the chaotic whirl of my thoughts.

I shake my head. "Talking about the situation won't change the outcome." That, at the very least, is the truth.

When Demi opens her mouth in protest, I raise my hand and cut her off. "I'm sorry, I need to change and get ready for class." Not waiting for a reply, I slip inside my room. Once the door is closed behind me, I lean against it and squeeze my eyes tightly shut.

It feels like I'm making the biggest mistake of my life, and there's not a damn thing I can do about it.

My relationship with Brayden is yet another casualty of the last decision Peter ever made.

Chapter Thirty-Six

BRAYDEN

I strip off my practice jersey and pads before shoving them in my locker. One would think that my head would be focused on football. We have a conference rivalry game coming up this weekend. There shouldn't be room for anything else. Certainly not Sydney or the way she annihilated my heart.

I'd hoped that with enough time and space, she would eventually come around, but so far, that hasn't happened. When I showed up to class on Wednesday, Sydney refused to look at me and then slipped out the door before I could track her down for a conversation. A couple hours after that, I broke down and texted her. She opened the message and never bothered with a response.

Can you believe that shit?

It's been three days since I dropped her off outside the apartment. The ride home from the cabin had been brutal. So many thoughts had run through my head as I poured over every minute interaction, trying to pinpoint where it had all gone wrong. It had to be when I declared my feelings. It's the only thing that makes sense. Okay, so she's not there yet. Why axe our entire relationship?

Is it possible that she was faking her emotions the entire time? The thought of her doing that is enough to make my gut twist into a painful knot. Or was this entire thing more casual for her? And the way I'd gotten serious freaked her out?

I don't know.

And that's the problem.

A heavy hand lands on my shoulder, forcing me out of the depressing thoughts I've become mired in. It's both a relief and an embarrassment. I don't need people to see that I'm handling this breakup like a little bitch. There has always been a revolving door of girls coming and going from my life. It's never been a big deal. Most of the time, I was the one holding the door open for them to walk through.

Sydney has turned out to be the exception to that rule.

Concern fills Rowan's eyes. "You doing all right?"

Laughter gurgles up in my throat.

Hell no, I'm not all right. Do I look remotely okay?

But I'll be damned if I allow those words to escape from my mouth.

I jerk my head into a tight nod. "Yeah, I'm fine."

There's no way I'm going to break down and have a Dr. Phil moment in the locker room. Can you even imagine? Maybe all the guys can crowd around, and we can take turns sharing our innermost feelings and expressing ourselves. We can turn it into one of those cheesy counseling videos they force you to watch in high school.

Hard pass.

Deep down, I feel like enough of a jackass for believing that we ever had something special. Clearly, I was the only idiot thinking long term.

His brows pinch together.

My guess is that Rowan doesn't believe me. Can't say I blame him. I've caught a couple of glimpses of myself in the bathroom mirror. I look like shit. My eyes are hollowed out and there are purple smudges beneath them that make it look like I haven't been sleeping at night because guess what?

I haven't been.

Instead of catching some much-needed Zzzz's, I stare sightlessly at the ceiling and rehash every second of the time we spent together. Play by play. Frame by frame. It's like I'm pouring over game film in my head, trying to figure out if I was faked out by a mastermind or if there's something else going on that I have yet to pick up on.

Know what's even more disturbing?

I've been stalking Sydney's social media. Not that I've found anything worthwhile. She's been laying low and not posting.

Yeah, I've become *that* guy.

It's just another kick in the ass as far as I'm concerned.

"Have you tried talking to her?" he asks.

I blink out of the sneaky thoughts that have tangled around me like jungle vines. It's disconcerting how easy it is to get sucked back into the whirl of them.

There's no need to elaborate on who the *her* in question is.

We both know.

"It's a little difficult to do that when she won't respond to my texts." I snap my teeth together, irritated with myself for revealing even that much. It's not like I'm gunning to look like any more of a lovesick pussy than I already do.

It's official—I've jackhammered to an all-new low.

If there were a way to shake myself out of the stupor I've fallen into, I would do it in a heartbeat. Unfortunately, there's no easy fix. For a brief moment, I'd considered hooking up with one of the groupies who are always hanging around at the house, but the thought of touching another girl turns my stomach. Plus, I don't want to do anything to fuck up our relationship if she changes her mind. Now, if that doesn't solidify my pathetic status, I don't know what will.

With nothing else to say on the topic, we lapse into silence before heading to the showers. I do a quick wash and try to concentrate on the game. The moment my mind begins to wander to Sydney, I give myself a quick mental slap and refocus my attention. I need to pull it together by Saturday or I'll be fucked. If I'm not playing to the best of my abilities, Coach will pull me off the field and bench my ass before I can blink. I could feel him scrutinizing me during the scrimmage this afternoon. He knows I'm off. There's no fooling Coach Richards.

I pull the towel from around my waist and run it over my face and hair before drying off.

As much as it sucks to admit, I've come to terms that Sydney and I aren't going to magically get back together again. Whatever reason she cut and run isn't going to disappear. And there's nothing I can do to reel her back in. That being said, a few answers would be nice. Maybe then I could move on from this place where I'm constantly spinning my tires. We're fucking grown-ass adults. We should be able to sit down and have a conversation. At the very least, she owes me that much.

Once Rowan is dressed, he grabs his athletic bag from the bench and hoists it onto his shoulder. Only then do I realize that it's Thursday night and the women's soccer team has a match.

"Are you heading to the game?" The question tumbles out of my mouth before I can stop it.

Guilt flickers in his eyes. If I hadn't asked, he probably wouldn't have mentioned it. I can appreciate that he doesn't want to rub salt into a fresh wound. Rowan is a good friend. One of the best I've made at Western. I have a shit ton of acquaintances. And there are a lot of people who want to hang out with me because of my status on campus. Sometimes it can be difficult to ascertain who actually likes you for the guy you are and the ones who are there because of your position on the team. It's one of the reasons I've always downplayed who my father is. I saw the way people reacted when I was a kid, and when he coached my football teams. Or in high school when he would show up to the games. Since we don't have the same surname, most people at Western don't realize that I'm Jake Winchester's son.

"Yeah. I wasn't sure if you wanted to go or not."

"Actually," I say, making a split-second decision, "I do." It's probably one I'll end up regretting in the not-so-distant future.

His brows rise. "Really?"

I jerk my shoulders. "Just because we're not together doesn't mean I shouldn't show up and support her and the team."

Rowan nods as he studies me. "I'm sure she'll appreciate that."

Yeah, well...that's doubtful, but who knows?

Maybe afterward we can sit down and finally hash shit out.

Chapter Thirty-Seven

BRAYDEN

As soon as I walk through the door of my accounting class, I glance around to see if Sydney has beat me here.

Nope. She's nowhere to be seen.

After the way she evaded me last night, it's not a total surprise. Although, it does irritate the crap out of me. I don't understand what her deal is. She and Ethan are still on speaking terms and they went out for half a year. We were together for way less than that, and I'm like a communicable disease she's deathly afraid of contracting.

Her behavior doesn't make a damn bit of sense. This isn't the same Sydney I've gotten to know over the last three years. That girl is brash and doesn't skulk around, hiding from anyone. And yet, that's *exactly* what she's doing.

It's tempting to confront her and talk out our issues for no other reason than to move past them. I'm constantly searching for her around every bend and corner. There are going to be times when we're forced to come into contact. Our roommates are still going strong without an expiration date in sight.

And you know what?

Good for them.

No, really. Good for fucking them. I hope they live happily ever after. They can get hitched and populate the world with little Demis and Rowans.

I squeeze my eyes shut and pinch the bridge of my nose before inhaling a deep breath. The urge to slam my fist through the wall thrums through me. It takes effort to shake off the fury attempting to take root deep inside. I haven't felt this out of control of my emotions since my father died.

That's not a place I want to find myself ever again.

My eyes snap open when Dr. Millhouse shuffles around a few papers at the podium before clearing his throat and launching into today's lecture. I take another inconspicuous peek around the room, surprised to find that Sydney is a no-show. Have we seriously reached the point that she'd rather fail a class than be in my general vicinity?

A mixture of disbelief and anger crashes over me. It's almost enough to stomp out the hurt flooding through my veins. Even before we dated—fake or otherwise—she didn't go to such great lengths to avoid me.

A full five minutes tick by before the classroom door creaks open and Sydney slinks into the small lecture hall. There's a pink ball cap pulled low over her eyes, which makes it impossible to get a good look at her face. But still...I know it's her. The moment she stepped inside the room, my body went on high alert, vibrating like a live wire. No matter how much distance she attempts to place between us, the gravitational pull I feel for her refuses to be denied. I don't understand how emotions this strong can be one-sided.

Doesn't she feel it as well?

Once she's settled as far as she can possibly get from me, Sydney pulls out her laptop and fires it up before staring straight ahead as if she's hanging onto every syllable that comes out of Millhouse's mouth. Like it's the most scintillating shit she's ever heard in her life.

Let me be perfectly clear—it's not. It's boring as hell. Millhouse is yammering away about something that has to do with decentralized firms. I'd probably understand it better if I were actually paying attention, but that's impossible now that Sydney is here.

I keep my gaze trained on her. I'm burning holes into the back of her head. If she can feel the intensity of my stare, she doesn't bother to acknowledge it. It only serves to piss me off even more.

By the time our professor wraps up his lecture for the day, I have no idea what was covered, which is problematic, considering there will be a quiz next week.

Before I can pack up my shit, Sydney bolts from the room like her ass is on fire. If she thinks for one damn minute that she can avoid me for the remainder of our senior year, she has another thing coming. I shove everything in my bag and take off after her. A few people try to capture my attention, but I refuse to make eye contact when they call my name. Instead, I barrel past like a locomotive. Most have enough common sense to stay out of my way instead of taking a chance on getting mowed over. At this point, I don't give a crap about collateral damage. All I care about is reaching Sydney and forcing her to have a conversation.

I have no idea what I'm going to say if I actually manage to catch up with her. Guess I'll burn that bridge in a blaze of glory when I get to it.

What I do know is that I'm seething inside.

I push through the throng of students plodding through the cramped corridor like cattle. I keep my eyes peeled for her pink hat but don't see it anywhere. Just as my gaze makes a second sweep of the area, I catch sight of her blond head as she rounds the corner. Her hair is scraped back into a ponytail. The ball cap is now conspicuously absent.

Did she take it off in hopes of losing me in the mass of bodies?

The thought is almost enough to knock the air from my lungs.

Is she seriously that desperate to escape my evil clutches?

My hands tighten until the knuckles turn bone white. Instead of backing off, I pick up speed and fly around the corner. The last thing I want to do is lose her. If a few people get shoved in the process, too fucking bad.

"Hey," someone grumbles when I knock into them.

"Dick!" another person shouts at my back. "Watch where you're going!"

I motor past without apologizing. The exact moment I reach for

Sydney's arm is the same one she tosses an apprehensive glance over her shoulder. It's like she can sense my presence the same way I do hers. Her green eyes widen as they lock on mine.

"Brayden," she gasps as if not expecting me to chase her down.

"Yep," I bite out grimly, steering her into a dark classroom and slamming the door shut behind us. In the echoing silence of the empty room, the lock clicking into place sounds like a gunshot.

She flinches. "What are you doing?"

When she attempts to break loose, I release my hold but stay positioned in front of the exit. I'll be damned if she escapes before we hash this out. As soon as she's free, she cautiously backs away. Her gaze stays pinned to mine as she puts more space between us.

"Making it possible for us to have a private conversation." My gaze searches hers, sifting through the emotions in her eyes. Normally, I know exactly what's going on inside her head. This time is different. No matter how much I probe, I keep coming up empty handed. Sydney has totally closed herself off. It's like she flipped a switch. I want to know what changed between us.

Even though her face turns ashen, she draws herself up to her full height. "There's no need for that. We've already talked about everything that needed to be discussed."

Is she joking?

"That's funny, because I don't feel the same way." I cock a brow. "I'm still confused as to why you ended things in the first place. And you won't return my texts or calls. You've been skulking around campus in an attempt to avoid me."

"I haven't been skulking," she says, lifting her chin in defiance.

"The hell you have, and I want to know why. I've never known you to be a coward, Sydney. Why are you being one now?"

Anger cracks through her eyes like a bolt of lightning, banishing the hunted look that had flared to life as soon as she realized I was intent on talking with her. "I'm not a coward."

"Under normal circumstances, I would agree with that statement. But you've been doing a damn good impression of it lately. I've seen you throw down with the best of them and get into fights and yet, here you are, running from me with your tail tucked between your legs. You know what? I really expected better from you."

A hot rush of color stings her cheeks as I stalk closer. That's all it takes for fear to flicker across her face as she stumbles in retreat. It doesn't take long for her back to hit the far wall of the classroom. Panic and regret flash in her wide eyes. I don't know if it's directed at me or herself, but I'm damn well going to find out.

Sydney flattens against the wall. Her fingers curl, clawing at the paint. She's doing everything in her power to avoid my touch, which is fucking hilarious. It wasn't so long ago that she couldn't get enough of it.

Of me.

My forearms settle on each side of her head, effectively caging her in with my body. I'm so close that she has to crane her neck in order to keep her gaze fastened on mine. When her tongue darts out to moisten her lips, my attention drops to the movement and a punch of arousal slams into me. I've never been so furious with a girl and still wanted her so desperately.

Only now do I realize what a potent concoction those two emotions are.

I loom over her until my chest is pressed against her breasts before lowering my face to hers. The scent of her warm breath ghosting over my lips is nothing short of intoxicating. We haven't been this intimate in almost a week.

There is nothing I don't miss about this girl.

My lips ghost over hers. Not only am I teasing her, but myself as well. It won't take much for my tightly leashed control to snap, and then I'll be lost. No one has ever pushed me the way she does. "I want to know why you broke up with me."

A whimper breaks free as she attempts to turn her head. Except there's nowhere for her to go. No way for her to escape. For the time being, she's trapped and completely at my mercy. And I'll use every weapon in my arsenal to reach her.

If I honestly thought that Sydney didn't crave my touch, I would back off, but that's not the case. She's anything other than calm, cool, and collected. Her heart is racing, and her breath has picked up its tempo. Even though she's doing her best to lock away the need that courses through her veins, the hunger is visible in her eyes. It's there in the way she shifts against me.

I've been with enough girls to know when one desires me. And every physical sign indicates that Sydney wants me just as much as she ever has. So why the hell is she so intent on lying about her feelings and pretending they don't exist?

All I want is her honesty. If there's not a future for us, then I'll have no other choice but to pick up the shattered pieces of my heart and move on. I can't force her to love me. But I deserve more. I deserve the truth.

Instead of responding, she presses her lips into a tight, thin line.

Does she really want to play a game of chicken?

That's fine. She might not realize it, but I'm a fucking pro.

I press even more into her physical space. I'm close enough for my erection to dig into the softness of her belly. The contact has her pupils dilating. All it takes is one shift of my hips and the head of my cock is lined up with her core. The only thing standing in the way of me screwing her against the wall are a few thin layers of clothing. It wouldn't take much to yank them out of the way and thrust deep inside the warmth of her body.

My lips drift over hers. "I want answers, Sydney. We're not walking out of this room until you give me something that makes sense. You want to continue to jack around, go right ahead. I think we both know how it'll end."

She swallows thickly, the delicate column of her neck working furiously. "I don't feel the same way as you do."

These are the same words that she threw at me at the cabin. They were like a knife to the heart. Four days later, they still sting, but I'm now able to see past my own pain. I search her gaze and realize there's something going on that she's attempting to conceal from me. I've never been so sure about anything in my life.

"You're lying. The question is why."

"I'm not." She shakes her head. Fear has slammed back into her full force. "This isn't working for me."

My tongue darts out to trace over her perfect cupid's bow of a mouth. She tilts her chin upward as if to grant me better access. "Tell me what's not working for you, baby. I'm curious."

Arousal floods into her eyes at the endearment. Or maybe it has more to do with the way I roll my hips, thrusting between her legs.

"Come on, tell me," I push. I refuse to back off until I break her down. It's not something I ever thought I'd have to do. "I want to know."

When I flex my hips again, a whimper escapes from her parted lips. Misery wars with desire. It's such a strange concoction.

"Please, Brayden," she whispers. "We can't do this. You have no idea."

Anger crashes through me. "You're damn right about that. I don't understand why you're so intent upon keeping us apart. And you know what? I won't allow it. Everything was perfect until this weekend. I don't understand what happened to turn everything to shit, but you're going to tell me." I'm so fucking furious that I can barely hold it in check. "Do you understand?"

"I can't."

The answer that bursts free is nothing more than a choked cry. But it's exactly what I needed to know. There's a method to her madness. And right now, that's exactly what it feels like.

Madness.

I'm all but consumed by it.

"Yes, you can. Haven't you realized that you can tell me anything?" I drive my erection against her core one last time, deciding to employ a different tactic to elicit the information I'm after. The only way we'll move past this issue is if I crack her open until she has no other choice but to spill the contents she's withholding.

But to stand there and try to tell me she doesn't want me?

That she's over this?

That she doesn't feel what I do?

I'm calling bullshit.

And that's exactly what I'm going to prove. Maybe my tactics are a little underhanded and cross a line, but I don't really give a damn. I'll do everything in my power to break through the walls Sydney's resurrected to keep me at a safe distance. This girl is going to realize real quick that all her efforts are for naught.

As I pull away, she releases a shaky breath. Sydney might think she's being given a reprieve, but she couldn't be more wrong. The moment air escapes from her lungs, my fingers drift to the waistband of her jeans. With her attention fastened on me, I unsnap the button and lower the zipper. The sound of metal teeth grinding against each other shatters the silence.

"You want me to stop?"

God knows that I don't want to. I'm not even sure if I can. The need to touch her thrums through me like an insistent pulse, blinding me to everything else.

Her teeth scrape against her lower lip as conflict erupts on her features.

That's all the prodding I need to take the decision out of her hands. My fingers skim over the muscles of her belly before delving into her panties. With one smooth motion, I thrust them inside her soft heat.

Fuck, but I've missed this more than I realized.

A garbled sound escapes from her parted lips as her eyelids lower to half-mast. As reluctant as I am to drag my fingers from her body, I pull them almost all the way out before driving them inside for a second time. Her pupils dilate with pleasure as I repeat the maneuver.

If I were a better man, I could resist taunting her. "For someone who doesn't want me, you sure are wet." I press closer, nipping at her plump lower lip before growling, "Soaking wet."

Embarrassment stings her cheeks as she rips her gaze away. My fingers settle on her chin before turning it so she has no other choice but to meet my knowing stare.

"If I'm going to get you off, you're damn well going to watch me do it. I want you to know exactly who's touching you when you fall apart. Do you understand me, baby?"

The harsh demand coupled with the steady rhythm of my fingers driving into her softness are all it takes to send her careening over the edge. Her orgasm comes on so hard and fast that it racks her body.

Even when she tries to fall forward and rest her forehead against my chest, I keep her pinned to the wall until every last shudder has faded.

It takes a handful of minutes for her breathing to even out. My fingers are still lodged deep inside her body where they belong. "Tell me again that you don't want me." There's a pause. "*Tell me*," I urge.

For the first time since she smashed my heart into pieces, I'm hopeful that there's a real possibility of reaching her. How can she stand here and look me in the eye, all the while insisting that she doesn't want me when I've just proven her to be a liar? All I have to do is touch her body and she shatters.

How can she deny it?

Or me?

You know what?

She can't.

End of story.

With fingers that tremble, she removes my hand before hastily buttoning up her jeans. Sorrow fills her eyes as they flicker toward me. "I'm sorry, Brayden. You need to trust that I'm doing what's right for both of us."

Frustration bubbles up inside me as I realize that this little demonstration has changed nothing. We're exactly where we started, and that's back at square one.

Unable to release her, I yank Sydney into my arms before wrapping them around her body. For a sliver of a moment, she stiffens before melting against me. It's yet another confusing piece of evidence that doesn't make sense.

"You have to know that I won't give up without a fight."

The disheartened rush of air that escapes from her lips tells me that she does.

Chapter Thirty-Eight

SYDNEY

Lucus speed walks into the ice cream shop and beelines for the counter to stare at the blackboard of flavors written in colorful chalk. Since they haven't changed from the first time we came here and my brother never deviates from his favorite, most people would find this behavior odd. I don't, because I realize that it's all part of the ritual. Instead of hurrying him along, I stand at his side and pretend to peruse the menu as well. I'm more of a wildcard when it comes to ice cream. One Tuesday, I'm rocky road, and the next I'm strawberry chocolate swirl. It used to drive Lucus a little bit crazy. He likes consistency and routine. When circumstances abruptly change, it can throw him off and agitate him. Although, I think he's come to expect this behavior from me, so it no longer bothers him.

When Brayden and I were together, Lucus was the one who invited the handsome football player to join us. Even though I wanted him to tag along, I wouldn't have imposed someone on Lucus. At least not so early in our relationship. And Brayden understood that. Just like he understood everything else about my life. A little bubble of grief bursts inside me like an overinflated balloon. I don't think the sorrow will ever go away. Not fully.

What transpired on Friday in the classroom after accounting shouldn't have. All it did was give Brayden false hope that it's possible for us to find our way back to each other. In the end, it won't help either of us move on with our lives.

After approximately five minutes, Lucus places his order for triple chocolate fudge brownie. He'll be a little hyped up afterward, but that's all right, since I'm dropping him off at home for Mom to deal with. The thought brings a slight smile to my lips. Before each outing, she sits down with Lucus and shows him a menu of all the different flavors he can choose from. None of which have chocolate.

It never works.

I order pistachio. Once we're handed our cones, Lucus eyeballs mine with disdain.

"It's green."

"Yup." I take a lick. "Tastes pretty good." I hold out my waffle cone. "Want to try?"

His face scrunches with disgust. "No, it's green and you've already licked it."

I shrug and take another swipe with my tongue before pointing toward a booth in the back corner. It's the one we always gravitate to. Once settled, Lucus tells me all about his week. Everything that happened at work along with the girl he's now in love with. His eyes spark with genuine happiness as he reminisces about how much he enjoyed tossing around the ball with Brayden at the stadium. For him, it was a highlight he won't soon forget.

He shifts impatiently on the bench seat. "When can we do that again?"

Unsure how to respond, my gaze drops to my ice cream. Even though the answer is never, I'm reluctant to admit it out loud. At least not yet. "I'm not sure."

"Can Brayden come over and visit?"

It's been more than a week since the breakup, and I've been hesitant to mention it to my family. I'm hoping they'll just forget about him or assume our relationship fell by the wayside. It's not like it hasn't happened dozens of times before. My brothers like to joke that I go through guys like most people go through underwear. Another fan favorite is that they both have milk sitting in the fridge that's lasted longer than some of my relationships.

Ha-ha.

Those two are a real comedic duo. They should take their act on the road.

It's not that I don't think Lucus will be able to process what a breakup means. I'm more afraid of the blunt questions he'll fire off in an attempt to understand. I was hoping that with enough time, my brother would forget about Brayden. I should have known better. Lucus finds a way to work him into almost every conversation.

The thought of telling my parents the real reason we broke up makes me sick to my stomach. There won't be a choice in bringing up the accident. Under normal circumstances, it's something we all go to great lengths to avoid. When we reminisce about Peter, we talk about the good times, not the mistake he made that ended his life. My parents would be heartbroken if they ever discovered Brayden's connection to our family.

"I'm not sure, Lucus. You know," I say, trying to manufacture a believable excuse, "Brayden is really busy with school and football. He doesn't get much time off."

"I know," he takes a lick of his cone, "but he promised he would visit soon."

My guess is that Lucus is talking about the last time we all had ice cream together. "That was a while ago," I point out.

He shakes his head as a stubborn light enters his eyes. "No, it was the other day."

Every muscle goes whipcord tight as my head snaps up. "What do you mean?"

"Brayden gave me his number." Lucus continues to lick his cone before adding like it's no big deal, "Sometimes we text." His brows pinch together. "He's my friend, too."

"Of course he is," I soothe.

"I told him that he could meet us for ice cream."

Icy cold tendrils of panic tangle around my heart and squeeze until it feels like I can't suck in a full breath. "You invited Brayden to have ice cream with us?" There's a pause before I add, "Tonight?"

"Yeah. I wanted to see him." Lucus frowns, unaware of the chocolate smeared around the corners of his mouth.

I fumble with my phone before glancing at it. We've been here for at least fifteen minutes. It usually takes half an hour for Lucus to finish up before I drop him back off at the house. Normally, I love spending time with my brother.

Now, however?

I'm an anxious mess.

I swivel around and glance at the entrance. No one has come in or out the entire time we've been here. If my luck holds, it'll stay that way. Plus, it's doubtful Brayden was actually planning on making an appearance. This place is totally out of his way. And it's not like we left on the best of terms the other day. I inhale a deep breath in an effort to keep my emotions under control and not hyperventilate.

My brother points to my cone. "Your ice cream is dripping."

I grimace, no longer wanting the melty mess in my hand. Any craving I'd had for a frozen treat has vanished. All I can focus on is getting out of here before—

"Hey, Lucus. Sorry I'm late. I got held up at practice." Brayden smiles as he slides into the booth next to me. His dark gaze flits to mine. It's just as friendly as when he was talking to my brother. "Hi."

It takes effort to paste the smile on my face as I carefully inch away from his body. The more physical distance I can place between us, the better off I'll be. I need to keep my wits about me, and that's difficult to do when the scent of his aftershave assaults my senses.

"We're almost done with our ice cream," Lucus says by way of greeting.

"Yeah, I can see that." His lips quirk at the corners. "You seem to be enjoying yours."

"Are you going to order a cone?"

"Nah." Brayden shakes his head. "Maybe next time."

Next time?

I swallow down the nerves steadily rising in my throat. Any moment, I'm going to vomit them all over the table. There is no way in hell this can become a weekly occurrence. It's already difficult enough to steel myself against him on campus. I can't take much more. I'm precariously close to breaking. Only now do I realize that I'll have to explain to Lucus that Brayden and I are no longer together and that we're not really friends. He can't just invite him to tag along on our outings.

My heart plummets. The smile now curving Lucus' lips already tells me that the news won't go over well.

"What kind of ice cream did you get?" Brayden asks. "It looks pretty good."

"Triple chocolate fudge brownie." A bit of happiness dims in his eyes as he adds, "It was my brother's favorite."

Everything in me freezes as the air gets clogged in my chest. I need to put an end to this disastrous conversation before it can careen any further out of control. Brayden's expression softens as he nods in understanding. Without further explanation, he realizes that Lucus isn't talking about Court or Ryan. He's referring to Peter.

My lungs burn as I force the words from my mouth in a rush. "You should probably finish up so we can get moving, Lucus. I need to drop you off at home. I've got a lot of work to finish up for tomorrow."

My brother frowns and rears back just a bit. One thing we never do on ice cream night is rush. We take our sweet damn time and enjoy our dessert while catching up. "You never want to talk about Peter."

His comment catches me by surprise and makes me feel like I've been sucker punched in the gut. It's a challenge not to double over with the pain that ricochets through my body.

"I—"

I'm at a complete loss for words. My mouth opens and closes like a fish out of water, gasping for its last dying breath. I probably look ridiculous. "Finish up so we can go," I finally whisper in a strangled voice. It feels like I'm watching a car crash in slow motion, and there's nothing I can do to prevent it from occurring.

Lucus scowls as his expression turns obstinate. "No."

Brayden's cautious gaze bounces between us as if he's attempting to puzzle out the sudden change in my behavior before shifting his attention to Lucus. "Hey," he says softly, "it's all right if you want to talk about your brother. I know what it's like to lose someone you love." He reaches out and tentatively lays his hand over my clenched fingers. "Even though it can be painful to talk about the people who are no longer with us, it can also help make them feel like they're not so far away. For a long time, it felt like there was a giant hole in my heart when I thought about my dad."

Oh, god. Please tell me this isn't happening.

Lucus stares at his ice cream as chocolate slowly crawls down the waffle cone and onto his fingers. "I miss him a lot. He was my best friend."

Hot tears prick the back of my eyes. My heart pounds so harshly that it becomes almost unbearable. Any moment, it'll explode from my chest.

"He made a mistake." Lucus' expression becomes pinched. "A terrible mistake. That's what Mom says."

"Lucus," I croak, only wanting him to stop.

Confusion flickers across his features as he glances at me from across the table. "That's what Mom says, Sydney."

My brother realizes that what Peter did was wrong because it's been a constant refrain, but he doesn't understand that the brother he loved killed someone else because of a poor decision on his part. It breaks my heart, because Peter really was Lucus' best friend. He was two years older than him and was the epitome of a protective older brother. It was always the two of us who flanked Lucus. As much as I miss my brother, he misses him more. Peter's disappearance left a void in his life that is impossible to fill.

"I know," I whisper.

Brayden's bewildered gaze continues to bounce between us.

"He shouldn't have been driving." He parrots my mother's words.

I blink away the tears that have filled my eyes. For the first time since we instituted our Tuesday night tradition, neither of us finishes our ice cream. Both cones have turned into a runny mess.

"Wait a minute...Peter died in a car accident?" Brayden asks. His voice sounds as if it's traveling over a long distance.

I force myself to remain calm, even though I feel like I might throw up all over the place. "Yes."

"When?" Tension fills every line of his face. I can almost see the wheels in his head turning.

He'll figure it out.

That is, if he hasn't already.

Dread explodes inside me as I force out the response. "Four years ago."

His eyes widen as he sucks in a sharp breath before slowly forcing it out again. "Your brother is Peter Daniels."

It's not a question. More of a statement.

I jerk my head into a nod.

Emotion crashes over his features. Shock. Anger. Hurt. Heartbreak. And then it dawns on him. All of the questions that have been swimming around in his head for the past week. "When did you figure it out?"

I press my lips into a tight line, not wanting to give him an answer. Although, my acknowledgment isn't necessary. I can almost see him mentally tripping back in time to when everything changed between us.

"The cabin," he whispers. "That's when you started acting so distant. At the time, I couldn't figure out what was going on," he murmurs, eyes unfocused as if he's become sucked into the past. "I've been kicking myself for coming on too strong and frightening you away." Hot color rushes to his cheeks and his eyes turn steely. "Instead of telling me the truth, you let me believe that."

Tears pool in my eyes as I reach for him. The need to explain myself bubbles up inside me like a geyser. As soon as my fingers make contact with his flesh, he flinches, shoving away from the booth before stumbling back a few steps. He can't get away from me fast enough. This is exactly what I knew would happen if Brayden ever discovered the truth.

"Don't touch me," he growls.

I raise shaking fingers to my mouth to stifle the cry of anguish fighting to break free. "I'm so sorry."

He shoves his hand through his short hair. "I don't want to hear your excuses. You could have told me the truth at any time. Instead, you chose to lie." A rough chuckle slips free from his lips. "And here I'd been so intent on winning you back." He shakes his head. "I'm such a dumbass."

Before I can apologize again, Brayden swings around and slams out the door of the shop before disappearing down the street. Paralyzed, I can only stare as the sharp jaws of grief swallow me alive.

Chapter Thirty-Nine

SYDNEY

"Hey, Syd?"

It takes effort to blink out of my thoughts and refocus my attention on Demi as we hustle across campus for our one o'clock classes. "Yeah?"

She raises her brows as if waiting for an answer. When she doesn't get anything more than a vague look, her voice softens. "Did you hear anything I've said?"

I rack my brain, dredging it for the previous threads of our conversation. It comes up blank. My teeth scrape across my lower lip in embarrassment as I slowly shake my head. "Sorry. What did I miss?"

Instead of becoming frustrated with my distracted behavior, my bestie wraps her arm around my shoulders and tugs me close. "We're planning to check out that new action movie on Saturday. Do you want to come with us? Maybe grab something to eat afterward?"

"No, I'm not really interested, but thanks for asking."

She cocks a brow. "You don't even know what movie it is."

Doesn't matter. Third wheeling it with Demi and Rowan is the last thing on my to-do list. After what happened with Brayden, I feel awkward around her boyfriend. My guess is that he shared all the ugly deets with Rowan. Only now in retrospect do I realize how poorly I handled the situation. I should have been straight with him when I figured out the connection. No matter how I thought it would impact our relationship. I owed Brayden that much. Instead, I hid the truth and pushed him away.

Once I'd dropped Lucus off at the house and returned to the apartment, Demi had immediately sensed that something was wrong. Unable to hold back the truth, I spilled the ugly story. All of it. Afterward, I'd braced myself for the worst, preparing to see the accusation in her eyes. That never occurred. Instead, she pulled me into her arms and held me close. Her unwavering support had me breaking down and sobbing like a baby. I don't think I've cried that hard since the accident. It was exhausting and yet, at the same time, cathartic.

"I'm not really in the mood," I mumble.

"Sydney—"

"I'm fine," I say, cutting her off. I can already tell by the tone of her voice which direction this conversation is moments away from swerving in, and I can't do it. Not now. Probably not for a while. Maybe not ever. All I want is to move on so that life can once again return to normal. Whatever the hell that looks like.

"Are you really?" she asks quietly, probing me further.

I draw in a breath before forcing it out. "I'm trying to be." That, at the very least, is the unvarnished truth.

She squeezes me again. It's like she's trying to absorb some of my pain, and I love her for it. "I wish there was something I could do to help you."

"I don't need help." I just need to be left alone. I need people to stop bringing up Brayden. Every time someone mentions his name, it's like jamming a knife into a fresh wound. It stings like a motherfucker.

Demi glances at me. "It breaks my heart to see you hurting like this."

As much as I appreciate her offer of assistance, there's nothing that will take this pain away. I need to work through these lingering emotions on my own, and hopefully, with enough time and distance, I'll forget all about Brayden and the way he made me feel.

What other choice is there?

I either suck it up and carry on or fall apart. The last thing I want to do is come undone. Although, I would be lying through my teeth if I didn't admit that every day is a struggle.

"Hey," Demi says, unexpectedly steering us toward a fork in the path, "we've got a little extra time. Let's go this way. Maybe we can stop and grab a coffee before class."

Coffee?

Now?

"Huh?" I frown, not understanding why we're suddenly veering to the left. "We never go this way. It takes almost twice as long, and we'll have to cut across the quad."

It's only when she jerks her shoulders that I notice the nervous energy wafting off her in heavy waves. When her gaze flickers to the right, mine automatically follows the movement. That's all it takes for my feet to stutter to a halt as I catch sight of Brayden. He's standing around, talking with a couple of teammates. If there had been an easy-going smile wreathing his face, it's long gone. The intensity that fills his gaze as it locks on mine is enough to knock the air from my lungs. It's as if all of the oxygen has evaporated from the atmosphere and I can no longer breathe.

It's excruciating.

My lungs sting and my heart aches. As much as I want to bridge the distance that separates us, there's no way to do it. The yawning chasm is so much more than physical. At this moment, it feels insurmountable.

"Syd?" Demi squeezes my fingers, reclaiming my attention.

"Yeah." It's a relief to jerk my eyes from his direction.

As I do, oxygen once again rushes in to fill my lungs. It still hurts, but it's so much better than not being able to breathe. This is always how it feels when I catch sight of his dark head. The class we have together is torture. Most days, I slink in late and sit as far from him as possible. The moment Millhouse dismisses us, I shoot out of the room, escaping as swiftly as possible. It sucks. I need this semester to be over with. It'll be so much easier when Brayden and I don't come into contact with each other three times a week.

"Maybe you should try talking with him again." When I remain silent, she adds, "It can't hurt, right?"

Is she kidding?

Of course it can!

I shake my head. "No." Just remembering the shock and anger that had filled his eyes when he'd puzzled all of the pieces together makes me sick to my stomach. "Nothing I say will alter the past." I force out the rest through lips that are numb. "And it will never change what my family stole from his."

As painful as it is to acknowledge that sentiment out loud, it's the indisputable truth. I can't bring his father back. In this instance, an apology is woefully inadequate and won't make it better. The best thing I can do for Brayden is to stay out of his way until graduation. My presence is a constant reminder of what he lost.

"Oh, Syd," she whispers, voice filling with heavy emotion.

I blink away the moisture that pricks the backs of my eyes. "Let's just go the long way, all right?"

"Yeah."

As much as I want to take one last look over my shoulder, I can't summon the courage to do it.

And honestly, it's best for both of us if I don't.

Chapter Forty

BRAYDEN

My gaze stays focused on Sydney until she disappears into the crowd of students marching across campus like ants. There's a part of me that wants to take off after her and make this right. Instead, my feet stay firmly planted to the earth. Staring at her for any length of time is gut-wrenching. It makes me feel as if my chest is being constricted. Like there's a thousand-pound weight sitting on it, slowly squeezing the life out of me.

Catching sight of her unexpectedly on campus is always like a punch to the gut. It's one thing when I can mentally prepare myself to see her in class and another to turn a corner and find her standing in front of me. When the latter happens, the urge to grab hold of her and never let go crashes over me. A couple times, I actually took a step in her direction before coming to my senses and grinding to a halt.

The broken look in her eyes all but kills me. I understand why it's there, and I also realize I'm the only one who can dull the pain of our shared trauma. I just can't bring myself to do it. I can't tell her that everything will be all right. There are too many volatile emotions churning inside me. Ever since I figured out the truth, I've asked myself a million times how I didn't realize it sooner.

Peter Daniels.

The twenty-one-year-old kid who struck my father in a head-on collision. One poor decision is all it took to wipe him clean off the face of this Earth. The thought is like falling to the ground and getting the wind knocked from my lungs. That first moment you lie there, feeling paralyzed. Tears sting your eyes as you attempt to suck in breath. For a second or two, you wonder if you'll ever draw air into your lungs again. It's a helpless and painful sensation.

That's exactly how this feels.

All of our lives would all be different if Peter hadn't been drinking that night. If he hadn't decided to climb behind the wheel of his car, I would still have my father. And Sydney would have her brother.

My mind tumbles back to that fateful Sunday morning when we'd met up at the diner and realized that we'd both lost people who were close to us. Maybe I should have dug deeper at that point. At the very least, our conversation should have set off warning bells inside my head. If I had realized the connection sooner, none of this would have happened. I sure as shit wouldn't have gotten involved with her. I would have forced myself to steer clear. It would have been painful, but nowhere near this level. There's no damn way I would have fallen in love.

Because yeah, I still love her. I wish there were a way to rip these feelings from my chest, but there isn't. All I can hope is that with enough time, they'll lessen until finally dissipating.

After a couple of minutes, the group I'm standing with splinters apart. Most of these guys have to hustle to class. I take off for the library to squeeze in a little studying before my two o'clock. It doesn't make sense to go home for twenty minutes before heading right back again. The plan was to cram for an upcoming test, but after seeing Sydney, there's no way I'll be able to focus.

I drag a hand through my hair as I cut across campus. It's about a five-minute walk to the sprawling, three-story brick building. If I'd been holding out hope that it would be enough time to clear my head of her, that doesn't occur. She's still at the forefront of my mind. I've yet to figure out a way to permanently evict her from my brain.

I don't realize that I've unconsciously made my way to the third floor until I'm gravitating to the table Sydney and I usually park ourselves at when we work on our accounting project. I swear under my breath and swing around, deciding to head down to the second floor. Once there, I survey the area, looking for a free table to camp out at for the next forty-five minutes. At the rate I'm going, this will turn out to be a total bust, and I won't get jack shit accomplished. Just as my gaze coasts over the stacks, I catch sight of a familiar face. Relief fills me as I take off in that direction.

"Hey," I say in greeting before pulling out a chair and dropping onto it.

The moment my sister glances up, surprise fills her dark eyes. "Hi. I didn't expect to see you here."

I shrug. "I've got an hour between classes. There's not much point in going home." I glance at the stack of books across from her and realize she's not alone. "Who are you here with?"

"Just a friend," she says evasively.

Interesting. This might be exactly what I need to get my mind off Sydney.

I quirk a brow. "Oh yeah? Tell me more."

"Come on, Brayden," she grumbles, rolling her eyes. "Are we really going to do this? I'm nineteen years old. If I'd known you would be up in my business all the time, I wouldn't have agreed to come here."

I almost snort but catch myself at the last second.

Maybe Elle doesn't realize it, but there was no way she was attending any other university. People know me here and respect my position on the team. The majority understand not to fuck with my sister. And I mean that both figuratively and literally. Hell, most won't even glance in her direction, much less sniff around her. There are about eighty guys who play football, and most look out for her as if she were their own family. Trust me when I say that I have eyes and ears everywhere on this campus.

Had she attended a different college, that wouldn't be the case. I'd have no idea what was going on, and that would have driven me crazy. Even after I graduate in the spring, there'll still be younger teammates here, watching out for her.

Four years ago, I became the man of the house. It's not a responsibility I wanted or was in any way prepared for, but I stepped into the role nevertheless. Our father was always so protective of my mother and sister, and I've tried to emulate that, knowing it's what he would have wanted.

"Exactly what kind of *friend* are we talking about here?" I settle back on the chair before crossing my arms over my chest. What I really want to know is if this is a dipshit that needs to have the crap scared out of him. Considering the mood I'm in, I'd be more than happy to take out my anger on some hapless victim.

Before she has a chance to respond, movement catches the corner of my eye and my gaze flickers to Carson. Surprise and guilt flash in his eyes before being snuffed out. It's there and gone before I can decipher the reason for it.

"Hey, man." I raise a hand in greeting. "Are you studying here, too?"

Excellent. Reinforcements. Not that I need help kicking some dude's ass. But I like the intimidation factor.

Shuffling his feet, Carson clears his throat. "Yeah. I was helping Elle with a math assignment."

I frown as my gaze darts to my sibling.

What the fuck?

Why all the subterfuge? If she'd told me from the start that she was here with my teammate, I wouldn't have bothered with the third degree. Instead, she'd acted like she was here on a date. Clearly, nothing could be further from the truth. Elle has known Carson forever. He's like her big brother.

My eyes narrow.

Hmm. It would appear that Elle was attempting to mess with me. This must be payback. I realize that she wants me to back off and give her some space. She doesn't like that I keep a constant eye on her. You know what I gotta say to that?

Tough shit.

"You could have asked me for help," I tell her. I've always aced my math classes and she knows it.

Elle jerks her shoulders in response. When a strange silence falls over the three of us, my curious gaze bounces between the two of them. I'm just about to ask what's going on when Carson clears his throat and beelines for his books before shoving them into his backpack.

"I should probably get moving." He glances at my sister before hastily looking away. "If you need any more help, just shoot me a text."

She nods. "Thanks, I'll let you know."

"Sounds good." Carson glances at me for a brief moment. Another odd expression flickers across his face before disappearing. "I'll see you at practice."

"Yup." My brows pinch together as he strides away. A weird feeling settles in the pit of my gut, and I'm not sure what to make of it. My attention slides back to Elle. "Were you two just working on math?"

Her eyes become shuttered. "What else would we be doing?"

That's an excellent question. And before this moment, it's not one I would have entertained.

"I don't know," I say carefully. I can't tell if the whole Sydney thing has knocked me so out of whack that I'm creating issues where there are none. It's a disturbing thought on so many levels.

"Give me a break," she mutters before nodding to the math book splayed open on the table. "Look, as much fun as this interrogation has been, I don't have time for it. There's an assignment I need to finish by three."

I blow out a steady breath and realize that I'm way off base. There's no way in hell something is going on between Elle and Carson. Even the idea is absurd. He would never betray me by hooking up with my little sister.

"You know what?" I don't give her a chance to respond. "I'm sorry. I didn't mean to piss you off."

Her expression softens, and the tension filling her shoulders drains away. "Don't worry about it. I just wish you would back off a bit and give me some space to live my life."

As much as I hate to admit it, Elle is probably right. Maybe if I give her a little breathing room now, I won't feel so out of control when I'm gone next year.

"I'll try. That's the best I can do."

"Thank you." There's a pause as she searches my eyes with more care. "Are you okay?"

I drag a hand over my face, not bothering to lie. If there's one person who knows me well, it's my sister. We've always been close, but the death of our father made us more so. "I ran into Sydney on the way here."

Elle's eyes flare as her voice drops. "Did you talk to her?"

As loath as I was to tell her about the connection to the blonde soccer player, there was no way I could keep it a secret. I didn't want to hide the truth the same way Sydney attempted to keep it from me. How hypocritical would that have been?

To say that she'd been shocked and saddened is an understatement. Strangely enough, she hadn't blamed Sydney for what happened. Elle might only be nineteen years old, but she's wise beyond her years. She's the one who reminded me that it had been a tragic accident and that Sydney had in no way been responsible for her brother's choices.

Honestly, I hadn't expected her to respond in that manner. I'd assumed she would be as angry as I was.

I shake my head. Even the thought of being close enough to converse with her makes me feel like my heart will crack wide open. Once that happens, there'll be no shoving everything that spilled out back inside again. "No. I can't."

She reaches across the table, laying her hand over mine. "It's not her fault, Bray. You know it isn't. You can't punish her for something she didn't have anything to do with."

"I know." I really do. Sydney has no culpability in the situation. But still...

Every time I look at her, it's a reminder of the accident all over again. She's an unwanted tie to the most tragic episode of my life. How am I supposed to get over that? Or somehow overlook it?

"Okay, then what?" she prompts when I fall silent.

I jerk my shoulders, unsure what to say. The truth is that I'm fresh out of answers.

"It's obvious that you have strong feelings for her."

I'll do us both a favor and not bother denying it. "Yeah, I do." Sydney is the first girl I've ever truly cared about. Certainly the only one I could imagine a future with. The feelings I'd developed make the situation even more unbearable.

Sorrow fills her eyes before she says quietly, "Dad would hate it if you let this stand in the way of you finding someone who makes you happy. And Sydney does that."

Her words are like an unexpected blow to the gut. They knock the air from my lungs. My mouth opens but nothing comes out.

"He wouldn't want you to blame her for something she had no control over."

It's difficult not to double over with the pain and grief that flood through me.

"If you love her," she continues softly when I remain silent, "don't let her go."

Chapter Forty-One

SYDNEY

"Hey, hun," Mom says, pulling me into the warm comfort of her arms and holding me close. "Are you doing all right?"

"Yeah, I'm fine." Although we both realize if that were true, I wouldn't have come home to lick my wounds. I'd be at school, enjoying my life without a care in the world.

She pulls back to search my eyes. Whatever she finds is enough to have her expression faltering. "I'm so sorry, Sydney."

"Me, too." It takes effort to push out the response.

As much as I'd wanted to keep everything bottled up and to myself, it wasn't possible. Lucus had been upset after what occurred at the ice cream shop and it had taken a few hours to calm him down.

These past two weeks have been a nightmare with no end in sight. I can't say that it's been the toughest time of my life because for obvious reasons, that's not true, but it's becoming a close second.

After classes wrapped up this afternoon, I packed a bag for the weekend and decided to come home to decompress. I'm hoping a little time away from campus will help clear my head so I can get back on track. Not only do I need to finish out the fall semester, but I have to make it through the spring before I'm finally able to graduate. I've got to find a way to put what happened with Brayden behind me and move on. At the very least, I need to stop torturing myself about it every second of the day.

That, unfortunately, is easier said than done.

"What do you think about going to the mall and doing a little shopping tomorrow? Maybe we can grab lunch. There's a new Mexican restaurant that just opened up in town."

I think I'd rather climb into bed and sleep the entire weekend away. Maybe when I wake up, I'll realize that this was nothing more than a horrendous nightmare.

Instead of saying that, I force a smile. "Sure, that sounds good, Mom."

She returns the expression, but, like mine, it doesn't quite reach her eyes. "Why don't you put your bag in your room and then help me with dinner? Ryan and Juliette will be over around six. They mentioned something about having news to share."

One brow climbs up my forehead. "Uh-oh. What do you think the chances are of her being pregnant again?"

The corners of Mom's lips twitch. "The last time she was over, I offered her a glass of wine and she declined."

Hmmm. That seems like a rather telling sign.

I shake my head and think about the two-year-old demon they already have a hard time controlling. "I'm gonna be completely honest, I don't know if they can handle another offspring."

"Sydney!" Mom admonishes. "That's not very nice."

My mouth tumbles open as I give her an *oh, come on* look. "What? We both know it's true." Caden runs circles around them. If he had access to rope, he'd probably hog tie both of them.

"That might be so," she says, which is the closest to a concession that you'll get from Jane Daniels, "but he's your nephew. And he's a real sweetheart."

A real sweetheart?

Caden?

More like the devil incarnate.

"I love him to pieces," I tell her, "but the kid has way too much energy. If he weren't such a handful, you would babysit more often."

She waves her hand, dismissing the accusation. "He's just a little boy. And boys can be bundles of restless energy. His father was the same way."

My parents like to joke that Ryan was hell on wheels. I have no idea how they had four more kids after that. I would have stopped at one and been done.

Allowing the conversation to fall by the wayside, I grab my bag from the floor in the entryway where I dropped it and point to the staircase. "I'm going to take a quick shower and change. Then I'll be down to help."

"Sounds good." She nods, pulling me in for another quick hug before padding into the kitchen to get dinner started.

As I move up the staircase to the second floor, I realize that coming home was the right decision to make. I've never been someone to run and hide from their problems, always preferring to tackle them head on. There have definitely been times when that tactic has blown up in my face. In this particular instance, I'm making an exception to the rule.

I don't want to worry about running into Brayden around every corner, and that's exactly what I've been doing. It's impossible to relax at Western, and it's throwing off my game on the field. I need to get my head on straight and figure out how I'm going to handle the rest of the year. What I'm doing obviously isn't working.

My childhood bedroom looks exactly the same as it did before I left for college. It's like stepping into a time warp, and there's something infinitely comforting about that.

One entire wall is decorated with photographs of family and friends. There's not an inch of space to be found. It's all the people who have come into my life and meant something to me. Like my room at school, there are fairy lights strung around the perimeter, giving it a whimsical quality. A fuzzy white rug covers a portion of the hardwood floor, and there's a queen-sized bed with fluffy white pillows piled high on top of it. A turquoise chair is arranged near the window where bright sunlight pours in during the early morning hours. Too many times to count, I've curled up there with my sketch pad and lost myself in my art. The shelves in the closet on the other side of the room hold dozens of sketch pads. Every single page is filled with doodles and drawings that I've been unable to part with. Each one feels like a piece of me that has bled onto the paper.

The wall opposite to the photo collage is covered with framed artwork that I've created from elementary on through high school. Every year there was a district art fair, and teachers would select several pieces to be displayed and judged. Afterward, they would end up on my wall or somewhere in the house.

A sigh of relief escapes me as I step inside my room and set the duffle bag on the bed. It's so tempting to crawl under the comforter and shut out everything that has taken place these past two weeks. Instead of giving in to the urge, I strip out of my clothes and leave them on the floor before walking into the Jack and Jill bathroom I share with Lucus. Since he's at work, I don't have to worry about him barging in on me.

Once enclosed within the small room, I lean into the shower and turn the handle. When the water finally warms, I step inside the tiled space and stand beneath the spray, allowing it to run over my body before washing and conditioning my hair. Ten minutes later, the world doesn't feel quite so grim. What is it about a hot shower that sets everything to rights again?

I grab a plush, navy-colored towel from the rack and dry my hair and body before wrapping it around myself. Then I run a comb through the tangled strands until they're nice and smooth. With the oversized towel secured over my breasts, I pad into the bedroom and grind to a halt when I find Brayden sitting on my bed with his elbows braced on spread knees. His head is bent as if he's studying his clasped hands.

What's he doing here?

When the floorboards creak beneath my feet, his head jerks up until his gaze can collide with mine. That's all it takes for my heart to jackhammer into overdrive as I remain frozen in place.

"Hey." There's a subdued quality to his deep voice. One I'm not used to hearing.

It takes everything I have inside to return the greeting. "Hi."

A suffocating silence falls over the two of us as Brayden stares until I'm squirming beneath his intense perusal. Unsure what to do, I clutch the towel wrapped around me as if it's a life preserver. This is so awkward. It's almost impossible to imagine that two weeks ago, everything had felt near perfect with our relationship.

The stillness continues to stretch and lengthen until it feels like I'm going to jump out of my skin. I clear my throat and rip my gaze away. Staring at Brayden, being this close without being able to touch him, hurts my heart. "What are you doing here?"

"I needed to speak with you." There's a pause. "And it couldn't wait."

I steel myself before refocusing my attention on him. Already I know that whatever he wants to discuss won't be pleasant. "All right. I'm listening."

We stare for a painful heartbeat before his gaze drops to his hands. Thick tension radiates off him in heavy waves that nearly choke the life out of me. Even so, I want nothing more than to close the distance between us and offer comfort. I want to snatch away the heartache I've inflicted. But I have no idea how that would be received. He might have come here of his own volition, but Brayden wants nothing to do with me. He's made that perfectly clear this past week. And I can't blame him for it. I would probably feel the same if our positions were reversed.

The longer he remains mute, the more my anxiety ratchets up until it's excruciating. Until it feels like I might splinter apart at any moment. By the time he finally breaks his silence, my nerves have been stretched so tight that they're precariously close to snapping.

"I never expected any of this." Each syllable that falls from his mouth sounds like a struggle. As if he's thinking about every single one before allowing it to escape into the atmosphere.

Since I'm uncertain as to exactly what he's referring to, I press my lips together until they feel bloodless and wait for him to continue. My heartbeat feels like the crash of the ocean filling my ears.

His gaze lifts, impaling mine with his dark depths. There's so much turbulent emotion swirling through them that it's almost enough to bring me to my knees.

"I never expected to fall in love with you, Sydney."

Air gets wedged in my throat, making it impossible to breathe.

"If I'm being brutally honest, I've liked you for a while. We didn't really know each other but there was always something about you that caught my interest. It was more than your looks. It was just," he jerks his shoulders as if unsure how to explain himself, "*you*. Your personality. Your drive and determination. Your confidence and athleticism." The corners of his lips lift marginally. By no means is it a full-blown Brayden Kendricks smile. "You can be a real wildcard, and I like that. You're not afraid of anything or anyone."

His words catch me off guard as everything inside lifts, cautiously filling with hope.

"The more I got to know you, the more time I wanted to spend with you. You have this irrepressible energy that I find addictive. After you took me home to meet your family, I saw a different side of you. It gave me more insight to your personality and what shaped you into the woman you are today. I understand why you stick up for your friends and don't take shit from anyone. That afternoon only made me fall harder." His voice drops away for an agonizing handful of moments. "I honestly didn't think there was anything that could change the way I felt about you."

All of the hope that had been cautiously rising within me crashes to the ground before bursting into flames. It's so painful and unexpected that it nearly steals my breath away.

Brayden's gaze skitters from mine before landing on a framed photograph on my nightstand. His body stills as he sucks in a sharp breath before reaching for it.

I take a cautious step toward him. "Brayden, don't," I whisper brokenly as he stares at the picture. The last thing I want to do is cause any more despair. He's been through more than enough at our hands. We need to end this now before more damage can be wreaked.

"Is this him?" His attention remains fixated on the photo.

I nod before forcing myself to respond. "Yes."

It's one that was snapped of us five years before he died. He's dressed in his high school soccer uniform and I'm wearing a travel team jersey. His arm is slung around my shoulders and we're both beaming at the camera as if we don't have a care in the world. I suppose, at that particular moment in time, we didn't. It's crazy how life can change in the blink of an eye, never to be the same again.

Our brightly shining happiness is a painful reminder of that reality.

"You look like him," he murmurs, gaze pinned to the picture in his hands.

My heart feels like it's going to thump right out of my chest. This moment feels especially raw and painful. And there's nothing that can be done to soften it.

Peter and I were both tall with blond hair and vivid, green-colored eyes. Our personalities were similar, and we were both athletic. Always moving. We liked to laugh and have a good time and were equally protective of Lucus. At the beginning of each new school year, he would remind me that it was my responsibility to watch out for our brother. It never felt like a burden. I was happy to do it.

Brayden and I fall into another suffocating silence as he stares at the photograph. I'm tempted to close the distance between us and rip the silver frame from his hands. But I don't. My legs are paralyzed, refusing to obey the orders of my brain. The only thing I'm capable of doing is watching the pain as it flickers across his face.

"I'm sorry that Peter took your father away," I force myself to say. Hot tears sting my eyes, clouding my vision. "I loved my brother more than anything, but I hate him for what he did."

When Brayden wrenches his head up, I see the wetness shining in his own eyes. Carefully, he sets the photograph where he found it before quickly rising to his feet. It only takes three long-legged strides for him to swallow up the space that separates us. My breath catches as he wraps his fingers around my arms and tugs me to him. The moment my cheek makes contact with his chest, the floodgates open, and my heartache pours out in a burst of pent-up emotion. His arms tighten around me as if he's holding on for dear life.

I have no idea how long we stand there, clinging to each other in the middle of my bedroom. It could be minutes or hours. All I know is that when the tears finally subside, I'm drained of all the emotion bottled up inside me. Even with the daunting history that stands between us, nothing has ever felt as right as being in Brayden's arms.

I've missed it so much more than I allowed myself to realize. I want to stay in their comforting strength forever.

That's not something I was ever able to imagine before Brayden came into my life. Not even with Ethan. As much as I liked him, our relationship was filled with too much drama to last for the long haul. But the dark-haired football player was different. More than that, *I* felt different when I was with him.

I keep my face pressed against his chest, realizing that if I risk a glance in his direction, this fragile interlude we've managed to discover will shatter into nothingness. All of the heartache that triggered this gulf will rush in and leave us on opposite sides.

I don't think I could bear that.

Not now.

Not when his arms are wrapped protectively around me.

His hands loosen from my body before settling on my cheeks as he attempts to lift my face. Instead of allowing him to do it, I fight him, refusing to glance up.

"Sydney," he whispers, "look at me."

I give my head a little shake. "I can't."

"Please, baby?"

The endearment has my heart shattering into a million jagged pieces. It takes everything I have inside to force myself to meet his gaze.

"I love you, Syd."

I didn't think it was possible for more tears to flood my eyes, but I was wrong.

When I remain silent, unable to give voice to all the thoughts circling through my head, he says, "Did you hear me? I love you."

"Why would you tell me that?" I whisper brokenly. Doesn't Brayden understand that he's only shoving the knife in deeper and inflicting more damage? Is that his intention? To bring me to my knees? To cause as much heartache as possible?

His thumb gently swipes at one cheek as wetness continues to trek down it. "Because it's the truth. No matter how much I've tried to fight it, there's no changing how I feel about you."

His palms fall away from my face before he sweeps me up into his arms and carries me to the bed. As he settles on the mattress, I can't resist burrowing against the solid strength of his chest.

Even though I'm terrified to give voice to the question, the words are out of my mouth before I can rein them back in again. "How can you love me now that you know the truth?"

"I didn't have a choice in losing my father. The circumstances were beyond my control. Beyond yours. I refuse to lose anyone else that I love," he says simply. "I won't allow that accident to steal any more of my happiness. Or yours."

My heart feels like it's caught in a vise. "How can you forgive me so easily?"

"There's nothing to forgive. You didn't do anything wrong, Sydney. And neither did your family. What happened..." his voice trails off. "It was a tragic accident. I'm not going to hold that against you or them. I can't even hold it against Peter. He was a kid who made a terrible error in judgment."

A hot rush of tears stings my eyes. "I should have told you the truth right away instead of keeping it a secret. I'm sorry for that."

"Now that I've had time to process everything, I understand why you handled it the way you did. I'm sorry for how I reacted when I found out. I felt terrible about walking out of the ice cream shop the way I did. I texted Lucus the next day to make sure he was all right."

"*Really*?" I blink, unable to believe that he would put my family above his own.

"Yeah. The last thing I wanted to do was hurt him. We talked about it and had a good conversation."

If I hadn't already realized that I was in love with Brayden, this would have pushed me over the edge.

My expression remains somber. As much as I don't want to hold back, I can't help it. "Are you sure that we can move forward so easily?"

Brayden lowers his forehead to mine as our gazes stay locked. "I've never been more certain of anything in my life. I love you, Sydney. More than I thought possible. Maybe this shook us a bit, but that's all it was. A tremor. One we can move past."

Everything inside me melts into a gooey pile. "I love you, too."

As I release what's been in my heart, the heaviness weighing me down finally dissipates, leaving me feeling lighter. There's no way for us to change what happened in the past, but we can do our best to rewrite the future and make it what we want.

What we need it to be.

EPILOGUE

Brayden

Two years later...

I stroll into the exhibition hall and glance around the wide, open space. It's three stories high with a glass ceiling that allows the sun to pour in, bathing the artwork in incandescent light. It's almost enough to take my breath away.

Almost.

The sight that does leave me feeling slightly knocked off kilter is the woman curled up on a metal bench with a sketch pad in one hand and a charcoal pencil in the other. Her long blond hair flows in soft waves over her shoulders and down her back. The strands glow under the light. The red tank she's wearing clings to her curves and the tiny, white shorts make her sun-kissed legs look like they go on for miles. Sydney has the most amazing legs. There's nothing like the feel of them wrapped around my waist as I bury myself in her slick heat. Every time I catch sight of her is like a punch to the gut. There are times when I can't believe this woman is actually mine.

After she walked out of the bathroom this morning dressed for the day, the urge to rip off every shred of clothing and fuck her senseless pounded through me. Actually, that's precisely what I did. No matter how many times we make love, it's never enough. I'm always left wanting more. It's been that way since the very beginning, and I don't see it changing anytime soon.

At least, I hope it doesn't.

For a handful of moments, I hover near the threshold and watch her work. I could do this all day long. Especially when she's immersed in her art. There's an intensity that overtakes her features as her pencil flies across the paper. I'm always blown away by what she's able to create. She's so damn talented, which is exactly why I couldn't allow her to waste it, sitting behind a desk for forty hours a week. Not when accounting wasn't her passion.

After about five minutes, she glances up and searches the area before her gaze collides with mine across the room. I raise my hand in silent greeting as a smile flits across her face. My heart speeds up. There's nothing better than when her attention fastens onto mine and her expression softens with love.

It makes me feel like the luckiest bastard in the world. And to think that we came so close to allowing the past to tear us apart. I almost shake my head at the memory before eating up the distance that separates us. It's impossible to imagine my life without Sydney filling every single part of it. We've only been together for two years, but she has quickly become my everything. She fills all the emptiness I didn't realize was lurking deep inside.

My goal is to do the same for her.

Once I've reached the bench, I lower my face until we meet somewhere in the middle. The moment I capture her mouth, I stroke my tongue against the seam of her lips. Almost immediately, she opens. I don't give a damn if we're in the middle of the art museum and people are milling around. The need I have for her is like a living, breathing entity. One that will never be fully quenched.

When we finally break apart, we're both breathless. Her eyes have turned heavy-lidded, and I know that once we return to the apartment, we'll be tearing at each other's clothes until I can sink deep inside her heat where I belong.

Where I was always meant to be.

"How were your classes this morning?" I ask, willing down the growing erection in my shorts.

"They were great." She beams a smile at me. "I'm really loving this program."

"Good. I'm glad to hear it." Her lips are already swollen from my kisses, and I'm unable to resist swooping in for another.

After graduation, Sydney returned home to work for her father. Since I ended up getting drafted by Dallas and moving halfway across the country, there was no other choice but to make a long-distance relationship work. After everything we'd overcome senior year, living without her wasn't an option.

It took about four months for my girl to realize that accounting wasn't going to make her happy. So, we talked about it and she explored a few different options before eventually deciding to return to school for graphic design.

In Dallas.

We rented a kickass apartment downtown that has amazing views of the city and we've made this our home.

And you know what?

I couldn't be happier.

I've got the woman I love and the career I've always wanted. Once the season is over and Sydney wraps up the semester, we'll return home to spend a couple of weeks at the cabin. One of these days, when we're both ready for that next step, I'll propose and make this relationship legit. We've talked about the future, and we both want a couple of kids. When I imagine what our life together and a family would look like, I think about taking our children to the cabin and teaching them all the things about life my father taught me. It'll be through them that Jake Winchester lives on.

"Are you ready to go home?" Sydney asks, her fingers drifting across my cheek.

"Yup." I press one last kiss to her mouth before pulling her to her sandaled feet.

The truth of the matter is that this girl is my home, and no matter where she is, that's where you'll find me.

Want more of Brayden and Sydney? Subscribe to my newsletter and get a bonus epilogue for free!
https://BookHip.com/SJNCQJC

Pre-order Campus Hottie, the next book in the Campus Series!
https://books2read.com/campushottie

ABOUT THE AUTHOR

Jennifer Sucevic is a USA Today bestselling author who has published nineteen New Adult and Mature Young Adult novels. Her work has been translated into German, Dutch, and Italian. Jen has a bachelor's degree in History and a master's degree in Educational Psychology. Both are from the University of Wisconsin-Milwaukee. She started out her career as a high school counselor, which she loved. She lives in the Midwest with her husband, four kids, and a menagerie of animals. If you would like to receive regular updates regarding new releases, please subscribe to her newsletter here- Jennifer Sucevic Newsletter (subscribepage.com)

Or contact Jen through email, at her website, or on Facebook.

sucevicjennifer@gmail.com

Want to join her reader group? Do it here -)

J Sucevic's Book Boyfriends | Facebook

Social media links-

https://www.tiktok.com/@jennifersucevicauthor

www.jennifersucevic.com

https://www.instagram.com/jennifersucevicauthor

https://www.facebook.com/jennifer.sucevic

Amazon.com: Jennifer Sucevic: Books, Biography, Blog, Audiobooks, Kindle

Jennifer Sucevic Books - BookBub

https://www.tumblr.com/blog/jsucevic

https://www.pinterest.com/jmolitor6/

Made in the USA
Monee, IL
29 December 2023